W9-CNA-167

RIVER
WHISPERS

OTHER BOOKS AND AUDIO BOOKS
BY KATHI ORAM PETERSON:

The Forgotten Warrior

An Angel on Main Street

The Stone Traveler

RIVER
WHISPERS

a novel

KATHI ORAM PETERSON

Covenant Communications, Inc.

Cover images: *Fishing Hook* © Mipan, *Octopus Rock* © ImagineGolf, courtesy istockphoto.com.

Cover design copyright © 2011 by Covenant Communications, Inc.

Published by Covenant Communications, Inc.
American Fork, Utah

Printed in Canada
First Printing: May 2011

17 16 15 14 13 12 11   10 9 8 7 6 5 4 3 2 1

ISBN-13: 978-1-60861-146-1

For my sister, Mustang Jo

ACKNOWLEDGMENTS

The idea for writing this book happened many years ago. My sister, Jo, and I were coming home from a fishing/camping trip. She asked what my next book would be about. Half joking, I said, "A woman who while fishing comes upon a dead man in the willows." The idea took hold, and I started writing the book. Of course, I had to have sisters become the main characters in the novel. Regi and Claudia are not at all like my sister and me. Jo has taken me camping, fishing, to rodeos, and on many adventures in our lives. I love you, sis.

The Wasatch Mountain Fiction Writers will always have my deep gratitude. I've been a member since we became a group many years ago, and I don't know what I'd do without them. I'd like to especially thank Brenda Bensch, Kathleen Dougherty, Charlene Raddon, Kerri Leroy, and Nikki Trionfo. They have become *River Whispers*'s guardians. Thank you, ladies.

I want to thank my publisher, Covenant Communications. They have made my dreams come true. Kathy Jenkins gave me great encouragement on this book. I appreciate her advice. To my editor, Samantha Van Walraven, thanks once again for keeping me on track and on message.

ONE

BLACK MOON

"Regi, I don't think you want to come in here." Stew Rankin, the owner of Twiggs Café, slung a towel across his right shoulder as he looked her square in the eyes. He leaned on the counter, his nutcracker face set in a stern take-me-serious gaze. Stew was in his late fifties and grass-blade thin. His fuzzy hair fit his head like a knit cap.

Cold and hungry, Regina Bernard had just walked in from the chilly October day. She knew it was cold enough to snow, which wouldn't be unusual in Idaho this time of year. She had no idea what was worrying her friend. All she wanted was something warm for her sore throat and empty stomach. Trying to ease the worry lines furrowing Stew's forehead, she said, "Is this how you greet your customers now? 'Cause I have to tell you, it lacks a certain kind of charm."

Regi saw a warm spark of friendship light his kind eyes, and then he grew serious again. "Samuel Tanner's in the billiard room shooting pool and watching a football game."

Her back stiffened. Regi got along with most everyone in town except for two people, one of whom was Tanner.

Stew's bushy brows bunched together. "Been here going on a half hour now. He's waiting for someone."

Regi inhaled deeply to stave her nerves. "Thanks for the heads-up." If she hurried, maybe she could sneak away without running into him, thus keeping her perpetual promise with God to control her temper. She'd learned from Elder Poole and Elder Crane, two Latter-day Saint missionaries, that God helped those who helped themselves. Her new faith had also taught her to avoid confrontation. And that's exactly what she was going to do. Stew knew she was allergic to Tanner. She smiled at her friend. "All I need is a hot cup of cocoa for my sore throat and a donut for Oscar."

In an attempt to change the subject and because she really cared, Regi asked, "How's Mark doing today?" Stew's brother had been fighting colon cancer successfully for years; but now, not only was the disease wreaking havoc with his body but it was also wreaking havoc on his life. His accounting firm had gone under, he was personally bankrupt, and his wife had left him. Desperate, he'd turned to Stew for help.

"As good as can be expected." Stew poured the steaming cocoa into a Styrofoam cup and squirted whipped cream on top, making it too full for a lid. He placed it on the counter in front of her. "Thanks for asking. And thanks for stopping by the house yesterday. Mark doesn't have many visitors." He slid a hundred-dollar bill toward her. Regi tried to appear surprised, but he didn't buy it. "I know you tucked it in the couch cushions." His right eyebrow rose as he gave her his Sherlock Holmes stare.

Regi knew Mark's treatments were a drain on Stew's income, but the café owner never complained. "Hey, I'd love to take your money. My Jeep needs repairs and all . . ." She hoped Stew would accept the gift without making a fuss. He merely shook his head. Not wanting to debate, Regi continued. "I know better than anyone what you're going through, and if you need anything, just call."

"See, now, there you go. You need money to fix your car and for the twins' college, but no, you're leaving a hundred-dollar bill stuffed in my sofa. You'd chop off your arm if you thought someone needed it, and that kind of thinking is what's got you beholden to Tanner." He tapped a knuckle on the serving counter as if to add emphasis to his well-intended statement. Then reluctantly, he picked up the Ben Franklin and stuffed it in his pants pocket.

Relieved that he was accepting her offer, Regi looked past Stew at the mirror behind him and saw the reflection of a football game on the television in the billiard room. No sign of Tanner. And despite what Stew said, she'd never been "beholden" to that man. Regi glanced down the counter and noticed a rather large mother-of-pearl-handled pocketknife. "Odd cutlery . . ."

Stew saw what she was staring at. "Tanner's. Gave me his knife when I couldn't unclog the nozzle." He nodded at the sink.

Regi looked at the knife's rather long five-inch blade.

"He's been watching the game since he gave it to me. If I put it there, I'll remember to give it back to him." Stew glanced at the knife.

This meant Tanner could return any minute. Wanting to leave as soon as possible, Regi asked, "So . . . where's that donut?"

She wove a stray hair into the waist-length braid that dangled down her back. Life had been wearing her down lately. She would be thirty-nine in two weeks, and her backbone felt every day of it. Who knew that an old injury from being bucked off a horse in her twenties would open the door for arthritis in her thirties?

Stew shook his head as he lifted the glass lid off the pastry plate. "It's cold enough to snow, and you left poor Oscar in the Jeep?"

"I left it running with the heater on. He'll be fine." Regi picked up the cocoa. This would feel good going down her scratchy throat.

Stew placed a plump, glazed donut into a white paper bag and handed it to her. "See, you just proved my point. Who leaves a vehicle running with the heater on for a dog?"

Regi feigned shock as she took the bag. "Anyone who buys them donuts, of course."

Stew rolled his eyes and cleared his throat. "How's that ol' mutt doing?"

"The vet in Madison said he has cataracts, which explains why he can't see very far, and that his leg is fine, but I don't know if I should listen to the vet." Regi's ten-year-old Irish setter had been hit by a truck a year ago. As a result of a crushed bone, the animal's left hind leg had a pin in it.

"Well, as I live and breathe, if it isn't Regina Bernard." The low, gravelly voice was unmistakable. Regi glanced again into the mirror behind Stew and saw Tanner directly behind her. The skin on the back of her neck prickled like a rash, proving to her all over again that maybe she really was allergic to the man standing behind her.

She glanced at Stew. He clenched his teeth, tilted his head, and cocked that Sherlock eyebrow of his, warning her with his stare that any person with a lick of common sense would avoid talking with Tanner and aggravating the rash.

Paying for the cocoa and donut, Regi nodded thanks to Stew. Intending to leave without confrontation, she turned. Samuel Tanner's six-foot-four-inch frame stepped in front of her. The Stetson atop his head made his chiseled face even more foreboding. Seemed he'd staked out his territory and was not about to budge.

Regi had to leave, yet she *had* to say something. "Tanner, excuse me, but you're in my way." She dodged around him and almost made it to the door.

"You were talking about not listening to what someone said. That's so unlike you." He'd followed her. Regi knew his comment was a dig about their past, but she didn't want to argue with him. She'd made that promise to God.

She didn't even turn around. "I don't have time for this." She reached for the doorknob.

"No? Maybe you have time to talk about the river property you've wanted to buy back for years."

Regi spun about. Was he serious? After all this time and everything that had happened, did he really think he could dangle that carrot in front of her and she'd bite?

Tanner gave her a country smile that would probably melt the heart of most every woman in town, but Regi knew that smile. Tanner pulled it out whenever he was about to spring a trap. He continued. "See, I've had another offer."

A chill snaked down her spine. He wouldn't sell that land to someone else, would he? Years ago when Regi's late husband, Earl, had been forced to put it on the market because of financial troubles, Tanner had bought it but had promised to sell it back when Earl was better off. When things turned around and Earl had money, Tanner had refused to deal. He'd put up a fence and wouldn't even allow Earl to herd his cattle across it to reach open grazing land near Trailhead Park.

After Earl had died five years ago and Tanner had learned Regi was having more financial trouble, he'd swooped in again and bought all her cattle at a rock-bottom price. Then to add salt to her wounds, six months ago Regi'd been desperate for money to send her twins, Jack and Lisa, to college. She'd already mortgaged the ranch to start a bed-and-breakfast business with her newly widowed sister, Claudia. Tanner had heard of her situation and offered to help, saying he'd take Regi's prized filly off her hands. So she'd sold her beloved horse and had missed it every day since.

The livestock was one thing. Earl's land was quite another. Regi'd do anything to get it back . . . even pretend to forget the past and play nice.

For a second.

Trying to keep her anger in check, she felt like a wild horse stuck in a trap corral. Regi forced herself to relax and smile. "Tanner, no one else wants that land. You are so full of . . . baloney!"

Tanner tipped back his Stetson and leaned against the door frame. "I can sell to anyone I want, and there *is* someone interested. But I'll hold off selling if you'll do me a favor."

Regi stared him in the eyes. He glared back. Tanner was serious. Just what was he up to? "You'll really hold off selling it to someone else for a favor?"

"Yep." His poker face didn't flinch.

"What do you want?"

"I won't sell it if you'll go out to dinner with me." He rubbed his thumb along his chin. "Just a harmless dinner, nothing else."

Regi could not believe the nerve of this man. They'd dated when they were young, but that was before he'd broken her heart and before he'd treated her husband so badly. Was he purposely trying to make her angry? She wouldn't put it past him, not with the history they'd shared. "Been there. Done that!" She could tell by the devilish look in his eyes he was not going to back down, so she added, "I'll go out with you again when trout start walking up Coffee Pot Rapids and swan diving into my net."

Tanner cleared his throat. "I'm meeting the buyer today. He's making an offer."

Regi's insides wiggled into knots like fish with whirling disease. Her cheeks heated. Her skin bristled. Oh, how she disdained Tanner.

That was not a Christian thought. The Almighty must think my promises very fickle. Then a notion struck her. *What if dealing with this man is merely a trial for me to overcome?*

The elders who had taught Regi about The Church of Jesus Christ of Latter-day Saints a few months after Earl's death had also told her that God allows folks to live through trials to make them stronger.

Was Tanner her trial? Maybe she needed to deal with him head-on and do something unexpected, something that would make Tanner think bygones were bygones, and maybe, *just maybe*, after a while, somehow, she could forgive him. She remembered a scripture that said to forgive everyone and that the Lord would deal with injustice. And wouldn't Earl want her to do everything she could to get his land back?

What if she went out with Tanner? What could it hurt, especially if Tanner would finally keep his promise? She took a deep, cleansing breath. "Okay."

The gleam of victory and the "gotcha" tilt of Tanner's head snuffed out Regi's good intentions as fast as a blizzard would smoke. "You . . . I . . ." *Curb your tongue; be succinct.* "Tanner, it's so sad you have to revert to extortion to get a woman to spend time with you. I've changed my mind."

"Can't take it back. I'll be calling." He smiled.

He could call all he wanted, but that didn't mean she'd pick up the phone. It was time to hightail it out of there. As Regi stepped outside and walked down the path to her Jeep, she wondered why Tanner would want to go out with her in the first place. It didn't make sense.

And *why* did she let him rile her so? Silently she prayed. *If I'm supposed to get over these bad feelings by meeting them head-on, Father, You've got to help me.*

She knew that if she had faith enough, a miracle could happen. Though, she wondered if she deserved one. Regi believed the missionaries had been guided to her door and that she and the twins, Jack and Lisa, were meant to become members. Lisa had embraced the gospel, but Jack was skeptical and hadn't joined. For a while, Regi had felt accepted in the ward. But when the old bishop had moved away, and Lisa's troubles had begun, things had changed, and Regi had had a hard time attending church. Yet, she still went as often as she could, though she sat in the back by herself and left as soon as the closing prayer was said. She prayed every morning and every night to hang onto her faith and to feel God's guiding hand in her life.

Diverting her attention, she licked the dollop of cream on her cocoa. Oh, how she loved whipped cream. It made her think of Earl. Every day with him had been a day topped with cream. She missed that man. He was so very different from Tanner. A shiver overcame her. Was it from memories or the frosty air? But then she decided against the memories. The cold had chilled her hands and face. This winter would be a bad one.

She heard voices coming from the direction of the dumpster. Turning, Regi could hear someone rummaging through the garbage. Wakanda— the nomadic woman of Trailhead—believed she was a descendent of Chief Joseph of the Nez Percé, despite the fact that she was Caucasian. She was a woman of mystery and had a hidden past that she shared with no one. Standing beside her, quoting verse from the ranger codebook and writing a ticket, was Park Ranger Curtis Romney. What were the odds that on one trip to town Regi would run into two of her least favorite people? First Tanner and now Romney. Must be a record. However, Romney was on a different plane from Tanner. While Tanner was a rash to Regi, Romney was boils.

Six months ago he had abruptly dumped her daughter, Lisa. Then he'd spread a lie around Trailhead that he'd stolen Lisa's virginity. Regi knew her daughter. Since she and Lisa had joined the Church, Lisa's main goal in life had been to marry in the temple. When Lisa heard Romney's lie from a friend, she was devastated that he would do such a thing and that people would believe him. Then, to add insult to injury, Romney had married the park superintendent's daughter.

How was it that this man could crush her daughter's heart, smear her good name, and then marry into a prominent family? Life wasn't fair.

Regi was grateful Lisa was away at college, away from the gossip and this horrible man who had never received what he truly deserved.

In Regi's heart, she wanted to make him pay for the pain he'd caused her daughter, but she knew the Lord would take care of him in good time. Regi's job was to forgive.

Forgiveness. There was that word again.

Even though Lisa was a grown woman, she would always be Regi's little girl. Her little girl had been hurt and humiliated by Romney, a tough grievance for a mother to overcome, let alone forgive. And now seeing him pick on poor Wakanda . . . Regi had to come to her friend's rescue.

"Leave her alone," she told Curtis through clenched teeth, stepping between them. Regi startled the ranger enough that he nearly dropped his pen.

Curtis moved back. And then that cocky, arrogant disposition of his took over. "She's breaking park law thirty-four-twenty, which plainly states that no one can pilfer in the park's garbage." He tugged tightly on the hem of his jacket and straightened his Smoky Bear hat.

"You're in the *town* of Trailhead, not the park, so you can't ticket her. *Leave her alone.* She's hungry." Regi handed the sack with the donut to Wakanda. The old woman's rawhide face brightened as she looked inside and spied the treat.

"We rangers have an agreement with your sheriff. We help each other enforce the law." Curtis madly scribbled on his ticket pad. Finally, he tore off a sheet and handed it to Wakanda, who glared at him as if he were animal droppings on her moccasin.

"You really are a sorry piece of work, aren't you?" Regi wasn't going to let this little rodent bully an old woman. "She probably hasn't had a decent meal in days."

Curtis huffed and clenched his perfect white teeth, making his jaw jut out. "Any money she finds, she uses to buy brew for her ceremonial potion. She thinks she's an Indian, when all she is, is a drunk who should be run out of town. And I'm going to do just that." He pulled out his handcuffs and reached for Wakanda's arm.

Forgetting her promises to the Almighty and seeing her friend in danger, Regi pushed him away. "Look, you brown-nosing, pencil-pushing . . ." Still holding the cocoa and without truly thinking through her actions, Regi faked a stumble and spilled the entire cup on him. He flailed backward, pulling at his soaked and steaming jacket.

"I'm so sorry." Regi reached to wipe him off. "Let me help." In an attempt to avoid her touch, Curtis tripped and fell to the ground.

Again, Regi reached to assist him. Ignoring her offer, he rolled onto his shoulder. She leaned over, clutched his jacket and gritted her teeth. "If I ever hear of you giving Wakanda a hard time, I'll make your life miserable, and believe me, I can."

"Regina, what on earth are you doing threatening this young man?" Tanner had evidently come out and been watching. He stepped over and picked up Romney's ranger hat that had rolled to the split-log steps of the café. Regi suddenly realized what she'd done. Remorse jumped her like a chute-crazed horse. She'd tried so hard not to lose her temper with Tanner, but with Romney, knowing his past and seeing him harassing Wakanda, Regi'd lost it.

She glanced at Romney, who had shot to his feet. He brushed dead leaves from his jacket and took his hat from Tanner. Before placing it on his head, Romney raked his fingers through his curly blond hair.

"I tripped was all. Ms. Bernard was helping me." Romney tugged on his hat as if to cover up what had really happened . . . that Regi had caught him picking on a poor, old lady.

"Not from what I heard, she wasn't," Tanner said. After studying the cocoa stain on Romney's jacket, he then gazed at Regi, the corner of his mouth quirking up in his old, familiar you-lost-your-temper-again-didn't-you look.

"He was giving that poor starving woman a ticket. That's just plain mean and wrong, but . . ." Regi paused a moment. "I am sorry he's a klutz and fell down. I really am," she said, inflecting as much earnestness in her words as she could muster under the circumstance. She *was* a little sorry she'd allowed her temper to rule her actions; however, righteous indignation had been called for in order to come to Wakanda's aid.

"I'm sure you're as sorry as you can be, which isn't saying much," Tanner said. His words didn't match the joyful glint in his eyes, as if he took great pleasure in seeing her best a park ranger. He turned and patted Romney's shoulder. "Let's go in and talk."

Regi was confused. Was Tanner on her side in this incident? That couldn't be. Then she realized he was playing games with her mind. Her feelings were topsy-turvy when it came to that man, and that's why she could never fully trust him.

Watching Tanner close the door behind them, Regi couldn't help but wonder if Curtis Romney was the buyer Tanner had been waiting for. No, that couldn't be. No park ranger made that kind of money, especially a newlywed. Yet, Romney's father-in-law was Cameron Elliott, the superintendent of Trailhead Park, and he could very well give Curtis the money.

Trying to dismiss her suspicious thoughts, Regi turned to Wakanda. "I don't want you rummaging through garbage for food. You know you're welcome to eat at my place any time."

The old woman's attention centered entirely on the empty space where the men had stood before entering the café. "Those two walk under a black moon." Wakanda licked sugar glaze from her gnarled fingers.

Regi gazed at her friend. "Well, if their moon is black, mine must be . . . I'm at a loss."

The old woman's eyes glistened as though she were the bearer of profound knowledge. "My friend, you walk under an amber moon. Though you may have hardship ahead, the Great Spirit will keep you safe and send good things your way."

Despite her sore throat, early the next morning Regi headed for the river to fish. She needed to feel close to the Lord and her late husband. She ignored Tanner's "No Trespassing" signs and barbed-wire fencing. Samuel Tanner would not keep her away from land that had been—and would once again be—hers.

Standing in the middle of the Snake River with her hip waders on and her fishing pole in hand, she waited for that recharging of her soul she usually felt. But today it didn't come. All she could think about was the scene at Twiggs with Tanner. He was such an arrogant jerk, saying he would call her after she'd told him she'd changed her mind and wouldn't go out with him. That's what she got for trying to do the right thing. Water swirled around her legs. She heard the caw of an eagle in the distance. Looking at the snow-capped Rocky Mountains, she marveled at God's handiwork. Being here among Heavenly Father's creations usually filled her soul with peace. She remembered that long ago her friend Hannah had brought her here to soothe her frayed nerves when Earl had been in the hospital for days on end. Hannah had known this was a special place for Regi and Earl. Being here while her husband was dying had been just what Regi needed. The river seemed to heal the soul, lapping against the banks, the fresh scent of water and moss heavy in the air.

Regi made a mental note to call Hannah and see how she was doing. Hannah's doctor said she was going through the early stages of Alzheimer's due to a bad concussion she'd recieved in a car accident a while ago and years of heart disease. Regi vowed that one day soon she would bring Hannah here to refresh her soul. Hannah loved the river almost as much as Regi did.

On a whim before leaving home and because she loved the openness, Regi had taken the top off her Jeep. She saw storm clouds gathering in the north, but she'd worry about them later. Standing in the river with the warmth of the sun on her, she knew she'd found some of the peace she had been searching for.

Glancing about, she wished she could have brought her Irish setter, but swimming in frigid weather bothered Oscar's bad leg, though the dog loved the river. Regi would bring him with her next summer.

She cast her line forward and backward until the arc was just right, then she let it fly. The reel zinged as the line flew over the current and lazily floated onto the water's rippling surface.

Earl had taught her to fish. She remembered watching his large hands deftly tie the fly on her leader line as if it were an art form. He could have done it blindfolded.

On one fishing venture, he'd told her to kneel on the riverbank, close to the water's edge, and listen real hard. His face had lit up when he looked at the coursing river. She'd followed his gaze and watched the swirling water weave its way over moss-coated rocks and through eddies filled with cattails. She'd listened to the caw of blue herons and the rustle of tall river grasses tossing in the breeze.

Earl had leaned over her shoulder and softly told her the voices of nature whispered in the water's spray, spirits of long ago—of old fishermen, mountain men and Indians, even the animals. All of them depended on this bloodstream of water. He'd said that someday his voice would join the others.

Regi came to this spot seeking Earl's whispers and longing for his presence. She could almost see his craggy, angular face with the large Roman nose that only enhanced his hazel eyes. That day on the river with Earl, she had noticed his hair was graying, along with his mustache and goatee. She could envision him standing hip deep in the water, his wide-brimmed cowboy hat shading his face as he cast his fly line. He had a rhythm of his own, a distinct one-two-three cast as smooth as syrup spilling over flapjacks. Such fond memories . . .

Regi drew in her fishing line and picked her way downstream, making sure she stayed clear of the deep main current, closer to her favorite eddy where the water lapped up to the willows lining the bank. Since Earl's death, she had come to believe river whispers were God's way of letting her know He would always be with her. This thought gave her great comfort.

She wished her older sister, Claudia, could find comfort. Since her husband's death, she had not been herself. Regi tried to talk to her about faith in God and the Church. Regi's new faith had given her some much-needed answers after Earl had died, but Claudia wasn't interested. That was all right. Regi wasn't going to force the matter. All she wanted her sister to know was that she loved her. God would take care of the rest when the time was right and when Claudia was ready.

Speaking of Claudia, she would have a conniption if Regi didn't return soon to help with breakfast. Even though in the morning rush at the Raindancer Bed-and-Breakfast Regi's help merely consisted of washing dishes and making sure the guests were entertained, Claudia would still want her there.

Time to go back. But just then, what looked like a seven-pound rainbow trout rolled in the water not far away. One more cast . . . just one more. Regi pulled her arm back and flipped the rod, but the line caught behind her. She turned to find the hook stuck among thick willows. *Of course. Just because I need to leave, this had to happen.*

Frustrated that after all these years she still managed to tangle her line, Regi sloshed through the water and laid her graphite pole and wicker creel on a lip of grassy bank. She tugged on the nylon line. The hook had a strong hold on whatever it had caught on.

Regi parted the willows and tromped up the bank. Stumbling over rocks, she followed the line and found the end—caught on the sole of a boot. Her eyes trailed up brown denim pants, over a cocoa-stained jacket, a discarded Smoky Bear hat, and a ranger patch.

Bile rose to her throat.

Gooseflesh swooshed across her skin.

She was looking into the lifeless eyes and mud-plastered face of Park Ranger Curtis Romney.

TWO

ILLUSIONS

CLAUDIA OSBORNE STARED AT THE capsules in her shaking hand. Depression meds. She needed these. They were her crutch, what kept her from totally losing sanity. She had to put on a good face for her sister. Claudia had always been the stable one who had her "good sister" act together. It would not do to fall out of character. Though her younger sister, Regi, had grit that had seen her through Earl's death and the last five years of raising teenage twins by herself, she had always turned to Claudia when the going got rough because her older sister was stable.

But Claudia felt like a fraud.

True, she had always been the one with good grades, the sister who took on responsibility, and the sister with the "ideal" marriage to a congressman. She'd played the part of the grieving widow. She had to. It was expected. And Claudia tried to always do what was expected of her. Except now she was paying the price for that image.

Adding to her façade, Claudia had become the sister who did all the cooking, cleaning, accounting, and any other menial chore that needed to be done at the Raindancer. She had to. This was her penance. Although cooking really wasn't a chore. Claudia loved to cook. Always had. Cooking was a comfort that had helped soothe her frayed nerves on those lonely nights when Morris hadn't made it home. However, in the last few months as she'd tried to heal from her grief and mental torment, she'd needed the additional help of pills.

Tossing the capsules into her mouth, she swallowed them with a glass of water. Closing the medicine chest, she checked her face in the bathroom mirror. Though she would always have high cheekbones, she could see a little sagging of skin along her jawline. And though her eyes were still the color of a clear morning sky, tiny fracture lines creased her skin at the corners. She had hidden the threads of gray hair with a good blond dye. She was only forty-one, but she felt much older. Setting the empty glass on the counter, Claudia was ready to greet yet another day.

She left her bathroom and was crossing the bedroom to the door when she realized she'd forgotten to set Morris's picture in its prominent place. Going to the dresser, she hesitated and then pulled open the drawer. Regi would notice if the picture wasn't on display. There would be questions, questions Claudia didn't want to answer.

Why did she let his picture bother her so? Her husband was dead. Why did she put herself through this every night when she hid his face and every morning when she had to look at him again? Silly. Yet, that stomach-wrenching feeling of his betrayal stirred her insides whenever she felt his eyes on her.

Taking a deep, cleansing breath, she pulled out the frame and set it on the dresser top, a place where a grieving widow would rightly display it. There, staring at Claudia, were his kind "Gary Cooper" eyes. He had been tall and lanky and had that down-home look of a summer sunset. Morris Osborne, man of the people. He'd betrayed not only Claudia but most of Idaho as well. She had attempted to right the wrongs of the past last night, but once again, fate had stepped in and stopped her.

Claudia's hands bunched into fists as she turned away. She stopped at the door before leaving the room, feeling his gaze on her back. If only she'd known before . . .

Before? What would she have done? She had no idea, nor did she want to dwell on it now. Breakfast needed to be cooked, beds changed, and guests greeted. She had to step into the role she had made for herself. Feeling the effects of her pills kicking in, she opened the door and left the room.

Staring down on Curtis Romney's corpse, Regi's heart jackknifed. Her breath choked in her sore throat. She staggered backward, fighting the willows as her world spun off kilter.

Once free, she turned to run and tripped headfirst into the river. Ice-cold water swallowed her face, filled her waders, and coursed over her body.

The jolt brought her to her senses. Struggling to stand, she grabbed for her straw cowboy hat before it floated away. Automatically, she tugged it back on. Water dribbled over her face. She was thoroughly drenched. Yet, she knew she must go back and make sure Romney was truly dead. What if he were barely alive and needed CPR?

Shivering and wiping water from her face, she sloshed to the bank. Unhooking her waders from her belt, she folded them down, allowing most of the water to escape as she climbed up. After a deep inhalation for courage, Regi elbowed through green willows until she stood over him. Mud coated the top of his curly blond head and his right cheek. His left cheek was scratched and caked with dried blood.

"Curtis?" Regi knelt on trembling knees. More water escaped her waders, spilling near the body. Reaching out a shaky hand, she felt his wrist for a pulse. His spongy skin was cold.

Her heart shuddered. Stopped. Then tripled its beat. "Oh, Curtis, I may have wished you'd never met my Lisa and that life would get even with you, but I didn't wish you dead. What happened to you?"

Shivering, Regi rose and walked around his rigid body. His head seemed turned in an odd angle as though his neck were propped up. She squatted for a better view and spied a knife lodged to the hilt in back of his neck. Blood had seeped into the dirt, but some had puddled beneath him. She focused on the knife's handle again. It seemed like she'd seen it somewhere before, but she couldn't recall where.

Reaching for the blade, she stopped. She'd watched enough movies and read enough books to know better. No way was she leaving her fingerprints on the murder weapon.

Regi's gaze fixed on Romney's face. The dried mud caked on the right side made her think he'd probably fallen when he was attacked and turned as he hit the ground so his entire face didn't end up in the mud. But his eyes were open. He must have fallen and tried to get up when someone stuck a knife in his neck, piercing an artery.

It bothered Regi that she couldn't remember where she'd seen the knife. She stared at the handle, most of it covered with blood. Maybe she merely thought she'd seen it before. No matter. Regi had to find Sheriff Morgan.

If she'd owned a cell phone, she could have called from the spot, but Regi had never purchased one. Reception was impossible in this region. Nope, she would have to find Morgan the old-fashioned way . . . using her Jeep. But find him she must. He'd know what to do. Regi prayed that the Lord would guide her.

Cold and wet, she backed away and tripped over her fishing line, falling to the ground. More water escaped her hip waders. If she had had time, she would have taken them off, but Romney was dead. Someone had murdered him, and she had to get help. She hooked the waders to her belt to cross the river. Trying to step free of the fishing line, Regi became as graceful as a long-legged pony tangled in rope. Her wet braid swung about as she struggled to get out of the mess. She mined fingernail clippers from her denim jacket and snipped free. Grabbing her graphite pole and wicker creel, she splashed across the river to the other side.

As Regi crawled onto the bank, she glanced at the stand of willows where Romney's body lay hidden. For a moment, she thought of yesterday, how she had stood over him in front of Twiggs, threatening him.

And Samuel Tanner had heard every word.

Samuel loved his ranch. Sitting atop his tall roan, Rufus, he rode among his cattle in the crisp morning air. The Herefords had been his world, until yesterday. He had finally decided to take a stand and throw a rope for the filly he'd loved all his life.

He'd known Regi since grade school, admiring her from afar until they were teenagers. It was then that she had started to look at him differently, and their friendship had turned into something more. And though he loved to see anger ignite the fiery sparkle of her green eyes, that was nothing compared to her smoldering gaze just before she was kissed. But he had tasted only a few of her kisses before making the mistake that had changed the course of their lives forever.

Finally, yesterday, he had decided to take matters into his own hands. Samuel had had enough of being patient. Too much time had been wasted nursing misunderstandings and resentments. He had to do something drastic to right the wrongs of his past, something that would get her attention and make her talk to him. The time had come for them to move forward to a brighter future—a future where he and Regi could be happy . . . together.

At that moment his horse stopped, interrupting Samuel's thoughts. Scanning their surroundings, he saw why. A dead cow lay only a few yards away. Samuel swung down from Rufus and walked over to the animal. She'd been shot. It must have been hunters. Once they realized they'd shot a cow and not an elk, they'd hightailed it out of there, leaving the meat to rot. This time of year hunters roamed about the borders of Trailhead Park and many times trespassed on his land. Problem was, every year this happened at least once or twice. Samuel walked back to his horse, grabbed a hunk of mane and climbed into his saddle.

"Let's see if there's others," Samuel said to his horse as he kneed the animal forward. As he rode, Samuel couldn't help but think of his father and how angry he'd been when this happened. Isaiah Tanner had been a bitter man whose wife had died shortly after their second son was born. When his boys were old enough, he'd worked them from sunup to sundown, which left little time for a social life. Samuel's father loved his alcohol, and he was a mean drunk. One fall night after finding that hunters had once again killed one of his cows, he'd taken his anger out on Samuel, blaming him. He'd called Samuel a liar, told him he was a worthless dog and that Regi would never love him. He'd see to it.

At the young age of seventeen, Samuel had thought that if Regi married him, his father might abuse her too. That night Isaiah Tanner nearly beat Samuel to death while quoting scripture and swilling beer. As a result, Samuel'd developed an aversion for a God who would allow a man to be such a tyrant.

After that last brutal beating and while his father had slept, Samuel had run away. He had to leave before his father did something drastic that Samuel could never recover from. He ran away, leaving not only his father behind but his younger brother, Jedidiah . . . and Regi, the love of his life.

It wasn't until Samuel had been gone a couple of months that he realized he could have taken Regi with him. He could have kept her away from his father. He'd resolved to send for her, but every time he tried to write a letter explaining what had happened, no words seemed adequate to describe his cowardice, no words could express the sorrow he felt in his heart for leaving her and the love they'd shared.

At first he thought as time went by his guilt over his actions would diminish. But guilt grew and was always with him, riding on his shoulder, whispering in his ear.

A cold breeze awakened Samuel from his ugly memory. He gazed up at the mountaintops. Snow had already fallen on the highest peak. Snowcapped mountains reminded him of Alaska.

Samuel had sought refuge from his father there, working on a fishing boat, cleaning fish, and swabbing decks. Big Jake, the owner of the boat, had taken Samuel under his wing and had treated him more like a father would have than a friend. During that time, Samuel grew in stature—six more inches—and maturity. He formed a plan that he thought would make everything right again back home. He saved money for ten years, and then Big Jake died, leaving his fishing business and cabin to Samuel. A note tucked inside a raven statue given to Samuel explained that Big Jake didn't care what Samuel did with the business, but the cabin and land were sacred. He wanted Samuel to keep them. So Samuel sold the boat, kept the land, and returned to Idaho. He planned to first make things right with his father and then turn his attention to the woman who held his heart. He bought the ranch next to his dad's. Samuel wanted his father to see he was successful and not a lowly dog he could abuse.

But things had changed by the time Samuel returned home. Isaiah refused to even see the son who had deserted him. Surprisingly, when the old man died, he left his entire ranch to Samuel and nothing to Jed. The attorney gave Samuel a letter from his father. Two words were written in shaky scrawl: "You win." No "Have a good life; I love you, son" or "I'm sorry for being such a rotten father."

To set things right with his brother, Samuel tried to pay Jed for half of their father's estate. But Jed refused the money. Was that his father's plan all along, to keep his sons enemies? Samuel wouldn't put it past him. Jed's resentment for Samuel grew deeper, uglier. Their relationship would never be what Samuel had hoped for.

And Regi—

She was happily married and had children. Samuel knew the hope he'd had that she'd never married was ridiculous, but that didn't stop him from being jealous of the man who had taken his place in her arms. *Ridiculous* described how he'd treated Earl too. Buying his land and then refusing to sell it back just to get even with him for stealing Regi's heart. Yeah, it had been a low blow. And Samuel had dug his heels in more by putting up a fence. At the time, he had wanted Earl to suffer in any way possible for being the man in Regi's life.

And then Earl had died.

Seeing how deeply Regi grieved for her husband made Samuel ashamed for how he'd treated them both. So when Regi started selling off parts of her ranch, he bought whatever she was selling, hoping that would show her that he cared.

Samuel's plan backfired. Regi grew even more suspicious of him. Yesterday he'd decided bribery was his next option, and though he felt uneasy about using such a tactic, it had worked. She was going out with him. That woman was forever a surprise.

Abner, a prized breeding bull, bellowed not far away, awakening Samuel to his surroundings. The huge creature lumbered across the path. Frosty breath billowed from the animal's nostrils. "Cold, are you? Go find yourself a woman. That's what I plan to do, and not just any woman." The slack season of winter was the perfect time for Samuel to make his move on Regi. He couldn't help but feel they were about to face the foe that had haunted them for years, lay to rest the hurt, and somehow, despite themselves, come out loving each other.

Granted, yesterday he'd made the task a bit more difficult with the idle threat of selling the land, but seeing the fire in her eyes had been well worth it. True passion drove that woman, and though she thought she hated him now, Samuel knew from years ago that he could change her mind.

The image of Regi standing over Curtis Romney and threatening to make his life miserable came to Samuel. Though Samuel had rescued the ranger, he'd chuckled under his breath at Regi's tenacity. And when her eyebrows had drawn up like teepees as he'd pretended to have business with the clueless ranger and gone inside, Samuel knew she had been worried. He felt bad about that and planned to confess everything when they had dinner *and* when the moment was right.

Truth was, Romney was an officious, nasty, lying little punk. In Alaska Samuel had learned how to deal with men like him. Alaskans had their own brand of justice, and though most folks wouldn't agree with such crude methods . . . they worked.

Feigning friendship after going inside Twiggs, Samuel had pinned Romney's ears back in a game of eight ball. Romney was a sore loser and had started a fight. *Idiot kid.* With no other customers in the café and with Stew busy in the back room, Samuel had wised Romney up fast. The punk would never again pick a fight with Samuel.

Or Regi.

Or anyone else, for that matter.

Regi sped down the winding road, desperate to find Sheriff Morgan. She popped a honey-lemon lozenge in her mouth to soothe her sore throat and try to calm her nerves. Glancing between the thick pines lining the highway, she hoped to catch a glimpse of his patrol car in the campgrounds.

Shivering from the cold, she cussed herself for taking the top off her Jeep. At the time, she had no idea she'd come away from her fishing trip sopping wet. All she had thought about was feeling the sun on her face and the breeze blowing through her hair. Right now, the sun had abandoned her, and she could swear her hair had turned to icicles. The threatening storm clouds had moved in, and with them came bone-chilling weather.

Taking her mind off her own discomfort, she remembered that this time of day Morgan stopped by Jedidiah's Gas-N-Grub for a cup of coffee and a bull session with Jed Tanner, the owner of the gas station and Samuel Tanner's younger brother. Jed was famous for telling stories about the locals. His place wasn't far.

As she rounded the curve, Regi saw Morgan's cop car and a Trailhead service truck parked next to the building. With great relief, she pulled into the parking lot, slammed on the Jeep's brakes, and skidded to a stop on loose gravel. The engine hissed, sputtered, and died. She sprinted inside the building, letting the screen slam shut behind her.

All eyes focused on Regi.

A group of men stood toward the back, next to the counter where Jed sat day in and day out. He glanced at her and nodded hello. His hatchet face barely cracked a smile. Sheriff Morgan stood in front of the counter. He turned as he was about to take a sip of coffee but froze when he saw Regi standing there sopping wet.

"Morgan, I need to speak with you." She tried to remain calm. No sense telling everyone. They'd find out the gory details soon enough.

Sheriff Thomas Morgan set his steaming cup of joe on the counter. "What is it?"

She motioned to the door. "Outside."

Morgan nodded good-bye to Ranger Knutson, a gangly Barney Fife look-alike, who stood beside him. What would the ranger think when he learned Regi'd found Romney murdered down by the river? All the rangers knew how he'd jilted her Lisa. They also knew that at the time, Regi's motherly instincts had boiled over. She'd made her disdain for the man more than public. Would Knutson and the other rangers think she had something to do with Romney's death?

That's exactly what they'd think.

Electric shivers tingled her skin. The world around her moved in slow motion as her mind tried to take in the reality of her precarious situation. She nervously chewed the remains of her honey-lemon throat lozenge.

Morgan walked toward her, but he seemed so far away. Blinking hard to keep a mental grip and turning her attention elsewhere, Regi noticed

Ida Peck, Jed's aunt, minding the till. The grandmotherly woman had been studying her. Ida had worn the same moss-green sweater for twenty years. On top of her head sat a nest of graying hair held in place by overburdened hairpins. She glanced to her side as if someone stood next to her. No one was there. Ida turned back and said, "Reg, Isaiah wants to know if the big one got away?"

What was wrong with Ida? The woman's brother, Isaiah, had been dead for years. Ida must have been joking around. Regi weakly smiled and shrugged. She knew she looked like a drowned river rat. For Pete's sake, she still had on her hip-waders! No wonder Ida had cracked a joke. The old woman had a kind heart and was always willing to listen to a person's problems. Though she did have a reputation of spreading rumors. Actually, Ida had confirmed to Regi the lie Romney had spread around about Lisa on the pretext of concern . . . or was it really? Following the prompting to not say anything to the woman, Regi bit her tongue.

Clifford, Jed's mentally challenged son, was sweeping the warped wooden floor, blocking the sheriff's path.

"Clifford, get out of the sheriff's way," Jed barked.

Regi hated how Jed spoke to his son. At least Clifford had Ida to shield him from his father's wrath. Jed's wife had left him years ago.

Sheriff Morgan smiled and patted Clifford's shoulder as he passed. "Good job, Cliffy." Clifford beamed from the small praise with a smile sweet as honeydew.

Morgan finally reached Regi. They stepped outside. With her teeth chattering from the wind cutting through her damp clothes, Regi led the way to her Jeep. Even though they were well out of earshot of the people who were practically pressed against the store's weather-spotted windows, she hesitated.

"What's up?" His lean body held a no-nonsense stance with his hands planted on his hips, his sheriff's cowboy hat hiding his bald head. Morgan's face and hands wore a deep tan from the summer's road patrol. He studied her with a stern police stare. Though Morgan was only three years older than her, she still looked to him as an authority figure.

Regi finally cleared her sore throat. "I was fishing on the Snake."

"Oh, don't tell me. Tanner caught you on his place and threw you in the river."

"Would you listen to me?"

Morgan's eyebrows pinched together. "What?" He zipped up the jacket he wore with the emblazoned word *Sheriff* on it.

This was going to be harder than she'd thought. She couldn't blurt out that Curtis Romney had been knifed in the neck. Precious time would be wasted while Morgan questioned her. They must go to the scene of the crime. "I found a dead man in the willows."

Morgan's face grew more serious, but he said nothing.

"Did you hear me? I found—"

"I heard. Get in my car. You can tell me the rest on the way."

"So do you know who the dead man is?" Morgan kept his eyes on the highway ahead of them. Before Regi could answer, Thelma Watts's nasally voice blared on the radio. "Sheriff, someone phoned a complaint I think you'd best check into. Said that old tramp, Wakanda, is walkin' naked down Highway 89 and shootin' at passin' cars."

The sheriff jerked the receiver into his hand. "I'm on it." Depositing the radio back on the hook, Morgan glanced at Regi. "If Wakanda is shooting at people, that takes precedence. Now, you were about to tell me who the dead man is."

Still reluctant, Regi defended her friend. "Wakanda is not shooting at people, and she wouldn't walk naked down the highway!"

Morgan exhaled. "It's not like she hasn't done it before."

"Wakanda doesn't own a gun!"

"No, but remember when she first came to town. She sat in front of the 'Welcome to Trailhead Park' sign dressed in only her underwear." Morgan tilted his head to one side, waiting for Regi's next rebuttal.

She remembered that day. Morgan had called Regi to see if she could help. He played the scene pretty cool for a man embarrassed enough that his tanned face turned red, so red that Regi thought a saddle sore couldn't be any brighter. Poor Wakanda had been disoriented from lack of food, plus she'd been feverish. No way could Morgan make her move. She'd planted herself next to the signpost and claimed she was a sacrifice. Half of her was painted red and half black. She was going to stay put until someone shot an arrow through her heart or until the white buffalo appeared.

Bringing herself back to the here and now, Regi again defended her friend. "That doesn't count. She was not herself that day."

"Well, I wonder who she is today." Morgan pressed his foot down on the gas. As he drove, he asked again, "So, do you know the dead man or not?"

Regi felt a sudden chill breathe over her. She had to tell him. "It's Curtis Romney."

"*The* Curtis Romney?"

"The one and only." Regi nodded.

Morgan groaned. "Good night nurse! Are you sure? I just saw him yesterday fueling up at the Gas-N-Grub."

"Believe me, I'm sure." Did he think she made it up? Regi couldn't help but bite her lip.

"And *you* found him?"

Regi nodded, again. She knew the sheriff was aware of the bad blood between her and Romney. Morgan's jaw muscles flexed at the sides of his face as he ground his teeth together. She wondered if he'd heard about the run-in she'd had with Romney yesterday, but she wasn't about to bring it up.

As the sheriff drove down Highway 89, they could see no sign of Wakanda. Morgan yanked the radio receiver into his hand. "Thelma, Wakanda isn't out here. Did the caller leave a name?"

"Nope, Chief. 'Tweren't a voice I recognized, either."

"Okay, I don't want to be called for an hour or so."

"You got it. Mail's coming in anyway." Thelma Watts was not only the police dispatcher but the postmistress as well.

After flipping a U-turn, Morgan headed toward the river road. Once Regi explained how she came across the body, the conversation stalled. She stared out the car's window, wondering who could have killed Curtis Romney.

And why?

Regi clenched her teeth as Morgan pulled up to the barbed-wire fence near the river and opened his door. "Show me where he is."

They made their way through the wire and down the slope to the riverbank. Regi pointed to the clump of willows in her favorite fishing eddy. "Over there."

Morgan splashed into the water, trudging to the other side.

Regi didn't follow, nor could she watch, knowing that at any moment he would find the body. Her hair and her long-sleeved shirt were nearly dry now; still, she was cold as though the chill came from within. Regi turned her attention to the river flow and tried to listen for the whispers Earl had told her about. She could only hear the rushing sound of water.

Her sore throat was growing worse, and her muscles were beginning to ache.

The sheriff came trudging back, a grave expression on his face. "You still have on your waders? Come with me."

Morgan led the way through the river. He climbed up on to the embankment, then offered his hand. Grabbing hold, Regi climbed beside him and parted the limber, green branches in the exact spot where she'd found Curtis Romney a little over an hour ago.

The body was gone.

THREE
EXCUSES

"HE WAS HERE. HONEST!" REGI searched the willows, trudging over river grass, pushing her way through branches down to the swampy area where the cattails grew close together. What had happened to Curtis Romney's body? He'd been dead! Stone cold! Rigor mortis had set in. He couldn't get up and walk away with a knife sticking out of his neck.

Suddenly, from behind, a hand pressed Regi's shoulder. Terror surged through her. For one frenzied, irrational moment, she thought Romney had risen from the dead. She screamed and spun around.

"Hey! It's only me." Morgan hugged his arm around her shoulders like a big brother.

Regi sucked in long, deep breaths and willed the panic bubbles gurgling in her raw throat to quiet. She'd never acted like this before.

"Calm down," Morgan said. "You're tromping on the evidence. I believe you. There's blood on the ground." He brought her back to the spot and squatted near the blood-soaked dirt. Pulling a paper bag out of his jacket pocket and using his pocketknife, he dug into the ground and carefully placed the sample in the bag.

Then he pointed to footprints that had crushed down long river grass and reeds. "Those yours?"

"No . . . yeah . . . I guess so." Regi knew better than to walk on evidence, but when the body had vanished, clear thinking had gone with it, as well.

Morgan didn't look at her but searched the ground. "I don't see any other tracks. Do you?"

"No."

"And all that's left are your footprints." Morgan sighed.

Concern pinpricked her skin. "What are you implying?"

Morgan rose and walked around the area to the other side. "Nothing, just that when you first came upon the body you probably walked right where the killer did. And whoever carted Romney off must have stayed in the water and dragged the corpse to him. You can see where the body was pulled. Then the murderer probably walked up the river a ways. He certainly wouldn't go downstream where the current is deeper. Let's see what we can find."

The willows were too thick to walk on the bank. Morgan made his way up the lazier-flowing section of river, splashing through cold water.

"Aren't you going to call for help?" Regi asked, following. "I mean, someone killed Curtis Romney! The killer could be out here somewhere. He could be watching us this very minute."

"No, I'm not calling for help. I need to find the body first. And I hope the killer *is* watching us. Make it easier to catch him or her."

Her? Why had he added "her"? Taking her mind off the troubling thought, she surveyed the area. The swaying pines swished in the air. Bare limbs of cottonwood trees, whose golden leaves covered the ground, were jagged and lifeless. She followed Morgan onto the bank. "This is Tanner's land, for the time being. The way he patrols his property, he might have seen something."

She remembered Tanner didn't like Romney any more than she did. In fact, Tanner intensely disliked the park rangers. It went back to the time the government had seized his grandfather's land for the park. And then with striking clarity, Regi remembered where she'd seen the knife before.

It had been sitting on the counter at Twiggs. Stew had said it was Tanner's. A cold, grave feeling spiraled through Regi. Tanner was no murderer, but she knew without a doubt that the knife in Romney's neck had looked exactly like Tanner's knife. Again her reality shifted, just like it had when she'd laid eyes on Romney's corpse. Tanner wouldn't murder someone, would he?

All those years ago when she'd thought herself in love with him, she'd known him pretty well until he'd up and left without saying a word. They'd made plans, were going to get married and grow old together, and then he was gone. Cold silence had trailed him.

Tanner had a side to him that no one, not even his own father or brother, understood. All that time in Alaska had changed Tanner. Still, before voicing such a concern about him to Morgan, Regi had to be certain. And darned if she would ever admit it, but she knew she did have feelings for the man. Deep, hidden feelings she didn't want to examine or think about.

Still, she wondered, and despite her well-meaning intentions, she asked, "Do you think Tanner could have had anything to do with this?"

Morgan turned to her with a put-out look on his clean-shaven, lawman's face. "Don't make accusations you can't support. See, Tanner told me about the little tiff you and Romney had yesterday. So if anyone should be a suspect, it's you."

Her question had turned into something ugly. Defending herself, she said, "Hey . . . I wasn't the last person with Romney."

"Weren't you? You told me you found his body."

Regi couldn't believe the sheriff was accusing her. Morgan was her friend. Surely he knew she could never kill someone. Speechless, she didn't know what to say and stopped walking.

"Look," Morgan motioned for her to keep up. "I know you didn't do it, and neither did Samuel. I know more about that man than his mother. He wouldn't murder anyone."

"Thanks for the vote of confidence." The familiar, gravelly voice came from behind.

Regi spun around to find Samuel Tanner sitting on top of his roan horse, lazily leaning his forearm on the saddle horn. How in the world had he sneaked up on them riding a horse? But they had been deep in conversation, trying to figure out what had happened to Romney. Tanner chewed on the end of an unlit matchstick. A smug smile pulled at his long, angular face. From this distance, his eyes, black as tar, glistened with—of all things—humor.

How dare he smile at a time like this? Romney was dead, and Tanner was *smiling?* Maybe he hadn't overheard their entire conversation.

Tanner tipped his Stetson to her in his cavalier, macho way and then nodded to Morgan. "What's this talk about murder?"

Morgan shot Regi a glare that meant *be quiet.* He casually walked over to stand next to Tanner's horse. He stroked the gelding's forehead. "Regi found a dead man down the river a little ways."

"No kidding?" Tanner appeared genuinely surprised. Or was he faking? He shifted in the saddle.

"She found him early this morning and then came searching for me." Morgan continued. "By the time we made it back here, the body was gone."

Tanner gave a concerned glance at Regi and then turned more serious attention to Morgan. "If the body was missing when you two returned, that would mean the murderer must have been watching Regi and took it when she left."

Was Tanner right? Had the murderer seen her discover the body? Staring up at him, she remembered moments ago saying how Tanner watched over his land.

Had he been watching her?

Could he have knifed Romney in the neck? The weapon certainly looked like the blade he had left at Twiggs.

Anger replaced her doubts. She was angry that he'd left her so long ago, angry that she didn't know him as well as she thought she did, and angry that she was in this horrible situation. Regi clasped her hands together and bit her lips. *Please, God, help the sheriff handle this.*

Morgan halfheartedly chuckled. "I also wondered if the killer had stuck around." He paused a moment and then said, "Let me ask this and get it out of the way . . . where were you this morning?"

"Overseeing my cattle. You can ask Abner if you don't believe me."

Everyone knew Abner was Tanner's prized bull. *Very funny. How dare he make light of what was going on.* Romney was dead! And though Regi didn't like the guy, this was serious business. She could not stay quiet a second longer. "I saw a dead man!"

Regi watched Tanner's reaction. She knew from firsthand experience the man was capable of masking his true feelings, but could he hide them if he'd actually murdered someone? He stared down on her, as if expecting her to say more. She had to choose her words wisely. "Tanner, the dead man was someone you know."

"Regi." Morgan glared at her. She nodded to him, trying to make him believe she was not going to say what she fully intended on saying. It might be the only way to get through to Tanner.

She stepped beside his horse to get closer. If he lied, she hoped she could tell. She fixed her gaze on him. "It was Curtis Romney."

She heard Morgan exhale heavily but kept her attention on Tanner. His dark eyebrows hiked up his forehead. "Romney, huh?" He seemed a little taken aback at first then added, "I saw him at Twiggs yesterday. Hard to believe he's dead, though he had an uncanny way of making people mad at him." He stared down on her.

Regi knew he remembered finding her standing over Romney and threatening him. Was this Tanner's way of telling her to keep quiet or he'd tell the sheriff exactly what he'd overheard? He'd already reported the tiff between them. Had he gone into detail?

Well, she'd put a stop to that. "I didn't do it, if that's what you're thinking. I found him dead in the willows. But you already know that, don't you?"

"Whoa! Don't pass this off on me." Tanner's scowl turned serious. "I'm not the one who's hysterical and running up and down the river. But, yeah, I always knew that smart aleck would come to a bad end."

Morgan finally came between Tanner and Regi. "Why would you think that?"

Tanner scoffed. "The little weasel tried to tell us ranchers how to run our cattle, where we could graze them, and how long. You know yourself, Morgan, those punk rangers graduate from their fancy colleges and think they can come here and tell us folks, who have worked the land all our lives, what to do. It riles me." Tanner took off his cowboy hat and ran his leather-gloved hand over his graying mop of hair.

Regi burst out, "Did it rile you enough to stick a knife in his neck?" She could hardly believe she'd made such an accusation, but now it was out there. Again, she kept her eyes on Tanner to see how he would react to the word *knife*, for surely now he knew she had seen the weapon.

"Regi." Tanner tugged his hat on. "I'm not the one with the hair-trigger temper." He chewed down on the wooden match between his teeth, no visible reaction to her words.

Okay. That was it. Regi's proverbial last short straw had been snapped clean off. So Tanner claimed he wasn't the murderer. That was a relief, but that didn't mean she wasn't about to pull him off his horse for his snide comments and for making the sheriff think she was a murderer! What was wrong with this man?

As Regi reached for Tanner's leg, Morgan grabbed her arm as if he knew her intentions. "Let's not blow things out of proportion." He kept hold of her. "I'm going to poke around your property for the next few days," Morgan told Tanner. "Hope you don't mind."

"Anything to be of service." Tanner looked as though he was about to ride away, when all at once he stopped and asked Morgan, "How's Hannah doing?"

"Has more bad days than good." Morgan's wife was Regi's good friend, Hannah. Regi felt bad that she hadn't asked Morgan about her before, but the murder and everything had her thinking all messed up.

"Sorry to hear that. Say hi to her." Tanner tipped his hat and spurred his horse. "Good luck."

Morgan waved good-bye and then guided Regi down to the river. "Let it go, Reg. Don't you think the man has paid enough penance for leaving you when you were young? He bought Earl's land years ago to help you guys out. After Earl died, Tanner bought the farming equipment. And then he bought the cattle and your horse, which he didn't need, so you could send your kids to college. Cut him a break."

Regi didn't care about all that now. "I'm sorry to hear Hannah isn't doing well."

Morgan gave a heavy sigh. "Me too." A quiet settled between them, and then Morgan added, "Could you at least try to get along with Samuel?"

"For you and Hannah, yeah," Regi said, without truly thinking through the commitment. She quickly added, "But to set the record straight, there's more to the story of Tanner buying our land. Just know that he wasn't helping us." Anger bubbled in her gut. "And then he has the nerve to accuse *me* of murder!"

"No, he didn't. He was only pushing your buttons." Morgan stared at Regi as if he wanted her to agree. She shrugged, and he continued. "And, of course, you didn't disappoint him, did you?" Morgan squeezed her arm in a friendly think-it-over sort of way.

Regi pulled out of his grasp.

Morgan's mouth set in a firm line and then, as if realizing no one would win this argument, he said, "Let's see what other evidence we can find." He began the tedious task of searching through cattails along the river bank.

Regi shivered, not only from the cold but from a case of nerves, as she guided Morgan to several eddies where a body could easily be concealed.

Finally, after they'd checked all the places Regi could think of and had gone a mile up and a mile down the Snake River with no results, Morgan headed back to his car. "I'm going to send this sample to the crime lab in Boise. See what those fellas say."

"And . . . you're going to call the FBI or someone, right?"

"Nope." He kicked the tires of his car to knock clinging river mud from his boots.

"Why?"

"Those boys would laugh their heads off if I called them to a murder scene without a body. It's hard enough to keep respect when I'm the only local police officer, besides park rangers, in a sixty-mile radius. I can't afford to give them half clues to a supposed murder." He sighed deeply. "I'm going to call Romney's place, see what his wife has to say. It's strange she hasn't filed a missing person's report, but if Romney had the night shift, she may think he's merely late getting home. After that, we'll have to wait and hear from the lab. Get in, and I'll take you to your Jeep."

Relieved that Morgan sounded as though he believed her, Regi quickly got in his car. As they drove toward town, she warmed her hands on the car's heater vents and noticed that snow had begun to fall. Large, lacy flakes. "This snow isn't going to help, is it?"

Morgan shook his head. "Nope. But I collected most of what I needed at the scene."

Regi didn't know why she hadn't told Morgan about the knife being Tanner's. If Tanner was the murderer, she couldn't prove it because there was no weapon . . . and no corpse! Tanner had been pretty calm stating that whoever had done it had probably watched Regi. How could he know that unless he had been watching her and, as soon as she left the scene, had himself moved the body? It made perfect sense. Knowing she had to tell the sheriff her suspicions, Regi opened her mouth to speak.

At that moment, static from the radio cued in. Thelma cleared her throat. "Sheriff, Karen Wilson called, said Curtis Romney's lyin' dead on her back porch. What the Sam-hill's goin' on today?"

Claudia glanced out the kitchen window over the sink to find that an inch of snow had fallen. She'd been so busy trying to run the Raindancer by herself that she hadn't noticed before now. She sprayed water over the sudsy frying pan. "Regi knows our busiest time is the mornings," she said to Wakanda, who never looked away from the breakfast and lunch leftovers she was eating. "This bed-and-breakfast is a partnership. We're supposed to share the load. It's after noon. Where in the world has she been for the last six hours?"

Claudia knew Wakanda didn't like her, and it probably irritated her that Claudia was talking to her.

The old woman grunted between swallows, which Claudia decided was an answer to her rhetorical question. In the months since Claudia had moved in with Regi, Wakanda had kept her distance and usually didn't come around unless Regi was home. The elderly woman must have been pretty hungry to have stayed once she found out Regi wasn't here.

Today Claudia didn't care if Wakanda liked her or not. She grabbed the dish towel and started wiping the stack of pots and pans, loudly putting them away in the oak cupboards. She glanced up at the clock. Two in the afternoon. Where had the time gone? Breakfast had been one mad rush. No sooner had Claudia finished cooking and clearing tables than new guests had arrived, so she'd dropped everything and made up some rooms. After which she'd started the laundry, vacuumed the reception area, and answered the annoying phone that incessantly rang off the hook.

The whir of the dishwasher beating a steady rhythm calmed Claudia a little. Darn her sister and her daydreaming heart. What ate at Claudia the most was envy. She envied Regi's ability to enjoy the simple things in life, to merely pick up and go off without a care.

The fact was—Regi enjoyed being alive, a pleasure Claudia hadn't had since the day she'd found Morris dead on the living room floor.

Shaking off the dreadful memory, Claudia said without thinking, "I don't know, Wakanda. Maybe I should sell Regi my share of our partnership. I don't fit in here. I'm used to going to the symphony or the ballet. Regi's idea of a good time is riding her horse or branding cattle."

Wakanda grunted as though she agreed.

Claudia shrugged, knowing she was right. She thought of going back to her old life. A cold emptiness shadowed her. "The problem is . . . I'd be alone if it weren't for my sister."

Glancing out the window as she reached for the upper cupboard, Claudia saw Sheriff Morgan pulling into the barnyard. Regi followed in her Jeep without the canvas top snapped on. Why in the world had she taken off the top? It had been on yesterday. Snow blanketed Regi like downy feathers.

"Oh, my stars! Now, she's going to have pneumonia and a whopping bleeding-heart story to go along with today's tall tale of where she's been." Her words masked her true feelings. Relief breathed over Claudia. Her sister was home and safe! Claudia slapped the dish towel on the counter.

"You want to come and hear it?" She glanced at Wakanda. The old woman steepled her hands together, closed her eyes, and began rocking back and forth, chanting some hocus-pocus prayer song.

Claudia shrugged. "I'll take that as a no."

Regi pulled up alongside Morgan's patrol car and turned off the engine. Cold as a freezer-burnt Popsicle, she didn't know if she shuddered more from the weather or the chaotic scene they'd left at Karen Wilson's.

Karen was the Dr. Quinn of Bowmount County. Everyone called her with their ailments. The nearest doctor was more than a hundred miles away and, with Karen being a registered nurse, she was the next best thing. Trying to keep her curious children in the house, Karen had wedged her foot on the bottom of the screen door while she'd explained that she'd tripped over the body when she ran out to take her clothes off the line because of the snow.

As Regi had gazed at the corpse, she had realized the knife was gone, but her fishing hook remained stuck in the sole of Romney's boot. Morgan had noticed too. He'd made a sign to say nothing then jotted down several notes and walked around the house to study the barnyard. About that time, several state patrol troopers and park rangers had arrived, lights flashing. Morgan had called them after Thelma had signed off.

Once they'd climbed out of their cars, Regi had been barraged with questions from disbelieving troopers and rangers. A shadow of apprehension had fallen over her as each answer cast blame her way. Regi had been glad to leave the officers' perplexed faces behind. Now she wasn't so comfortable having to face Claudia. At the moment, she seriously thought of returning to Karen's.

Morgan crawled out of his car as Regi slowly stumbled from her Jeep. Oscar galloped out of the barn and came over to her. She patted his head. With the dog and Morgan by her side, Regi'd be safe from Claudia's dressing down. Oscar often growled at her sister for no apparent reason, which was probably why he was outside in the cold. Morgan had been Claudia's sweetheart in high school, so she wouldn't say too much in front of him. Still, Regi inhaled a deep breath and told Morgan, "I think I'm in trouble."

"You ducked out of work to go fishing again. What did you expect?" Morgan smiled then wiped snow from Regi's cheeks. "You're going to be *so* sick. Too bad you didn't have the top for your Jeep with you."

With a big sigh, she said, "Maybe if I catch pneumonia, Claud will forgive me. Right now, she looks like she's ready to lock me up." As the words left her mouth, Regi felt their sting. Why in the world had she said *lock me up?*

Morgan didn't seem to notice Regi's discomfort over her word choice and turned to wave a greeting to the woman who stampeded toward them. "Hi, Claudia. She has a good excuse this time. Got hot chocolate on hand? She's going to need plenty of it."

"I'll make some." Claudia yanked down the sleeves of her Ralph Lauren shirt, her eyes on Regi. Snow dampened Claudia's designer jeans, but her gaze never left her sister's.

"Claud, I can explain everything." A giant shiver made Regi fold her arms around herself for warmth. Her teeth chattered.

"What happened this time?" Claudia's worried eyes quickly surveyed Regi's appearance. "Never mind. Don't answer that. I don't think I want to know. You need a hot bath."

Claudia glanced at Regi's Jeep. "Morgan, would you mind parking her car in the barn before it fills entirely with snow?"

"Need my fishing gear," Regi said, shivering as she followed Morgan to the driver's side. Oscar trailed after her. Earl had given Regi the rod and reel. Keeping the fishing gear close was keeping Earl near her.

Morgan reached behind the seat to retrieve the gear. Regi patiently waited . . . and waited. He was taking forever. Finally, he rose, no gear in hand. "Reg, what is this doing in here?" His expression was stern and bewildered at the same time.

She followed his gaze to the floor mat behind the driver's seat. There, partially covered with a film of powdery snow, lay the bloody knife from Romney's neck.

FOUR
MOTIVE

SAMUEL RODE HIS ROAN INTO the stable and shook the snow from his cowboy hat and Levi jacket. He shivered from the cold. Dismounting, he swung open the stall's gate and led the horse in. Taking off his leather work gloves and shoving them in his hip pocket, he looped the reins over the stall's top rail and tied a knot.

As he worked, his mind trailed over the afternoon and his close encounter with Regi and Morgan. Regi's face had flushed an angry pink. Sparks had shot through her gaze. Her malachite eyes had lit up as they had years ago when they had little spats. But today when they'd exchanged jabs over who could have killed Romney, fear had shown in her eyes. Samuel had never seen that look before.

His roan hoofed the ground impatiently. "Sorry, Rufus. Got a gal on my mind." Samuel looped the stirrup over the saddle horn, unbuckled the cinch, and pulled the saddle and thick blanket off the tired horse. Carrying them to the tack room, he grabbed the currycomb and brush and returned to the horse. "I hoped she could forgive the past and look at me as a guy she might care for again, but now . . . let's just say, I have my doubts." Ordinarily he enjoyed grooming Rufus, but tonight his mind was somewhere else.

The horse craned his head around, gazed at Samuel, and snorted as if to agree with him. At that moment, the pretty little pinto Samuel had bought from Regi stuck her head over the stall's railing next to Rufus.

"You too, huh, Gypsy?" Samuel stroked the filly's forehead. "Have my work cut out for me, that's for sure. But I like to fight the odds." He finished with Rufus and put the grooming tools away. Filling a couple of buckets with oats, Samuel dumped one in each of the horses' troughs. Next he checked the water barrel they shared under the stalls' fencing. Plenty for the night.

Making his way to the dark and lonely house, Samuel's mind returned to when Regi said she'd found Romney dead on Samuel's property. If word got out that a ranger's body had been found on his land, things could turn ugly quick.

Since Curtis Romney was the son-in-law of Superintendent Cameron Elliott, the media would latch onto the news, and it would be Buffalo Bill's Wild West Show all over again. The super would not pass up an opportunity to go before the press and show fake remorse for his son-in-law's passing. Everyone knew Elliott didn't like Romney. But even though he didn't care for the leech who had latched onto his daughter, Elliott would do anything for his precious little girl, even play the part of a caring father-in-law.

Elliott was a walking billboard for hypocrites. He'd set up environmental rules for tourists, yet secretly let the rangers ride four-wheelers in the backcountry. He promised the ranchers that their cattle could graze in certain areas in the park and then cited them for trespassing. Almost every rancher had had a run-in with the park's super and his rangers, though no one was as vocal as Regina Bernard.

Romney's untimely death, while tragic, was only the beginning of the ruckus that would be made over this mystery. Country folks were famous for their sharp memories, and it wouldn't take long for them to remember the bad blood between Samuel's grandfather and the park.

And then people would wonder about Samuel too.

He couldn't let that happen.

Transfixed, Regi stared at the steel-edged knife. Everything in her peripheral vision went dark as the blade seemed to mockingly gleam through the snow. A frisson raced up her spine as she remembered coming upon Romney's cold, lifeless body. His frozen stare suddenly blinked as the nightmare reached out and grabbed her, pulling her in deeper and deeper.

A shiver overcame Regi, bringing her back to her surroundings. How did the weapon get in her car? Was it possible that while she and Morgan were at the county nurse's, the murderer had gone to the Gas-N-Grub and placed it in her Jeep? The thought of such a diabolic act made her quiver inside and out.

Snowflakes continued to fall, sticking to Regi's lashes as she forced herself to turn her gaze to Morgan. "That is not my knife." She didn't want to point blame, but now she had no choice. "It's Tanner's!"

"What?" Morgan glared at her.

"Yesterday at Twiggs. There was a knife just like that on the counter. Stew told me it was Tanner's. Plus, don't you remember he owned one like it when we were teenagers?" She prayed he would.

The sheriff didn't answer. He gritted his teeth, making his cheek twitch. A furrowed forehead overshadowed his condemning stare.

"Morgan, I'm not making this up. Ask Stew! Besides, I think Tanner's father gave him the knife long ago."

The sheriff said nothing.

Regi nervously chattered. "I have no idea how that got in my Jeep. When I found Curtis Romney, I checked his pulse, but I didn't touch him after that, and I sure as thunder didn't touch the knife." Her cold lips tingled as she bit them together. If Morgan didn't believe her, no one would.

Claudia elbowed her way between Morgan and Regi. "Why in the world are you going on about a knife Tanner owned, and what's the deal with Curtis Romney? You're talking as if he's dead. Regi, you went fishing like you always do, right?"

"Yeah, but . . ."

Claudia glanced down at the blood-stained blade. "That's Earl's knife."

Nausea crawled up Regi's sore throat.

Claudia was right.

Earl did have a pearl-handled knife just like it. Why had Regi forgotten? Maybe because Tanner's had been at Stew's. And Earl rarely used his. Still, it didn't matter. Casting blame on Tanner while her late husband owned a knife very similar looked bad.

Real bad.

Feeling light-headed, Regi leaned against the Jeep and stared at Claudia. Without realizing what was going on, her sister had fingered Regi as the killer.

"That is not Earl's," Regi defended. At least she didn't think so. Regi hadn't seen her late husband's knife in years. Where the heck had she stored it? Claudia was staring at her, waiting for an explanation. Regi knew telling her sister about finding Romney dead would be hard, but now—with this mixed-up mess over the murder weapon—what could she say?

As they both stared down at the blade lying on the floorboards of the Jeep, Regi's mind froze. She could think of no easy way to explain this.

Morgan exhaled and dug out of his coat pocket a paper bag much like the one he'd put the blood-soaked dirt in at the river. From his hip pocket he retrieved a man-sized handkerchief elaborately embroidered with a very manly and bold *M*. Hannah's handiwork in her better days. The woman embroidered everything.

M for murderer, Regi thought and shuddered as much from her thinking as from the cold. *No, M is for Morgan.*

She knew Morgan used the cloth to keep his prints off the weapon. He leaned into the Jeep and picked up the long-bladed pocketknife. Blood had mixed with the snow and colored the weapon a watery red.

Claudia stared at the knife then at Regi.

Regi slowly shook her head. "Here's the deal, Claud. This morning I went fishing and found Curtis Romney dead in the willows with that knife stuck in his neck."

Claudia's disbelieving eyes grew as large as Rocky Mountain boulders. Regi could see her sister's mind adding up the facts: dead body, a knife that looked like Earl's, and Regi's bad temper. The problem was Claudia's figuring would add up to the wrong answer.

Regi needed to keep her sister calm and, at the same time, reason with Morgan. "I don't know what's going on. But Samuel Tanner had a knife like that at Twiggs yesterday."

Claudia shook her head while biting at her bottom lip.

"Well, believe me, he did!"

Claudia grabbed Regi's arm as though hanging on for dear life. Oscar growled at Claudia, and she immediately let go. Regi had forgotten the dog was there. His hackles had risen. Shivering, she patted Oscar to quiet him while concentrating on her rattled sister.

Then all at once Claudia's expression changed from shocked to understanding. She took a deep breath. "Don't worry, sis." Swiping at the snowflakes landing on Regi's face, she continued. "If you say the knife is not Earl's, it's not."

With her sister now on her side, Regi watched as Morgan carefully eased the wicked blade into the evidence bag and folded the top shut.

Regi followed him to his car, pleading. "You believe me, don't you?" She knew in her heart that he did, but she desperately needed to hear him say it.

He leaned on the door of his patrol car. "You have motive. Plus, as Claudia has so aptly pointed out, the knife could be Earl's. I'm quite certain the blood on the blade will match Romney's, so what appears to be the murder weapon has been found in *your* vehicle. It doesn't look good."

"Regi, we need to talk." Claudia bit at the nail of her index finger, reverting to the bad habit of her youth.

A bone-tired weariness crept over Regi. Gazing squarely in her sister's eyes, she said, "I didn't murder anyone." Regi didn't mean to sound angry, but she did anyway. "Claud, it's a long story, and I'll tell you everything in a minute."

Claudia nodded and tucked a lock of hair behind her ear as she fell silent.

Regi turned to Morgan. "You can't honestly think I'd kill someone. If motive and weapons were all anyone needed to become a murderer, I would have killed Samuel Tanner long ago."

Morgan tipped back his hat on his bald head and swiped his hand over his now whisker-shadowed face. He, too, looked bone-tired. "Tanner jilted you, *not* your Lisa. Hell hath no fury like a riled mother."

If a newly shod horse had kicked Regi in the gut, she wouldn't feel this badly. She folded her arms, trying to keep Morgan from seeing her shake, a dead giveaway that she was more than a little upset. If Sheriff Thomas Morgan doubted her innocence, everyone would.

"Look . . ." He brushed snow off the top of her head and took hold of her shoulders. "I wouldn't be a good police officer if I ignored such a glaring motive. The deceased spread lies about stealing your daughter's virtue and then left her to marry another woman. I know how that tore you up. The whole town knows how you felt about him. I won't sugarcoat this. We're in for a fight, but I'm going to try my best to keep you out of jail."

The word *jail* became a bullet pinging around in Regi's mind. *Jail.* Such a haunting word. This was not happening. The shaking left her, replaced by numbness that crawled down her arms and legs.

Claudia spoke up. "Thomas Morgan, after all these years, you can't honestly believe my little sister killed that man."

The old kindness of long-lost love gentled Morgan's stony face as he gazed at Claudia. "Doesn't matter what I believe." He let go of Regi. "When this evidence is known to the state troopers and the park service, well, let's just say it's not going to be a good day. Until I get a handle on this, I suggest you and Regi stick around the Raindancer and keep a low profile. I'll need to confiscate your Jeep for a while. You still have Earl's old one to get you by, don't you?"

Regi nodded, handing him her keys.

"I'll get help from state troopers. We'll go over it as closely as possible. Might take a while."

Walled in by fear, Regi looked to Claudia. Her sister put an arm around her, and together they went inside.

As soon as Regi entered the bed-and-breakfast, she saw Wakanda sitting at the table chanting, which was never a good sign. Regi was tempted to tell the old woman the black moon she thought was over Romney and Tanner had moved to Regi, but the look in Wakanda's eyes said she already knew. Regi left her in the kitchen, heading to the attic to search for Earl's old knife.

"You really should change," Claudia said, trailing her up the stairs to the musty, dimly lit room. "You're fighting a cold, you're tired, and you've had a shock." Claudia caught her arm. "Reg, it will still be here after you take a bath and eat something."

Regi knew her sister was right. With great reluctance, she followed Claudia to the bathroom. Sitting on the rim of the iron-clawed tub, Regi struggled to pull off her hip waders as she watched Claudia drop herbal bath bags into the water. "You know I hate your bathing do-dahs."

"Helps your muscles relax." Claudia swished the bags around.

Regi tugged off her flannel shirt and peeled off her damp jeans. She had avoided talking in depth about the murder, which was a landslide hanging above her head just waiting to drop. Even though Regi was scared to death, she didn't want her older sister to know her fear. Claudia had been through a lot in the last while. She'd come to live with Regi to get away from memories of her husband's death and start a new life. Regi hated that now Claudia would be pulled smack-dab into the middle of a murder investigation along with her, for what affected Regi was bound to affect her sister.

Before Claudia left Regi alone to bathe, she paused at the door. "Reg, you know I believe you, but you have to tell me everything up front. Sounds like we're in for a siege, and I want to be as prepared as possible. I hate surprises."

Regi stopped undressing and looked up at her sister. "Thanks, Claud. That means a lot. I had the feeling outside that you had something you wanted to talk with me about. I mean, besides this mess I've landed us in?"

Claudia gazed at her for a moment then shrugged. "No, I'm worried about you, that's all."

"I will tell you everything as soon as I get out of the tub." A shiver bristled Regi's skin as if a ghost walked through her. "Then maybe we can look for that knife."

Claudia nodded and closed the door.

Regi stripped and eased into the steaming bath water, letting it swallow her up to her neck. She snagged the herbal bags, squeezed the bundles, and put them on the rim of the tub. The earthy scent of pine and grass reminded her of the river and the willows—and Romney's corpse.

Lifeless eyes staring.

To keep the haunting scene at bay, she whispered, "Please, Heavenly Father, I'm going to need Your help to find Earl's knife and get through the next few days. I promise not to lose my temper with anyone." Regi thought for a minute then added, "'Cept when it comes to Samuel Tanner, and I won't lose my temper. Nope, I'm going to get the truth out of him before he up and does a Houdini on me again and disappears without a trace." She had a nagging feeling he knew something about Romney's death. She just didn't know what. Though at times she'd felt the Lord had abandoned her today, she knew He hadn't. She had to keep the faith. With God's help, she knew she would find a way out of this mess.

Seeking escape from frayed nerves, Regi pinched her nose and slipped under the water.

Leaving Regi alone in the bathroom, Claudia sidestepped Oscar. The dog growled as she retreated down the stairs. She found it curious that in the six months she'd been living here, the beast was still uncomfortable around her. She had the same problem with Wakanda.

Or was it the other way around? *They* didn't have the problem. *She* had the problem. That was a disturbing thought, and Claudia didn't want to dwell on it.

As she crossed the reception area, she thought of Regi and this new dose of trouble they had to deal with.

Murder.

Did Claudia have it in her to stand by her sister's side and not say anything? Claudia couldn't afford to become embroiled in a police investigation. Questions would be asked. Too many questions that could lead the police to the secret Claudia had guarded so well, a secret she would do anything to protect. She'd proved that last night. She had worked very hard to keep the past hidden. Now, her nightmare was in danger of being exposed.

Hadn't Claudia been through enough grief? Regi too? They'd both lost their husbands. Life was continually throwing bombs in their paths. But this bomb . . . this bomb was nuclear. How was Claudia going to keep the truth from surfacing and yet save Regi? Their lives were not supposed to turn out this way.

When Regi and Claudia were little girls, they'd made up stories about what they wanted to be when they grew up. Claudia's dream was to marry a politician and have twelve children. She wanted a large family. Regi never wanted to marry. The word *children* hardly crossed her lips and never when it pertained to her. No, Regi's main ambition was to herd cattle over the Tetons every summer.

Claudia had married the politician, but the children never came. Regi married and had twins with the man she loved, and, fortunately, he owned a cattle ranch. Though, after Earl's death, Regi had been forced to sell the livestock, and her dreams of herding cattle over the Tetons had ceased.

As Claudia headed toward the kitchen, she worried how their parents and Regi's children were going to take this news. Fifteen years ago, her parents, Jacob and Edie Priest, had moved to Canada. Father was a doomsday believer, always planning for the end of the world. Mom went along with him, supporting her man. Claudia was envious of the love they shared. Her parents rarely left the Canadian mountains to visit, and when they did, they were in a hurry to return home, never staying more than three days. Chances of their parents learning about the murder were slim at best. Claudia worried more about Jack and Lisa, Regi's children, finding out.

Richmond College was only two hundred miles away. The twins would likely hear something, especially if this little murder investigation turned its ugly head toward Claudia, the late congressman's wife.

Claudia didn't know if she could speak with news reporters again. Not after all that had happened.

The hot water helped soothe Regi's aching muscles and tempered her sore throat a little. But even the bath could not shake the chill-of-a-grave feeling that pulled at her. Plus, she was haunted by the fact that she had forgotten Earl had owned such a knife.

After her bath, she tugged on a long-sleeved turtleneck sweater, leggings, and a pair of wooly socks, trying to chase away the frigidness seeping back into her bones. She soon realized her efforts were pointless. The chilling sensation coursed in her veins. Once dressed, Regi dried her honey-colored hair, streaked with strands of white, and braided it into one long braid again. Now she had to deal with her sister.

If she told Claudia and Wakanda exactly what had happened this morning, maybe the chill in her blood would leave. Anxious to get it over, and with Oscar by her side, Regi headed downstairs.

She found Claudia checking in two couples dressed in new Eddie Bauer clothes they'd probably purchased especially for their vacation. The women were tall, slender, and looked as if their most serious worries were what hairstyles were fashionable. The guys appeared to be stockbroker or banker types, with chins tilted a tad higher than regular folks.

Claudia's gaze caught Regi's as she passed the registration desk. "This is my sister and partner, Regina Bernard. Regi, these are the Steinfelds and Mattiases from New York." Regi forced a smile then glanced at her sister and nodded toward the kitchen.

Claudia handed the keys to the guests and explained the Raindancer's rules and routine.

Grateful to leave them in Claudia's care, Regi pushed open the kitchen's swinging doors. Oscar went straight to his corner where a sheepskin doggy bed waited. He circled twice then settled down quickly, resting his snout on his front paws.

Braiding some type of animal hair, Wakanda sat at the pedestal dining table, clad in threadbare jeans, moccasins, and a black sweatshirt with ragged cuffs. Regi had given Wakanda new clothes countless times, but she hardly ever saw her wear them. They mysteriously disappeared.

"What are you working on?" Regi asked the woman, noticing the steaming teapot on the stove. Grabbing the cocoa can and a mug from the cupboard, Regi mixed powder with the hot water in her cup. She opened the bread bin, hopeful to find a leftover muffin and instead found homemade, whole wheat bread. She grabbed the loaf and began searching for the bread knife when she realized Wakanda hadn't answered. Regi stopped and turned around.

The woman's long, scarred face emphasized her accusing I-told-you-so eyes, although Wakanda's nimble fingers kept braiding the thin band of hair.

"What did I do?" Regi reared back.

"Shadow bundles rope your being. I asked the wind to send guardians for you."

"With your guardians and God's help, things should work out." Regi continued to search for the stray bread knife.

Claudia pushed through the doors. "The Steinfelds and Mattiases are staying a couple of days. I didn't want them to think we served dinner, so I emphasized that we only do breakfast. They seemed okay with that."

"Great." Regi found the knife in the dishwasher. For a second, it took on the appearance of the bloody knife. She blinked and rubbed her eyes. Pushing the murky image from her thoughts, she busied herself sawing off a one-inch slice of bread and slathering it with honey butter.

Claudia pulled a chair out for Regi, pointed to the seat, and then sat across the table. "Okay, time to tell us what's going on."

Regi eased onto her appointed chair, careful not to spill her cocoa. Taking a big bite of bread, and between chews, she told them of her hair-raising day and how each event had led to a bigger one. By the time she finished, she'd eaten another slice of bread and started to reach for more, when her sister put what was left away.

"Regi, I don't know what to say, except that I'm sorry. It must have been an awful shock for you, finding Curtis dead like that. Then I didn't help matters by saying the knife looked like Earl's."

"Don't feel bad about telling the truth." She didn't want Claudia fretting over what she'd said. "But we do need to find Earl's knife."

Claudia grew still. Regi knew the ordeal of discovering her husband dead in her living room had to weigh heavy on Claudia's mind right now. Claudia brushed a hair from her face. "It's frightening to think there's a murderer lurking in Trailhead. I mean, in this little town where everybody knows everyone, things like this don't happen. It's very disconcerting."

Regi knew that wasn't a stretch for her sister. Claudia had been very disconcerted almost every day since she'd moved to Trailhead. She was a hard worker, and Regi knew her older sister would do anything for her, but Claudia was a snob, and if truth be told, a wimp to boot. If a garter snake slithered from under a rock, she'd faint.

If anything was disconcerting to Regi, it was Claudia's late husband. Morris Osborne had put on a great performance for the people of Idaho, but something about the man had never set well with Regi. He had been good-looking, charming, and all that, but for some reason she could not put into words, she had never trusted the man.

"Regi?" Claudia said.

"What?" She had to keep her mind on track. Why in the world was she thinking of Claudia's dead husband at a time like this? Overload. Her brain was on overload.

Claudia picked up Regi's empty cup and placed it in the sink. "I asked you if you knew of anyone who would want to kill Curtis, other than yourself."

Regi's guard rose. "Hey, you said you believed me."

At that moment, a voice from the dining room called out, "Is anyone here?"

Regi didn't recognize the voice. She looked at Wakanda and then Claudia.

Her sister gave a knowing nod. "That's Mrs. Steinfeld." Claudia headed toward the door.

"How do you know? Could be Mrs. Mattiase?"

"Steinfeld has a nasal tone in her voice." Claudia paused. "And don't think I'm going to forget what we were talking about. I'll be back in a second." She pushed through the swinging doors.

Regi remembered that even when they were kids Claudia had an uncanny talent for recognizing voices. Came in handy before phones had caller ID. If Claudia answered first, she could warn Regi of who was calling before she picked up the phone. Regi sipped her cocoa as she remembered happier times with her sister.

All at once, Claudia was back. "She wanted extra towels." She looked at Regi then picked up their conversation as if nothing had happened. "Of course, I believe you're innocent, but last spring after Curtis and Lisa split up and you learned of the lies he was telling, I thought you were going to hunt him down and beat him to a pulp." Claudia pulled a casserole dish of lasagna out of the fridge, setting it on the counter. Then she turned on the convection oven. "I'm afraid other people who know you but don't know the soft side of you . . . well, I'm afraid they may think you actually killed Curtis, especially if word leaks out about the knife."

Regi's memory turned to last spring and the encounter she'd had with Romney at the Trailhead Ranger Station. "The entire park service knew I was upset with him."

"What did you say?" Claudia had been staring at the oven's little red light. As though forgetting she needed to wait until the light went out, Claudia put the lasagna in the oven and turned her full attention to Regi. "Why on earth would the entire park service know?"

The kitchen became stiflingly hot. Regi pulled at her turtleneck collar as she glanced around at the shining cherrywood cupboards and the modern touches Claudia had placed about: sleek chrome salt and pepper shakers, the clock with lines for numbers, and a basket of spiraling twigs that cost way too much when they could have collected some very similar weeds out in the field. Her sister liked things smooth and uncluttered, except for the twigs.

Claudia'd never understand how someone could let their temper get the best of them. How could she? The woman never became outright mad at anyone. She might become upset, but to be truly vindictive was not in her.

Unable to think of a way around the subject, Regi gave in. "Last April I stormed into Romney's office and told him he was a no-good jerk. As I recall, when I left, the rangers surged out of Superintendent Elliott's office like a river bursting its bank. Some type of rezoning meeting had been going on. I continued to tell them what I thought of their rezoning and where they could store it. Then I left."

Claudia turned her crestfallen face away from Regi. She picked up square place mats, stoneware dishes, and clear beverage glasses, setting them on the table. Claudia eased into her chair. Taking a deep breath, she said, "Spill the rest of it."

Shaking her head, Regi said, "Can't hide anything from you, can I?"

Claudia stared at her. No emotion.

"A little thing, really. Not even worth bringing up." Regi cleared her scratchy throat before going on. "I'm sure the rangers had a good laugh."

Claudia folded her arms and gave her *the look*. No escaping that *fess-up* expression: left squinty eye and flat-lined lips. Wakanda kept braiding, but Regi knew she was intently listening.

Resigned to her fate, Regi said, "What I did is really pretty funny. I'm sure you'll get a good chuckle. See . . ." Regi bit at her quivering lower lip. The memory of Lisa crying on her shoulder, saying that she'd been tempted, yet she'd kept her virtue intact, and she didn't understand why Curtis—who claimed he'd loved her—would lie. Her daughter's sobs had torn apart Regi's heart.

She pushed her thoughts aside. "Well, Claud, as I left the station, I saw his four-by-four truck with its fancy wheels, and I had to do something, so I flattened his tires and left." Regi'd said it all in one breath and now inhaled deeply.

Claudia rubbed her forehead. "While you were at it, why didn't you leave a dead chicken on his front seat?" She nervously swiped her fine blond hair away from her eyes.

"I probably would have if I'd thought of it." Regi smiled.

Claudia pursed her lips as if gathering patience. "Does Sheriff Morgan know about this?"

Regi remembered Morgan had visited the ranch the next morning. He'd told her Romney had filed a complaint, but Morgan had told Romney he probably got off lucky because if it had been his daughter that Curtis had lied about, he would have found himself working in a national park somewhere in the Arctic. Morgan had influence where it counted. And if Romney had pressed charges against Regi, the kid still might have found himself hunting polar bears. But Morgan had also warned Regi to stay away from Romney. And she had, until yesterday. "Morgan knows."

"No wonder he looked so grim when he left. Poor Thomas has such a burden with his wife's illness and being sheriff. I don't know how he does it." Claudia finished setting the table. Regi knew her sister would always love Thomas Morgan. They would have married if Claudia hadn't met Morris. And the odd thing was that since Claudia had returned to Trailhead, she'd become good friends with Hannah.

"Morgan mentioned Hannah wasn't doing well. I'm concerned about her." Again, Regi worried for her friend but didn't know what to do. The tickle in her throat grew worse; sniffles set in. Wiping her nose, she added, "Hannah's one of my closest friends. Morgan's personal life must be horrible, having to watch her go downhill and not being able to do anything about it."

Claudia grabbed a pitcher and filled it with water from the tap. Setting it on the table, she said, "You should know. You had to watch Earl suffer. Makes one wonder if there's something in the water around here."

Regi didn't want to remember those dreadful days. "Look, Morgan has his hands full. He's the only policeman who lives in the area, and he's the only one who knows I wouldn't kill Romney." She didn't mention that the state troopers and park rangers who had questioned her at the county nurse's had accusing eyes.

"But when people learn that the knife that killed Romney was found in my Jeep, I don't think Morgan can keep the authorities from arresting me." Regi didn't add that she'd had a tiff with Romney at Twiggs. That would only make Claudia worry more. Glancing at Wakanda, Regi caught the *tell her everything* stare. But she ignored her old friend.

Claudia reached across the table and patted Regi's hand. "It will be all right. Thomas will take care of it. You need to be patient and wait this out."

The burden of proving her innocence was more than a one-person job. And Regi was not going to sit around the bed-and-breakfast waiting for the state troopers to come knocking on her door.

Wakanda rose. With the finished braid in her hand, she walked behind Regi. Looping the hair around Regi's neck, she said, "Buffalo hair guards against shadow bundles." She tied it snugly. Regi felt honored her friend would give her such a thoughtful gift.

"Thanks. I don't know what I'd do without you two." Regi grabbed her friend's hand and patted it. Then she hugged her sister. And even though Claudia's wise words to be patient and wait were right, Regi knew she had to do something. She needed to investigate on her own. No way would she sit this out. She'd start tomorrow.

But she couldn't let Wakanda and Claudia know what she was planning, or they'd both have a royal conniption. Best to placate and make them feel as though she were leaning on them and that she was going to do exactly as Morgan had asked her to.

"After dinner, let's have a go at finding the knife in the attic," Claudia said as she pulled the lasagna out of the convection oven and placed it on a trivet in the center of the table. Regi nodded and watched as Wakanda and Claudia lifted up their plates.

Claudia took Regi's dish and gave her some food. Regi nodded thanks, even though her stomach had seized up tighter than a square knot. Taking a bite, she thought of Earl's knife. She was determined to find it tonight. Then tomorrow Regi planned to do some snooping around Trailhead.

FIVE
MISGIVINGS

THE NEXT MORNING WHEN SAMUEL Tanner walked into Morgan's office, he found his friend behind a large wooden desk with several opened paper bags before him. He was madly writing on a form and didn't look up. On the wall behind Morgan hung a gray, depressing picture of a lawman in the old west riding his horse in the pouring rain while leading two prisoners to jail. It mirrored the thankless job Morgan had dedicated his life to.

The sheriff looked up, blurry eyed. "What brings you to my office this early in the morning?" He rose and walked around to the front of his desk.

"Hunting season is starting. Thought you might want some help again." Samuel plopped down on a chair and pulled out a matchstick to chew on.

"Can't use you."

This was not what Samuel had expected. Morgan always called on him for help. "What do you mean?"

"I'm investigating a murder." Morgan folded his arms and leaned against his desk.

"Yeah, about that." Samuel needed to find out all he could—and what better way than to ply his friend with questions? "Don't you think Regi's getting too involved in this?"

"With good reason." Morgan tilted his head, watching Samuel a little too closely.

"What do you mean?"

"Found Romney's body at the county nurse's." Morgan rubbed his chin. "He'd been stabbed in the neck. At first I thought he might have been killed by poachers, but then when what looks like the murder weapon turned up in Regi's Jeep and she claimed it was your knife . . . well . . ."

"What!?" Samuel nearly swallowed the matchstick. "She said the knife was mine?"

"Said she saw your knife on the counter at Twiggs the day before yesterday. Stew confirmed that you'd lent it to him to work on the spray nozzle and that he'd left it on the countertop. He figured you'd picked it up when it was gone."

Samuel rubbed the back of his neck. "To tell you the truth, I forgot all about it. Someone else must have taken it." Samuel had a sinking feeling his life was about to become very complicated. Morgan stared at Samuel as though gauging his reaction. Samuel had to say something. "So you've run DNA tests on the blood on the knife and matched it to Romney's?"

"Working on it, but I'm pretty certain it's a match."

Samuel felt as though a noose was tightening around his neck.

"I strongly suggest you find your knife." The sheriff meant business.

"You're looking at me as a suspect?" Samuel couldn't believe this.

"I can't rule you out, just like I can't rule out Regi." Morgan folded his arms again.

"Half the guys in Trailhead have had a pocketknife like mine at some time in their lives." Samuel clenched his teeth on the matchstick.

"Half the guys in Trailhead weren't in the vicinity where the body was seen." Morgan stared at him.

"I wasn't near Karen Wilson's."

"Regi saw Romney on your property before he ended up at Wilson's."

"Come on, Morgan. If I'd killed the guy, I wouldn't have left him on my property."

"Which is why you moved him."

"You seriously think I did this?" Samuel stared at Morgan. The sheriff's expression remained unchanged. Samuel continued. "Half the people in Trailhead must have been in and out of Twiggs the other day. Anyone could have taken my knife." Right now, even Samuel felt his argument grow weak.

Morgan drew a deep breath. "You'd best find it, my friend." He paused a moment. "You're right, though, about that kind of knife being popular. Claudia even said Earl had one. I imagine Regi is tearing her house apart looking for it. Would set my mind at ease if I could account for both of your knives. Plus, then there won't be any more finger pointing between you two." He scrubbed his hand over his face. "Just what I need, a murder investigation in the middle of poaching season, I mean, hunting season." Morgan walked to a table and picked up a banana and a raspberry yogurt. "Breakfast. Want some?"

Samuel shook his head. He was far from hungry. He wasn't used to Morgan grilling him.

The sheriff sat down at his desk. He peeled the banana and took a bite. "Going to need you to stay as far away from this investigation as possible, so I can't use your help with poachers this year."

"The hunters are already causing trouble. Found a dead cow yesterday just before I found you and Regi wading in the river searching for Romney. Can't afford to have too many hunters mistaking my cattle for elk." Samuel paused a moment. "I'll tell you what. I catch a hunter on my property, I'll hold him until you show up." All sorts of hunters went to the woods outside the park to bag themselves a deer or an elk. The rangers took care of most of the poachers, but some hunters tried to get away and spilled into Morgan's jurisdiction.

"No! Call me or the park rangers, but don't take the law in your own hands. Got that?" Morgan once again had that serious glint in his eyes.

"You're treating me like a suspect instead of a friend."

Morgan gave a deep sigh. "Well, if luck is on my side, maybe I can wrap this case up quickly and things can get back to normal."

"Wish I could help." Samuel meant it.

Morgan paused a moment. "Me too."

Samuel changed the subject. "What's in the sacks?"

"Evidence." Morgan pointed at one. "This has a sample of blood-soaked soil. Taken from your place, I might add." He then pointed to the other one. "And this has the knife."

"Well, I can prove right now if it was mine or not." Samuel reached for the bag.

Morgan blocked him. "Not a good idea. Besides, it's covered with blood."

"Were you able to lift any fingerprints?" Samuel asked while nervously pulling at his eyebrow. "If the knife is mine, somebody else's prints will be on it, as well, which would clear me and Regi."

Morgan's eyes widened. "After all these years, I find it very interesting you're still worried about Regi. You need to look out for yourself." He stared at Samuel.

Samuel countered, "What? I didn't kill Curtis Romney."

"I'll make a note of that." Morgan smiled a little as though to ease the tension.

Trying to switch the topic again, Samuel gazed at the bags. "Why use paper bags when you could use plastic?" He had seen cop shows on TV. They used what looked like freezer bags.

"Old fashioned, I guess." The sheriff shrugged. "As for lifting prints from the weapon, it will take someone with fancier equipment than I have. Just putting it in the bag could have ruined the prints. Though with new technology, I'm hoping they can find something. I don't want anything or anyone, including myself, to screw this up. Too many lives could be ruined." Morgan glanced at the bags and then at the form he had been filling out.

Samuel chewed the matchstick, wondering if he should continue to ply Morgan with questions. He had to. "Think people will believe Regi had anything to do with Romney's death?"

The worried expression returned to Morgan's face. "When they hear the knife was found behind the driver's seat of Regi's Jeep, yeah, I think they'll believe she did it."

"Someone is doing a darn good job of framing her," Samuel said.

"Add to that the fact that she was the only one who saw Romney at the river and the plot thickens." Morgan rubbed his chin. "And there are witnesses who saw her at Jed's, soaking wet after her discovery."

"But the body wasn't at the river, so that might help."

The sheriff shrugged. "There will be those who think she took him to Karen's before she came to find me."

Shaking his head, Samuel added, "Come on. People are not going to believe she could heft a dead body by herself."

Morgan rubbed his chin. "We are talking about Regi, right? I've seen that woman wrestle a steer to its knees. She can do anything she sets her mind to."

"True." Samuel tried to think of another explanation. "But even if that's the case, why would she haul you out to the river?"

"To cast blame on someone else." Morgan leaned back in his chair, his attention entirely on his friend. He took another bite of his banana. After swallowing, he said, "You two have been arguing for years, though you've never accused each other of murder before."

Samuel didn't know what to say. Morgan was right. The squabbles between him and Regi were public knowledge and fodder for Trailhead's gossip mill, and Samuel's aunt was president of the club.

"Relax, buddy." Morgan set his banana down. "Once you produce the knife, you'll be off the hook. I confiscated Regi's Jeep, hoping that once she finds Earl's knife and the Jeep proves clean of any other incriminating evidence, she'll be off the hook as well." He shook his head.

"That's a relief. After hearing her threaten Romney yesterday outside of Twiggs, I . . ."

"What?" A big scowl shadowed Morgan's already grim face. "You told me they argued, not that she'd threatened him."

Wanting to explain further, Samuel said, "Romney was hassling Wakanda, and Regi, being Regi, told the kid if he didn't knock it off, she'd make his life miserable."

Morgan rubbed his eyes. "That's perfect. And you heard this?"

Samuel nodded.

The sheriff looked at the evidence bags again then crumpled up the forms.

"What are you doing?"

"I'm going to deliver these in person." Morgan threw the balled-up papers in the garbage. "If someone else heard her too, well, I can't afford to have something go wrong."

"You're going to take the time to drive all the way to Boise?"

"No. Need to stick around today." He rubbed the side of his head as though he had a headache. "Thought I'd go back and talk with Romney's widow again, give my condolences to Elliott, and see exactly what's going on at that house." He opened the small safe next to his desk where Samuel knew the sheriff stored confiscated property from people he'd put in jail. He placed the bags inside, locked it, and shoved the keys in his pocket. "I'll take the evidence to Bounty Falls tomorrow. Maybe their crime lab there can run some tests, but if not, there's a bigger criminal investigation unit in Monticello. Hopefully the folks there can help me so I don't have to send it to Boise. Like it or not, a storm's brewing. As careful as I've been, I can feel trouble all the way down to my tailbone. A lot of good people could get hurt."

"Let me know if I can help you out, at least with the poachers."

Morgan got up and grabbed his Stetson, tugging it on his bald head. "Like I said, stay away from this investigation."

"You're the boss." Samuel felt sorry for his overworked, underpaid friend. He knew Morgan was near out of his mind with worry for his wife. "How's Hannah today?"

"Worse. While I'm in Bounty Falls, I think I'll have a chat with her doctor." Morgan started for the door and stopped. "Whatever you do, stay away from Regi. We don't need any more flare-ups between you two."

"You got it." Samuel followed his friend outside. As they parted ways, he couldn't help but think of Regi and the trouble boiling around her. Somehow Samuel had to find a way to help her and keep himself out of the quicksand at the same time.

When Regi awoke, she had a pounding sinus headache, a three-alarm sore throat, and a mild fever. She'd stayed up half the night tearing through the boxes in the attic. Still, she couldn't find Earl's knife. But she wouldn't let her lack of sleep or her aching muscles stop her from doing her daily chores. She wanted to make up for taking off yesterday and landing them in this sorry fix. To convince her older sister that she was going to do what Morgan had said and stick around the ranch, Regi made sure she was at Claudia's beck and call, doing dishes, answering the phone, and changing sheets.

Finally in the afternoon as soon as Regi completed the chores, she downed a couple of aspirins, grabbed the tissue box, and headed upstairs on the pretense of taking a nap, making certain Claudia watched her go to her room. But instead of lying down, Regi tugged on her work boots, grabbed her sheepskin jacket and lucky cowboy hat—with the red-tailed hawk feather tucked in the band—and tiptoed downstairs. No sign of her sister. She had to be in the kitchen.

An eerie quiet befell the Raindancer. The New Yorkers had gone sight-seeing. These were the in-between hours, the time just after guests left for the day and before new guests checked in.

Regi steered clear of the kitchen and used the front door. Frosty crystals hung on the trees and in the air. Yesterday's skiff of snow still covered the ground. It crunched beneath her boots.

Bending over so no one could see the top of her head from the bay window in the reception area, Regi sprinted across the front lawn, down the small slope around the house, and toward the barn. Oscar raced across the yard to join her. Earlier, when Regi had been cleaning, she'd put the dog out, and he had taken off for adventure. Now he was back and ready for fun. She gave him a pat as she came to a stop at the barn.

She kept a watchful eye on the back exit of the Raindancer as she pushed up the heavy wooden plank that locked the double tongue-and-groove doors. Leaning the plank against the wall, she and the dog slipped inside.

"Just as I suspected." A condemning voice filled the cavernous barn and stopped Regi in midmotion. Squinting, she spied Claudia in the front passenger seat of Earl's old Jeep, all dolled up in her pink parka.

She drilled her long fingers on the dash. "Where do you think you're going?"

Regi could either waste time reasoning with her sister or she could prepare to leave. "Since you seem to know everything, why don't *you* tell me?" Not standing still for the dressing-down that would follow, Regi swung open the barn doors, allowing light to illuminate the rafters. The barn was Regi's pride and joy, along with the only two horses she had left.

This morning she had led her mare, Dusty, and her gelding, Copper, from the barn to the pasture so they could graze on tufts of grass poking through the snow. Regi had cleaned their stalls and even laid fresh hay in their feeding troughs for the coming night in case she'd be late returning. She kept the barn as organized as Claudia kept her kitchen.

There was winter hay neatly stacked in the south end. At the north end, there were bunk and tack rooms. When the ranch was in its prime, the bunk room was used by seasonal cowpokes. Now only Wakanda occasionally stayed there. Regi worked hard to keep the tack room orderly. She kept her saddles oiled and bridles and halters in prime condition. Guests of the Raindancer were not allowed in unaccompanied.

Regi gazed at Gypsy's empty stall as she passed and fought a pang of guilt. Every year since Earl had died, she'd lost a little more of her old life, and now because of Curtis Romney, she might lose it all.

Spirited on by a sideswipe of fear, Regi made her way past a small tractor, the snowmobile, and the welder until she stopped at the storage bin. She lugged out the heavy canvas top to Earl's old Jeep and carried it to the vehicle.

"You're not going to poke your nose into the sheriff's investigation, are you?" Claudia glared.

"What do you think?" Regi started to throw the canvas on top of the vehicle.

Claudia jumped out and stomped around to the front. "I know you don't listen to me, but Thomas? His instructions were quite clear. He said to stay put."

Oscar growled at Claudia.

"Knock it off," Regi said to the Irish setter. The dog looked up at her as if to say, *only trying to help.* "Go lie down." Regi motioned for him to leave. Oscar defiantly leaped up on a bale of hay and settled where he could keep an eye on them.

Returning her attention to her sister, Regi said, "I *was* listening and not only to Morgan. While you and I and Wakanda talked last night, I realized Morgan is overworked, his wife has been struck with a debilitating disease, and although I know he's going to run his tail off trying to solve this case, he doesn't have the manpower to do it. We're talking my life here, Claudia, real life, where an accused person is not always thought innocent until proven guilty. I've got to do something before this thing blows out of proportion and the entire countryside thinks I'm a killer."

Claudia leaned against the front bumper. "Speaking of people knowing, I'm concerned about the twins. Don't you think you should call Jack and Lisa? If they hear this news from someone else, they'll never forgive you."

Regi's children were always uppermost in her mind. "Thought I'd wait a day or so. The less they know, the better. They'd only worry. Besides, how does a mother tell her children she's being investigated for the murder of her daughter's ex-boyfriend? You do see my problem, don't you?"

Claudia slowly nodded. "Your kids have been through a lot. But you underestimate them. Besides, don't you think Lisa's friends will call her as soon as they hear what's happened?"

Regi tugged the canvas more squarely on top of the Jeep and started to latch it into place. "Hopefully I can get this solved today before that happens."

Claudia helped by climbing up on the vehicle's hood and fastening the top above the windshield. "I'll let you go on one condition."

The word *let* struck Regi as rather odd. Her sister was never one she'd worried about gaining permission from. Regi may have to sneak around Claudia to avoid confrontation, but she'd never seek permission. She chuckled and said, "What's that?"

"I want to help," Claudia replied. Regi knew Claudia could be tough when she needed to be, but she'd already been through so much with the death of her husband. She'd handled the press very well during that horrible time. But Regi wanted to keep her out of the spotlight. Why drag her sister through the dirt with her?

"To know you're in charge at the Raindancer will set my mind at ease. Taking care of this place by yourself is a big enough burden." Regi smiled at Claudia as she fastened the last latch.

"No." Claudia jumped off the Jeep. "No guests are checking in until tomorrow. The others have gone out for the day. Wakanda mentioned she'd be by later. She gets hungry around three, so I'll promise her dinner and ask her to stay. Though she gives a bad first impression, she can keep an eye on the place and we won't have to lock up. I have to do something to help you." Claudia grabbed Regi's arm. "Remember, we're partners. I can do this."

Regi couldn't deny she needed help checking out a few hunches, and there was simply no one else to turn to. If they could somehow straighten out this whole mess before she had to call her kids, it would be well worth getting her sister involved. With great reluctance, Regi agreed.

"Where do we begin?" Claudia went to the passenger side.

"There are two places I wanted to check. I should pay my respects to Romney's widow, and while I'm there, I'll see if she knows what Romney was up to the other night. Then I thought I'd head over to Samuel Tanner's."

Claudia had opened the door and was about to climb in but stopped. "Don't you think it would be rather awkward to meet with Romney's widow, being as he broke up with your Lisa to marry her?"

"Yeah." Regi knew that better than anyone. "But I know Romney was up to something, and his widow may be the only one who would tell me. The rangers and Elliott wouldn't."

"You're probably the last person Melissa would talk to. Let me go alone." Without getting into the Jeep, Claudia closed the vehicle's door and walked around to stand in front of Regi. "While I'm there with her, you can go see Samuel."

Knowing she'd have to face Tanner again made Regi's insides feel as though a bobcat had clawed the lining of her stomach. She really had no choice, just as she had no choice but to let Claudia go alone to meet Romney's widow. Desperate times called for desperate measures. The trite saying wasn't enough for what she felt right now. No, the saying should be *desperate times call for frantic, fly-by-the-seat-of-your-pants measures.*

"As much as I hate the idea, you're right. You go talk with Melissa. Be careful and keep an eye out for her father. They live with him, you know. He has an office at the ranger's station, but Superintendent Elliott runs much of the park's business from his home. Whatever you do, don't let him corner you. And if he happens to bring up the run-in I had with Romney the other day, well, tell him—"

"What run-in?" Claudia's face pinched with worry.

"Nothing really, a little misunderstanding about some garbage and Wakanda. Didn't I mention it to you?" Regi avoided eye contact with her sister and crawled into the Jeep.

"I don't think so, but there's been a lot going on. Don't worry, I can handle the superintendent." Claudia swept her gaze over Regi's clothes from the feather in her cowboy hat to her work boots. She pursed her lips together and then sighed.

"Now what?" Regi huffed.

"If you're going to Samuel's, you might think about changing. Make some type of effort to look nice. Whether you're willing to admit it or not, for some reason the man still has feelings for you."

Regi guffawed. "You know better than anyone that he can't be trusted. I cried on your shoulder after he left. And then what he did to Earl and me over the land . . ."

"Regi." Claudia pulled her hair behind her ears. "Did you ever think he did all that to annoy you? And that maybe he was taking out frustration on Earl because he married the girl who got away?"

"What?"

"Think about it. I'm sure Earl realized it." Claudia looked at Regi as if expecting an "ah-ha" moment.

"Earl would have said something to me. 'The girl that got away!' You're really going to play that angle?" Regi couldn't believe her sister would think such a thing.

"I'm just saying, after all this time, can't you find it in your heart to forgive him?"

"Nope!" Regi gazed out the barn doors, wishing she were somewhere else and not talking about the past that still stung as though it were yesterday. "Tanner's a liar, and once a liar, always a liar! He's proven that. Besides, Claud, you haven't had a man betray you like that." Regi glanced at Claudia. For a second, she thought she saw her sister flinch, but then she seemed to be herself again. "Tanner and I have spent the past few years picking fights with each other. There's no way—"

"Even so, Regina, he likes you . . . a lot."

"You've been drinking some of Wakanda's potion, haven't you?"

Regi's accusation didn't stop Claudia. "The man has tried countless times to talk to you. He's gone out of his way to help you—us—really. And why? There's only one answer, and you know it as well as I do. Think it over, sis." Claudia turned about and started for the barn door. The pink fur trim of her parka hugged her neck. She said over her shoulder, "I'm going in to make something to take to Melissa Romney."

Claudia was wrong about Tanner. Warm anger inched up Regi's spine as she thought of old wounds, and then she remembered what Morgan had said as he'd tried to calm her down at the river yesterday. He had told her Tanner had bought her land to help her. At the time, Regi thought Morgan was merely saying those things to keep her from taking a punch at the man.

But now . . .

Could Claudia be right? Could Samuel Tanner still have feelings for her? After all, he had bribed her to go out with him. Hmmm. Well, even if he did, she had gotten over Tanner long ago. Her marriage to Earl proved that.

Yet, if Tanner had old feelings for her, maybe she could use this to her advantage. Regi glanced down at her work-worn jeans and scruffy cowboy boots then looked over at Oscar. The dog sat up, ready to do her bidding. "Couldn't hurt to change clothes, could it?"

The Irish setter jumped off the hay bale and headed for the door. Regi followed. Walking back to the house, she continued to think about Samuel Tanner and that night so long ago when she'd waited and waited for him to pick her up. At first she'd worried that he'd been in an accident. She hadn't realized the truth until the next morning.

She'd learned a good lesson that day. She would never trust Samuel Tanner again. She thought of yesterday and how he'd stared down on her as he sat smugly on his horse. His eyes were as black as Satan's heart, and she shivered at the thought of getting too close to him.

Samuel Tanner was only interested in himself. But would he frame Regi for the murder of Curtis Romney? She thought of the knife—the pearl-handled pocketknife. Samuel had one and so had Earl. For the life of her, Regi couldn't remember what she'd done with it. Earl hadn't used it often, and she was surprised Claudia remembered he'd owned one. He must have used it when her sister and Morris were visiting long ago.

Regi scratched her neck. Her fingers touched the braided buffalo-hair necklace Wakanda had given her. At the time, Regi'd tolerated the woman's act of kindness, never believing in such nonsense. Now the necklace reminded Regi to say another prayer before heading over to Tanner's.

How she wished she could feel the Lord's help through this nightmare. Maybe she should call the new bishop and ask him for a blessing? Though, what kind of impression would she make, asking for a blessing to guide her to find a killer? He'd think she was some nutcase. No, it was best to keep this between her and the Lord for now. She hoped her faith in His guiding hand would give her the peace she needed to get through what lay ahead.

Claudia sat on the edge of the camel-backed couch, waiting for Melissa Romney to regain her composure. All Claudia had said to start the crying siege was "hello." She'd added how sorry she was to hear about Curtis's death, but the young woman would not be consoled. Melissa's reddened plump cheeks reminded Claudia of a tubby chipmunk's. The girl had a needle nose, and her thin-lipped mouth even came to somewhat of a point. Her feminine sobs were squeaks and sniffles.

The girl finally blew her nose in an already dampened tissue. "The sheriff just left. He's so thoughtful to come over to see how I'm doing. I miss my sister, Miranda. She's a photo journalist, you know. I spoke with her earlier. She's in China right now but will try to come to the funeral." The young woman glanced at Claudia. A faint smile of gratitude came to her lips. "It's so nice of you to visit, Ms. Osborne. You're kind of famous because your husband was a congressman and all. That you would take the time to come see me, especially since your niece and Curtis . . . Anyway your being here means a lot. Curtis's death has been a great shock."

Claudia knew firsthand how startling the sudden death of a loved one could be. She placed her hand on Melissa's shoulder. "I wanted you to know you're not alone."

Melissa patted her hand. "We do have something in common, don't we?"

Claudia hugged the young woman. "Sadly, we do. But you know, as I think about the days leading up to my husband's death, I realized there were signs that he wasn't feeling well. He suffered more headaches and wasn't quite himself. I know Curtis didn't have a heart attack, but did he say anything to you the night before? Was he worried over something?"

Melissa blinked cloudy-eyed at Claudia. Her brows bunched into a knot. "I don't know."

Claudia didn't want to press, but she was desperate for information. "Did he say anything about meeting someone?"

"He is always meeting people." Melissa spoke as if he were still alive. "But he never tells me who. Curtis has been so upset lately. He's hardly ever home; sometimes he stays out all night, and when he's home . . ." The new widow closed her eyelids tightly. "When he *was* home . . . he was mad." She opened her small, beady eyes, now filled with worry and . . . something else. Anger?

"Was he upset about work?"

"Dealing with poachers is upsetting, but I don't know. He seemed preoccupied. The thing is, before we were married, Daddy had him running errands all over. But after we moved in here, he didn't use Curtis as an errand boy anymore." A new storm of tears spilled down her plump, flushed cheeks.

So Romney had been dealing with poachers. Plus, he was mad all the time. Odd for a newlywed. Claudia needed more answers, but with the girl crying, she didn't have the heart. Melissa had been taken in by Romney's charms, just as Regi's Lisa had been. No more questions today. Melissa's grief was too fresh.

A new thought came to Claudia. Could Curtis have come upon a poacher on the river? He was on Samuel Tanner's land, though, not the park's. Still, he could have followed a poacher to Samuel's. It made perfect sense and might take the investigation away from Regi. Claudia decided to mention this to the sheriff in case he hadn't thought of it himself.

She stood. "Melissa, I'll drop by in a couple of days with more crumb muffins. You take care."

Melissa managed a glimmer of a smile and stood to show Claudia out. Understanding that the girl was having a hard time not sobbing, Claudia said, "I can find my way. Don't worry about me."

"Thanks." Melissa quickly left through the dining room, bravely making an attempt to hold back tears.

Claudia knew exactly how Melissa felt. Not a day went by that she didn't grieve for the husband she thought she'd known. But the reality of who he really was shadowed the memory.

She could not dwell on her sorrow. Not when so much was at stake. With head held high, Claudia left the living room, walking toward the front door. As she approached the exit, she heard voices coming from Superintendent Elliott's den nearby. Regi had warned her to steer clear of this man.

The door was slightly ajar. Despite strong misgivings, Claudia tiptoed closer and strained to hear.

"Not many people know this, but the park may soon get permission from Congress to sell parcels of land. That land is worth a fair chunk of change. It will be sold by auction. For those smart enough to manipulate the system, they stand to make a small fortune. So, let's keep a lid on it."

That was Elliott's voice.

Claudia wanted to see with whom he was talking. As she tried to peer through the crack, the door suddenly swung open. A surprised and disgruntled Superintendent Cameron Elliott stood before her.

SIX

DETERMINATION

AT FIVE O'CLOCK, REGI PULLED HER Jeep into Tanner's place. Gazing out the windshield, she saw the sky flamed with brilliant pinks and oranges. Tall pines silhouetted in shadows stood in a long line as a windbreak.

She'd never been to Tanner's before, had never had a good enough reason to visit. Tanner had built his two-story southern mansion shortly after he'd returned from Alaska and purchased the land. Rumor was he'd built the house for a woman he'd met while working on an Alaskan fishing boat. But she never came.

Oh, that's a big surprise. He probably left her in the middle of the night too.

Regi could hardly believe it, but she was now glad that a few days ago Tanner had manipulated her into agreeing to go out with him. She would use this to her advantage and on her terms: where no one could be a witness to the event—which could have Trailhead gossiping for days— and where she could snoop for information. Deep inside she didn't want to believe that Tanner had anything to do with Romney's death, but deeper still she worried that he did. When it came to Tanner, she had learned to expect the unexpected. To protect herself just in case, she'd strapped her Lady Smith .36 revolver to the calf of her leg before leaving home. She had a "concealed to carry" permit, so she was well within her right.

Before driving to his place, Regi had stopped at the Gas-N-Grub and bought what looked like good lean steaks, with no fat marbling the meat, a small bag of potatoes, and a can of creamed corn. Feeling guilty that in her thirty-eight years she'd managed to avoid developing culinary skills of any kind, Regi had no idea if she could cook what she'd purchased, but, really, how hard could it be? She could open a can, turn on a stove, and cook . . . maybe . . . hopefully.

Gazing at Tanner's house, Regi couldn't help but think that it somehow looked lonely. The fancy building with black shutters and white colonnades was intriguing and further muddled her mind about this man.

She must be crazy or *desperate*. There was that word again, though it applied. Only a desperate woman would cook dinner in the house of a man who had left her—and who was possibly a murderer—in order to prove herself innocent.

Sheesh, no, desperate *was not the right word.* Frantic *was more like it. Terrified, horrified, totally freaked out of her mind.* Yep, that's what she was. But she was here.

Get this over with.

Making sure her cowboy hat sat straight on her head, she glanced at her reflection in the Jeep's rearview mirror. Her nose was still a little red from her cold, but she'd taken a decongestant before leaving home. She would be all right for four to six hours. Quickly smoothing flyaway hairs back to the braid at the nape of her neck, she climbed out of the vehicle.

Maybe if she found the key to the house, she could snoop around and hopefully find evidence and avoid Tanner altogether. Reaching in the back seat, she drew the grocery bag out of the Jeep, turned, and collided with Tanner.

Regi let out a little shriek and nearly dropped the bag. "You scared me!"

"Didn't mean to." He smiled as he took a good look at her.

Despite Regi's knee-jerk reaction to Claudia's suggestion that she change her clothes, Regi had put on clean, tight-fitting Levi's and a long-sleeved T-shirt that clung to her body. Her leather jacket molded to her curves as well. By the look on Tanner's face, her sister might have been right about his taking a liking to Regi again. Did he *like* what he saw enough to become distracted and say something he shouldn't? She'd watched too many spy movies.

"I was walking back from my father's old place when I saw your car pull in." Tanner gazed at her skeptically. "After yesterday's quarrel on the river, I'm surprised you're here." His good-ol'-boy smile graced his face. He pushed his cowboy hat back from his forehead. He looked winded, as though he'd been running. His eyes trailed to the bag in her arms.

Regi shrugged. "Felt bad about what happened, so I'm here to keep my promise. Remember you said if I went out with you, you'd keep my land until I could buy it back?" Regi hoped she sounded innocent and convincing at the same time. Flirting did not come to her naturally, and she wasn't certain whether she was doing it right. Still, she gave it a stab. The word *stab* brought the image of the knife stuck in Romney's neck to mind.

Please, God, help me through this, she thought as she tried to appear cool, calm, and collected.

"That land must be mighty important for you to come to me." Tanner wiggled his eyebrows like he had when they had been young and in love.

"Do you want to do this or not?" Regi had half a notion to climb back into her Jeep. She thought of that day so long ago when she'd learned she could never trust Samuel Tanner.

On the morning after Tanner's no-show and no message, Regi had gone to his father's place, which she hated to do, but she had to make sure Tanner was all right. Jed had met her in the barnyard. He'd told her Tanner had run away and wasn't coming back, not after their father had severely beaten him. The old man had a bad hangover and was out of his mind with rage to find his eldest son gone.

Back then Regi could hardly believe Tanner had left without talking with her. She would have helped him. Her parents would have taken him in. Didn't he trust her? That morning Jed had given her a hug and told her he was certain Tanner would get in touch with her, but in the meantime if she needed anything, she was to let Jed know. Jed had been very sympathetic, understanding, and worried about her safety. He'd told Regi to go home and stay away from his father.

Oh, how everyone had changed since that time.

The years had not been kind. Isaiah Tanner had taken the wrath he'd had for Tanner out on Jed. Odd that when Jed finally married that awful woman—who'd run off shortly after Clifford was born—he'd become as bitter as his father. His resentment toward his brother had grown even stronger when their father died and left the ranch to the prodigal son who had returned. In many ways, Regi understood Jed, except when it came to how he mistreated his own son. That was a puzzler. Why did people repeat behavior they hated as a child?

For Regi, the memories of the past confirmed that Tanner would do anything to get ahead: leave the woman he adored, leave the brother he loved, and then take all the spoils after someone died. He'd done it to Jed and was working on doing it to Regi. She stared at Tanner. Funny how an avalanche of memories could hit a person in just a matter of seconds.

Tanner had been studying her as well. "There's something very wrong with this picture," he finally said. He stepped back, holding his hands to frame what he saw. "Regina Bernard coming to my house." He shook his head and peeked into the grocery bag. "And she comes bearing food. I didn't know you cooked."

"There's a lot you don't know about me," she said as she stepped into the role of a cool and collected woman out to have a good time. She walked past him on the way to his front door. "Now, do you want to have this *date* or not? 'Cause I have a ton of stuff I should be doing, rather than being here with your sorry caboose." The itch to start a fight with him caused her considerable pain.

"Well . . ." He paused as if thinking it over.

Of all the nerve! Regi yearned to give him a piece of her mind.

Then he grinned. "Come on in." He led the way.

Gritting her teeth hard enough to crack a tooth, she followed.

As soon as he shut the door behind them, he told her to make herself at home while he freshened up. Glancing over his tall, lean form, she noticed that despite the chill in the air and the snow on the ground, the T-shirt beneath his opened Levi jacket appeared sweat dampened at the neck. He smiled and dashed upstairs.

Surely the walk from his father's old place wouldn't make him sweat. What had he been doing? Unable to think of an answer and still standing in the marble-tiled entryway, Regi spied a coatrack. Setting down the groceries, she hung her coat and lucky cowboy hat on a peg. She glanced into the living room.

The decor was traditional, with Queen Anne chairs and cherrywood accent tables. There was an elegant mahogany, baby grand piano in the bay window. She'd always wanted to learn to play. The keyboard was open, waiting. Did Tanner know how to tickle the ivories?

Again, not what Regi had expected. Not at all. For one thing, he must make more money cattle ranching than she imagined. And for another, everything looked so clean. Regi and Claudia were constantly struggling to keep the bed-and-breakfast tidy. Tanner didn't seem the type to carry a duster and mop around. He probably hired someone.

Regi turned her attention across the hall to the brooding den. Why *brooding*? Could have appeared that way because of the darkly stained desk and end tables. The rest of the room looked like a dream den. Walls were lined with shelves of leather-bound books. A suede boxlike couch sat in front of an inviting cobble-rock fireplace with a Navajo rug lying between the hearth and the couch. On the end table near the couch was a carving of a raven.

Again her eyes were drawn to the desk holding a laptop computer and neatly stacked papers. On the corner was a Remington statue of a cowboy riding a bucking horse. Had Tanner placed the statue there because he felt the major decisions he made while sitting at the desk were like riding a wild bronc?

The sense of brooding changed to something more ominous, as if an impending storm were developing within the walls. She was really losing it, sounding like Wakanda and her black moon theory.

Shaking her head, Regi grabbed the grocery bag and headed toward the door tucked beneath the sweeping staircase Tanner had gone up. She guessed the kitchen was behind it. She stopped when she heard water running overhead. Tanner was taking a shower. The thought of him cleaning up for her brought a surprised smile to her lips.

But did that mean he expected . . . ? No way! Not with their history. The notion was absurd.

No, this was a . . . well, it wasn't really a date since Regi was going to use the opportunity to fish for information that might link Tanner to Romney's murder or at the very least see if he still had his knife. This was a hoax; that's what it was.

Regi glanced back at the front door and her chance for escape. Maybe she should leave the food and get out before the chute to this gate closed and she was locked in. She remembered seeing Romney dead in the willows and the knife on the floorboards of her Jeep.

No! If Tanner had done it and was framing her, the only way to find out was to play this through. She was certain Sheriff Morgan would not seriously investigate Tanner without more evidence.

Regi *had* to stay.

Besides, she had her gun just in case. Regi pushed through the swinging doors to a surprisingly homey kitchen. Cute little hand towels hung from the oven door. Matching blue Priscilla curtains draped the bay window of a cozy breakfast nook. Even the wallpaper was dotted with small bluebells.

When Regi had been a teenager, she'd liked bluebells and many times gathered the wild flowers that grew in clumps near the side of the road. In fact, if she remembered right, before their relationship had blown up, Tanner had been with her on one occasion when she'd stopped. He'd said he liked watching her pick flowers. She hadn't thought of that for a very long time. Being around Tanner and his things seemed to conjure up the past.

Gazing at the room, Regi knew that this kitchen had a woman's touch. Tanner must have all sorts of women waiting on him. Marjean Buttons and Dixie Sutherland were a couple of the rumored women he'd been seen with, though Regi tried to pay no attention to the gossip. Just because she didn't care for Tanner didn't mean other women couldn't like him.

Regi thought of the ominous feeling that had overcome her while she'd studied Tanner's den. What if he frequently entertained women who never left the premises because they were buried down in the basement beneath the den? She shook her head at the absurd notion. Then a teasing idea needled her. If Tanner were capable of killing Romney, he very well could kill others, including Regi.

To stop from thinking, she quickly set the groceries on the granite countertop and got to work. In the drawer below the stove, she found a frying pan. Placing the skillet on the largest burner, she retrieved the steaks from the bag, tore off the plastic wrap, and dropped the meat onto the cold stainless steel. Then she turned on the burner.

While that was heating up, she fished out two other pots, one for the potatoes and one for the creamed corn. She pulled the tab on the corn can and coaxed the kernels slathered in creamy goodness out with a spoon. Flipping the burner on high, she turned her attention to the potatoes. She poured water into a pot to cover the bottom of the pan and plopped two whole spuds into that. Vaguely remembering she needed to spear the potatoes before putting them in, she paused. Or were spuds supposed to be speared for baking? No! They were supposed to be peeled for boiling.

Regi retrieved the vegetables, mined a peeler out of a drawer, and quickly stripped the potatoes of their skins. Dropping them back into the pot when she finished, she placed the kettle on the back burner and flipped it on high.

Smoke from the skillet began to rise. Regi remembered Claudia had told her not to turn meat over too soon so it would become nicely brown, or maybe she was supposed to put a lid over the meat to help it brown. Deciding to leave the steaks alone, she snagged the lid out of the stove's bottom drawer. What would it hurt to do both? She put the lid on the skillet. Tails of smoke danced about the room.

Dinner was well on its way.

She snooped in the cupboards and found blue china dishes, blue embossed glasses, and blue-handled flatware. Tanner knew how to color coordinate.

Spreading a tablecloth over the oak table in the breakfast nook, Regi then set out the plates, glasses, and utensils. Something more was needed. *I should have brought rolls and a salad.*

As she finished setting the table, Tanner's tall, rangy form filled the doorway. His thick, wet hair was combed straight back from his angular face. He reminded her of Tom Selleck. Odd that she'd never seen the similarity before. He smiled when he saw she'd set the table but frowned at the smoke now madly escaping the frying pan. "What are you cooking?"

"Steak."

"Have you turned it over?" He went to the stove, immediately lowered the temperature, and lifted the lid. Smoke filled the room. Coughing, he tried to fan the fumes away. He rushed to open the door as the smoke alarm went off.

Holding her ears, Regi didn't know what to do. Tanner glared at her then grabbed a chair, stepped up, and disconnected the batteries from the alarm.

With the blaring noise shut off, she heard the potatoes and corn boiling away and knew the disaster was not over yet.

Tanner climbed down and rushed to the skillet, placing it in the sink, burned meat and all. Then he looked in the pot with the two whole potatoes in it. The small amount of water she'd poured in the pot had quickly boiled away, and the potatoes were burned to the bottom. "These are gonna taste like charcoal. Seriously, have you never cooked before?"

She stared at him. He had to be thinking, *how could a woman live to be thirty-eight and not learn how to cook?* And it wasn't that she hadn't tried, but after many disasters, Earl had decided her talents with horses and cattle were more important than cooking, so he had done the cooking or hired someone during hectic times at the ranch. When Lisa was old enough, she'd taken charge of the kitchen.

Regi wondered if God would allow her one lie. But she supposed if she were allowed one lie, she needed to hold it in reserve. Unable to form the word *no* on her lips, she shook her head.

"Holy mackinaw!" A smile creased Tanner's face. Small laugh lines crinkled beside each eye. "I've never seen you speechless." He began to laugh. And not a mere chuckle but a deep-chested guffaw that made his shoulders shake. His hearty laughter grew louder as he dumped the potatoes in the sink with the meat. The lid rattled on the pot of corn as it rapidly boiled.

Feeling that this would be her saving grace, Regi said, "I do know how to heat up corn." She grabbed a wooden spoon from the drawer, lifted the lid, and began stirring. Big brown scorch patches surfaced in the creamy sauce.

She hadn't noticed that Tanner had moved to stand directly behind her. He burst out laughing again. With her pride sorely bruised, she added the pot of corn to the rubble in the now overburdened sink. Tanner laughed so hard he wiped tears from his eyes.

Here Regi stood in the home of the man who had hurt her so deeply in the past and whom she believed may have had something to do with Romney's death—and she'd made a fool of herself.

How could she possibly have thought she could manipulate Tanner into a confession with her womanly skills that were really not skills at all but rather pathetic misfires? The entire situation was ridiculous. And then, to her utter amazement, she, too, began to laugh. "I can't believe I'm here trying to play nice to a possible murderer," she said between chuckles.

Tanner grew instantly quiet.

She'd hit her target. She'd had to say something drastic to catch him off guard. As she gazed at Tanner, she saw hurt cloud his eyes. Deep hurt. He turned to leave. She couldn't let him go, not now when his emotions were so close to the surface.

She grabbed his arm. "Well, you have to know after our confrontation at the river yesterday what I'm thinking. And, besides, you have nerve becoming all hurt and defensive after you implied in front of Morgan that I could be the murderer." His eyes widened as though he remembered. She went on. "But I probably shouldn't have said what was on my mind. Tends to get me in a great deal of trouble."

His gaze told her nothing.

She had to bite the lethal bullet that was killing this evening the only way she knew how. She took a deep breath. "I'm sorry."

Awkward silence chased her words. Tanner's eyebrows rose. "Wow, Regina Bernard apologized to me. That's one for the history books."

She let go of him. Tempted to defend her actions, she bit her lips together.

He took hold of her shoulders. "Listen to me. I know you didn't kill Romney. And neither did I."

Regi stared at him and stiffened in her stance.

"You can't honestly believe I killed him, or you wouldn't have come here."

As Regi saw it, she had two options: admit that deep down she had hoped he didn't do it or repair the damage she'd done by playing nice so she could snoop around and prove he did. "Let's just say I came here for convincing."

Tanner let her go and shrugged. "That's fair enough." As if to ignore the tension, Tanner chuckled a little. He crossed the room to the fridge, where he pulled out two prime-rib steaks. "While I'm *convincing* you, let me show you how this cooking thing works." He smiled, and in that moment, Regi knew she'd successfully repaired the damage.

Despite the uneasiness, she watched as Tanner cooked a delicious dinner of steak and garlic-sautéed green beans. He added a tossed salad. While he worked, he made idle chitchat about the weather, the town, and ranching but avoided any mention of Romney, making Regi ill at ease. Could he really dismiss what she'd said so easily? The man was either a darned good actor or he was innocent.

When they finished their meal, Regi washed the dishes while Tanner wiped and put them away. At times, his warm, cautious smile reminded her of Earl. The twinkle in his eyes—which she'd thought looked like black tar but now appeared to be the color of a rich, dark mocha—made her feel less awkward.

After the dishes were done, he asked her to step into his den for dessert. He wanted to share some chocolate-covered macadamia nuts.

Time had come for a serious talk. Remembering the eeriness she had sensed earlier in the den, Regi was hesitant, but wanting to dig down to the truth, she agreed.

She followed him to the ominous room. After lighting a fire, Tanner went to his desk and pulled out a candy box from the bottom drawer. He sat next to her on the suede couch and offered her a chocolate morsel. "How do the twins like college life?"

His question caught her off guard. But she supposed a little more chitchat might be good before diving into the subject of murder. "They're doing fine." Nervous, she eyed the tasty-looking treats and picked one. "I'm sure I miss them more than they miss me. Thank goodness Claudia cooks, or I'd starve without Lisa at home." She popped the candy into her mouth. The chocolate was creamy goodness, and the nut—heavenly crunch.

"You're fortunate to have family around." Tanner seemed to mean what he said.

"Jed doesn't live that far away from you. And there's your aunt."

"Aunt Ida? I'm sure you know as well as everyone else in Trailhead that she has no use for me. And things have never been the same between Jed and me since I returned from Alaska."

He picked up the raven statue from the end table. "I got this from Big Jake, the man I worked for up there. He treated me like a son. This statue reminds me that there are good people in the world. Too bad Jed didn't know him. He could have learned how to become a better parent." He took a chocolate. "I'm surprised Jed allows Clifford to come over." Tanner ate his nougat.

"Then you and your nephew get along?" Regi was surprised.

"Oh, yeah. He comes and helps me clean up the barn and my tack room." Tanner looked straight at Regi. "Many people underestimate him, but Cliff is smart. Jed treats him like our father treated us. Sometimes I wish he'd let the boy stay here permanently." Tanner grew quiet, and Regi realized there were layers to Samuel Tanner she'd never seen before.

"Have you asked him?"

"I know better than to ask. It would take a visit from the Almighty for Jed to say yes," he scoffed, as if God were a fable.

Regi couldn't let him think that. "If you seriously want your nephew to live with you, you might try praying about it."

Tanner chuckled and set the box of candy on the coffee table. "I heard you joined the Mormon church. Just don't preach to me. I learned all I want to know about prayer and scripture study from my old man." He grew solemn. "Praying is the last thing I'd do."

"Miracles happen," Regi defended her faith.

"Not for me."

"You didn't used to be so cynical."

"People change, just like everything else. Remember the big swell in the river where we used to swim?"

She nodded.

"That huge cottonwood that we jumped from is dead." His voice trailed off.

Regi remembered the tree and the times they'd gone swimming. "That was so long ago. If I remember right, one night when we'd stayed late, we roasted hotdogs. You whittled a couple of willows so we could roast them. I remember that old knife of yours. In fact, I saw it at Twiggs the other day. Stew said you lent it to him. Do you still have it?" Regi watched Tanner closely. She'd put the bait out, but would he take it?

He chuckled, scrubbed his face with his hand, then said, "I can't believe you."

"What?"

"Regi, you're always thinking."

"I'm remembering a good time we had, is all." She blinked at him, hoping the twisting feeling in her gut—that told her he knew she thought his knife killed Romney—was wrong.

Tanner folded his arms, shook his head, and sank back against the couch cushions.

Before Regi or Tanner could utter another word, the doorbell rang.

Samuel growled under his breath and rose to his feet. "Don't go anywhere. I'll be right back. We still have things to discuss." As he left, he shut the sliding doors, closing off the den from the entryway and blocking her view.

Regi's chance to find evidence had arrived. But she didn't move. Throughout this awkward evening, Tanner had been nothing but nice, even when she'd accused him of murder.

Could Sheriff Morgan be right, and Tanner hadn't killed Romney? After all, how could a man who worried for his mentally challenged nephew murder someone? The old wound of Tanner's betrayal reminded her of his deceptive ways. What she needed was proof of his guilt . . . or innocence.

She looked over at his desk and knew she had to take this opportunity to find some type of clue. Regi grabbed another chocolate and tiptoed to the desk. She rifled through piles of invoices and letters, searching for a familiar name or any little detail that would help her find a tie between Romney and Tanner.

She hadn't noticed before, but a picture sat on the corner of the desk. Regi picked it up. Within the frame was Tanner's father on a beautiful black horse. The man's face was full of pride as he surveyed his land.

Too bad he hadn't been as proud of his sons. Why would Tanner keep a picture of the man who had been so cruel to him?

Another layer to Samuel.

Whoa! Had she thought of him as Samuel? He was Tanner! Referring to him with his last name gave her the distance she needed.

Looking at the picture of Tanner's father turned Regi's thoughts to her own parents. She and Claudia were lucky. Their parents were never abusive. They loved their girls and fed and clothed them, and though much of their lives were filled with worries of the end of days, her parents had cared for her and Claudia. Besides, her father used to say, "To be prepared is to have no fear."

Except, how did one prepare to be accused of murder? How did one prepare for a spouse to die? Regi knew the answer. She could never be prepared for all of life's tragedies, but God had helped her when Earl had died by sending the missionaries to her door. And somehow He would help her again. Though she hoped it would be sooner than later. If only she could feel Him near and not so alone now.

Again she glanced at Isaiah Tanner's picture. Pictures were misleading and did not record the true soul: the good or the bad. Had Isaiah Tanner been so cruel to his son that he'd created a person who could smile like a movie star yet become a murderer?

After spending the evening with Tanner, Regi didn't know anymore. As she remembered yesterday when Tanner had come upon her and Morgan searching the river, he'd seemed surprised at the news of Romney's death. And tonight Tanner'd looked right at her and plainly stated he didn't do it.

Romney's body flashed before her, the knife in his neck.

She had to find more evidence.

She quickly glanced at the door and then flipped through another stack of papers. As she was about to give up, she noticed a note with the Trailhead National Park logo on it. Regi pulled it from the pile and read the cursive handwriting:

Meet me at Twiggs. I have some information you need to be aware of. Curtis Romney.

The murmur of voices behind the den doors drew her attention. Tanner's visitor must be leaving. Curious, Regi tiptoed to the sliding doors. On her way, she snatched another chocolate. She recognized Tanner's voice, but who belonged to the other one? The low, soothing tones were familiar. What were they talking about? Inching closer, Regi leaned over to put her ear to the wood.

The familiar voice plainly said, "I'll see you tomorrow. Remember, I don't want Regi knowing about this." Then as she heard the front door close, recognition set in.

Sheriff Thomas Morgan!

Why was he talking to Tanner about keeping something from her? She reached to open the door and confront Tanner but realized she still held the note from Romney, and there was a big ugly smudge of chocolate on it. *Blazes!* She may have ruined the best piece of evidence she'd found so far and now . . .

Regi's stomach nosedived. She couldn't let Tanner find her holding this note, and she couldn't very well put it back with a chocolate smudge on it.

His footsteps were coming. She quickly stuffed the note in her pants pocket, popped the uneaten chocolate in her mouth, and sat on the couch as the doors slid open.

SEVEN
COMPOSURE

CAMERON ELLIOTT WAS A TALL, dark-haired man. The type of man to draw a line in the sand, dare people to cross it, and then before they could move, snap their necks.

Claudia slowly stepped away from his door. Elliott's cheek twitched as he folded his arms across his barrel chest. He knew she'd been eavesdropping, but she wasn't about to admit it. She cleared her throat. "You're just the man I was looking for. I stopped by to give condolences to you and Melissa on behalf of the Raindancer Bed-and-Breakfast. It was a shock to learn of your son-in-law's death."

Elliott unfolded his arms. His face turned a brilliant shade of sunburned red. "How do you have the nerve?"

"Excuse me?"

"How do you have the nerve to come into *my* home the day after *your* sister murdered my son-in-law?" The man's eyes seemed to bulge.

Claudia was not prepared for such an accusation. She knew the state troopers and park rangers at Karen Wilson's must have been suspicious of Regi, but to actually hear someone call her sister a murderer was a different matter. Claudia had to remain calm. With an even tone, she asked, "Who told you such a lie?"

Before Elliott could answer, Ranger Knutson stepped out of the room. "I did." Of course there had to be another ranger close by. This was the ranger Regi had said saw her at the Gas-N-Grub yesterday after she'd found Romney dead in the willows.

Exasperated and fighting the world's grandest headache, Claudia continued. "Superintendent Elliott, you must believe me, my sister did not kill Curtis. She may not have agreed with how he handled certain situations, but she would never have harmed him."

A sniff came from the connecting archway of the living room where Claudia had sat with Melissa. There stood the widow. Her chipmunk cheeks were wet with tears. She stared at Claudia in disbelief. "Your sister . . . killed him?"

Claudia stepped toward Melissa to assure her that Regi was innocent, but Elliott blocked her path. She looked up at the man who at that moment seemed as tall as Paul Bunyan. With more courage than she felt, she said, "Tell your daughter that Regi did *not* do it."

Elliott folded his brawny arms and stood as erect as timber. He had already made his decision, labeled Regi a killer, and sentenced her. All he lacked was a key to lock the cell door. Realizing her only option was to retreat, Claudia decided not to skulk away but to leave with dignity. "I'm sorry I've upset you and your daughter by coming here. That was not my intention. But Superintendent Elliott, think about this. I've known Regi all my life, and I've seen her at her worst. She would never harm another person, no matter how upset she was." Claudia paused a moment, hoping what she had said would make him think. To make certain he understood that she would not tolerate him talking about her sister in such a manner, she added, "Regi is not a murderer. If I had the slightest doubt, I would never have come into your home. Though rest assured, if I hear that you and your rangers continue to slander my sister's good name, you will hear from my attorney. I still have connections."

Elliott's shoulders slackened slightly, but his features maintained a stone-faced stare. "My daughter and I appreciate your kindness, Ms. Osborne. I know you lost your husband six months ago, so I think your visit is sincere. However, what you said only heightens my resolve to convict Regina. You may well have 'connections,' but while I've served as park superintendent, I've learned that humans are animals when they're hurting. Mama bears will kill anyone who comes between them and their babies. I am well aware of my son-in-law's brief relationship with Regi's daughter before he married my Melissa. And, like you, I'm well aware of Regi's temper. If Curtis pushed her in any way, she would have killed him. See, I know your sister well enough to know that."

Numb from his rebuttal, Claudia turned and walked away. A nervous flutter pulsed in her heart. As she exited and hurried down the steps, she realized that man and those people in that house honestly believed Regi had killed Curtis Romney.

Her sister's reputation for a hot temper had already convicted her. How in the world could Claudia help her out of this mess? Surely Regi had friends who would vouch for her. Claudia immediately thought of Wakanda, whom Regi had been more than generous to. And Stew was a good friend; he'd back her up. Thomas and Hannah Morgan knew Regi very well, though Thomas was the sheriff and probably couldn't take sides, and Hannah—the poor woman—suffered from Alzheimer's. Who would believe her?

Claudia would find a way to help her sister, even if it meant telling the world what really happened to Morris and exposing the truth about her late husband and his shady dealings.

"Now, what were we talking about?" Tanner picked up the box of chocolates, offering Regi another.

She shook her head. "No, thanks. Who was at the door?"

"A friend needing a favor."

"Anyone I know?"

"Regina, I can't tell you."

He obviously didn't want her to know his visitor was Morgan. And by the few words she'd heard the sheriff say before he'd left, Morgan didn't, either. How dare they keep secrets from her? Especially if it had something to do with this murder investigation! A rash of anger frizzed her skin.

She had to maintain control. She needed God's help to stay her tongue and guide her out of this situation. *Please help me.* She felt no divine inspiration. Nothing. Regrouping her thoughts, she decided she could be forceful without getting angry. She stood and wiped her sweaty palms on her jeans. "Tanner, what's going on here?"

He looked up, as though pretending to be confused. "Not sure, but I think it's two friends eating chocolate. What do you think?"

Did she want to tip her hand and tell him she'd overhead Morgan, or was it better to keep it to herself and use that knowledge later? In a split second, she made her decision. "If that's what you think, then that's what it is. It's been an interesting evening, but I'd best go home."

He stood. His gaze met hers and held caring and concern. How was that possible? Caring and concern when he was keeping secrets? Regi's composure slipped a tad, yet her determination to walk away guided her.

Tanner reached over and took her hand. "You've shut yourself off again."

"What?" She tried to pull away, but he held on.

"After the blow-up in the kitchen, you calmed down. We actually started talking nicely to one another. I know you're peeved that I won't tell you who was at the door, but I can't. Regina, don't build the wall again. Tonight for the first time in years our relationship started to change for the better."

"Relationship?" She pointed first to herself and then at him. "We have no relationship. You closed the door on that when you left years ago." Again she tried to break free from his hold, and this time she succeeded.

"Regi, I'm a patient man." He followed her. "Haven't we fought enough in our lives?" He waited only a moment for her to reply. When she wouldn't answer, he said, "Look, I left when I was a teen. Granted, I was a stupid kid, afraid of my own father and what I might do to him if I stayed. Self-preservation drove me to run. And as a result, I hurt you."

"What?" Regi felt as though she were sliding on ice heading toward a hole with deep, dark water. In all these years, they'd never talked about that time. And she didn't want to now.

He continued. "My leaving had nothing to do with us. You don't know how many times I tried to write to you and explain, but I couldn't. And then I came up with a plan to make things right with my father and brother . . . and you, but I was too late."

"Stop it! You've been too late for a great many things." Leaving her behind was only part of the wrongs he'd committed against her. She was amazed at his oversight. He stood there as if bewildered. How could he look so clueless? She couldn't stand it. "Earl sold you land that you agreed to sell back to us, and then when we tried to buy it, you refused."

Tanner cast his eyes to the floor, shaking his head. "What can I say? I've been stupid. I suppose I wanted to strike back at you and Earl for finding happiness. But especially you for not waiting for me."

"What? Am I hearing right? I was supposed to wait for someone who left in the middle of the night without saying a word? I was supposed to wait for someone who never wrote?" Regi stepped away, overwhelmed by Tanner's ridiculous claim. "Tanner, I waited for years. Cried myself to sleep so many times I lost count, and then this wonderful man came into my life. A man you took advantage of and lied to. Earl Bernard did not deserve that and neither did I." This entire scene—*the entire evening*— was too much. Regi had come here in hopes of learning the truth about Tanner and *Romney*. She had no desire to relive their past and open old wounds best left alone.

No! She came here because Curtis Romney had been murdered. *She came here* to learn the truth. And that's exactly what she intended to do.

"You had a mother-of-pearl-handled pocketknife at Twiggs. Do you still have it?"

Tanner's face paled as though he was overcome with guilt. He rubbed the back of his neck. "Morgan told me you thought the murder weapon was mine."

"Well, show me your knife, and prove me wrong." Regi stared at Tanner.

He glared back. "Spent a good deal of the day looking for it. I must have left it at Twiggs."

"Convenient." Regi started for the door, but Tanner cut her off.

"Regi, you know me. How can you think I'd be capable of murder? Murder is the worst kind of act a human being can commit. Do you think so little of me?"

"I don't know." She shivered and bit her bottom lip but kept her gaze on him. "For self-preservation, people do strange things, like leave their loved ones behind."

"That's still a far cry from murder." Tanner swiped his hand across his chin and then huffed. "Be reasonable. If I had killed Romney, I wouldn't leave him where he could be found, where I know you would go. No matter what you may think of me, I'm not that coldhearted." He paused a moment as though realizing his argument was not having any effect on her. In a more calm tone, he said, "Look, anyone could have picked up my knife."

"Even you?" She waited. He was trying to make himself sound noble and cloud over the fact that his knife was missing.

"I wish I had it so I could prove to you that I'm innocent." He looked up at the ceiling and took a deep breath. "Regi, I'm sorry I've been a jerk all these years, but you have to believe me on this. I didn't do it." His voice softened as he stared at her.

For a second, she wanted to believe. She gazed into his dark, pleading eyes, begging her to trust him. An old forgotten feeling swirled in her stomach and sizzled over her skin. Her breath caught, and for a second she was a teenager, looking at the young man who meant everything to her. She remembered what it felt like to have his arms around her. It had been years since she'd experienced this longing.

The grandfather clock in the living room bonged and awakened her from the surreal trance. Reason flooded in, reminding her of his lies. She had to get away. Shoving her hand in her pants pocket, Regi felt her car keys and Romney's note she'd stolen from Tanner's desk. This was tangible proof that there was a connection between Tanner and Romney. She had to give the note to Morgan and let him investigate. Then she remembered the sheriff's visit only moments ago—a visit he wanted kept from Regi.

Why had the sheriff visited Tanner? And why didn't they want her to know? Her head throbbed. She had to breathe some fresh air and clear her thinking. She stepped around him, heading for the door.

"Life is messy, Regina." Tanner's voice followed her. "Remember, if you need me, you know where to find me." He reached the door before she did and opened it.

Grabbing her coat and hat from the hall tree, she raced to her Jeep, leaped into the front seat, and shoved the key into the ignition. As she peeled out of Tanner's barnyard, Regi realized his layers came in a variety pack: some good, some irritating, and some downright deceptive.

Upset after leaving Tanner's, Regi didn't feel like heading home and facing Claudia. Not right now. She pulled into Twiggs' parking lot and slammed on the brakes. Cars were crammed into spaces as if Stew were giving away million-dollar lottery tickets. Cowboys filled the place. The juke box was playing so loudly the building appeared to shake.

The perfect place—crowded with people—where hopefully no one had heard about the murder yet. With any luck, Regi could seclude herself in a corner. As she made her way into the café, Stew gave her a nod over the heads of hamburger-eating bronc riders. Some recognized her and waved, but luckily no one wanted to talk. So either word hadn't leaked out, or it had and no one wanted to talk with a suspected murderer.

Regi quickly found a booth in the back near a window where she could sit alone and people watch. As she wiped away the tailings of salt left by the previous customers, she thought about Tanner and what he'd said as she'd left. "If you need me, you know where to find me." Like she would ever go to him for help. The man was delusional, bringing up their past in the middle of all this mess. She had enough to deal with. Her hand went to the pocket where she'd hidden the note she'd stolen.

Only two days ago Romney had wanted Tanner to meet him here. And they had. As she thought about it, though, she realized the note, in and of itself, was not incriminating evidence that Tanner had murdered Romney; it only meant that they'd planned to meet. But the note combined with the knife and the fact that she'd seen the body on Tanner's place was enough for Regi to think Tanner was involved with the murder.

Sparkling, brown-eyed Julie Ann, who walked on the balls of her feet everywhere she went, sashayed up to Regi's table. "What can I getcha, Reg?"

She had to take her mind off the murder, so Regi forced herself to think of her favorite food. She was tempted to order an entire chocolate cream pie loaded with whipped cream, but knew she'd regret it in the morning. "How about some fries?"

"Comin' up." Julie turned around and made her way to the kitchen, dodging several wolf-whistling cowboys.

Regi watched another waitress carrying a single slice of chocolate cream pie to a customer. How much damage would one little piece do? Besides, wasn't there a saying about chocolate being good for you? Something like a piece of chocolate a day keeps the doctor away. That wasn't quite right. Whatever. When Julie Ann returned with the fries, Regi would order a slice.

Gazing out the window so she'd quit thinking of pie, Regi watched several cars drive past, and then a familiar large Ford truck rumbled into the café's parking lot and stopped.

Out stepped Tanner.

Had he already realized the note from Romney was missing from his desk? Regi ducked down, not wanting him to see her. No, wait. He was carrying a bundle of some kind.

"What the . . .?" she said under her breath as she watched him walk to her Jeep. "What is he doing?" He put the bundle inside the vehicle and did it like he knew exactly what he was doing. *Like he'd done it before with his knife.*

He headed back to his truck. Regi had half a mind to chase after him, but as she watched, he stopped, turned around, and walked toward the building.

"Shoot!" Regi really didn't want to speak with him.

Julie Ann arrived with Regi's fries and a piece of beautiful chocolate cream pie topped with a mountain of cream and little shavings of chocolate. Much better than the other customer had received.

"What are you, a mind reader?" Regi asked, as her mouth salivated.

"Stew said you looked like you needed chocolate." The waitress winked.

Regi chuckled and stared past Julie. Stew was gazing at her from across the crowded and noisy room. She mouthed, *thank you.* He nodded and set back to work. It paid to have good friends in high places who cook.

"Extra cream, just as you like it." Julie turned to leave.

"Wait a minute. Where's the bill?"

The waitress bent over so only Regi could hear. "It's on the house." She quickly trotted away.

The pie was almost enough to make Regi forget that Tanner was coming in. Almost.

She glanced over the bobbing cowboy hats, wondering if he'd already joined their ranks, but she couldn't see him. Maybe while she had been talking with Julie, he'd changed his mind and had left. Peering out the window, she found his truck still there. She couldn't see him in the crowd. She nervously ate a french fry as Tanner finally walked in.

Regi hunched down and peered around the end of the booth. She'd done all the talking she wanted with that man. He went to the counter and found Julie as she hurried by with an armload of plates filled with food. They talked for a moment, and then that sweet little waitress who had brought Regi the best looking piece of pie nodded in Regi's direction.

Darn it! She wistfully glanced at her dessert, knowing she'd have to leave it behind and flee out the back door. Picking up her fork to take one quick bite, she was stopped.

"We have a few more things to settle." Tanner nudged her over on the bench seat.

She should have left when she'd had the chance. She set the fork down and glared at him. "Really? And here I thought we'd said everything at your place."

"I want to know why, after Morgan found the murder weapon in your vehicle, you don't lock Earl's Jeep when you leave it? Someone could hide in it or plant a weapon." His eyes probed hers as if to make her feel guilty or something.

Ornery cowpokes had tried to intimidate Regi for years when she'd bossed them on cattle drives. Tanner would not best her. She scooted to the edge of the seat to give him room. "And you should know. That old roan of yours is pretty fast. How long did it take you after you'd left Morgan and me on the river to ride that poor horse to the Gas-N-Grub and plant the knife?"

Tanner stared at her in disbelief as if he were shocked by her conclusion. Or as if he'd been found out. Then his shocked expression turned to a grin.

And Regi knew this argument was far from over.

EIGHT
REASONING

WHEN CLAUDIA PULLED INTO THE Raindancer's barnyard after nine PM, two cars were in the parking lot. One she believed was the rental car the Steinfelds and Mattiases shared, and the other was vaguely familiar. An old Plymouth station wagon with wood panels on the sides and tailgate. Suddenly, Claudia remembered. That car was Ida Peck's.

What on earth did she want?

Claudia knew. Somehow word must have leaked out that Regi was a suspect in Romney's murder. Ida had come to poke around and discover new juicy gossip to spread. Even though Regi knew how this woman talked, she thought her harmless, even grandmotherly. But then Regi liked Wakanda, too, so her judgment of character was more than a tad off balance. However, Claudia had spent years in politics and had learned to be wary of people such as Ida. Gossip was a tool politicians used as a weapon, and Claudia was well trained at spotting snipers.

She inched out of her Cadillac and locked the doors. Tapping the keys against her hand as she made her way to the bed-and-breakfast, she realized poor Wakanda was in there with that woman. And what about the guests? Had Ida cornered them as well?

Entering through the kitchen door, Claudia was greeted by Oscar's growl. The arthritic dog slowly rose from his cozy sheepskin blanket in the corner. "Why aren't you helping Wakanda?" Claudia asked the Irish setter. The dog stared at her while issuing little grrrs, but he still wagged his tail as if he couldn't make up his mind whether to like her or not.

Claudia couldn't deal with the crotchety canine. She needed to collect her wits about her before actually confronting Ida. Glancing about the kitchen, she saw everything was as she'd left it. Nothing out of place. Heaving a deep sigh of relief, Claudia pushed through the swinging doors into the reception area.

Wakanda sat on the parson's bench close to the dining room door. Ida was asleep on the couch adjacent to the TV while an old western blared from the classic movie channel. A trickle of drool dripped from the old woman's receding chin. Trying not to disturb the dozing pariah, Claudia whispered to Wakanda, "So, is everything all right?"

Wakanda had probably weathered a vicious onslaught of probing questions. Since the woman rarely spoke to anyone except Regi, Claudia felt certain that answers had not been given. Wakanda gathered her animal-skin coat around her girth, nodded, grunted in disgust at Ida, then lumbered out as Oscar walked in.

The Irish setter sat by the dining room doorway, watching Claudia. What was the animal up to? Ignoring him, Claudia crossed the room and clicked off the television.

At once Ida awakened. She yawned. "Oh my! What time is it, dear?"

"Nine. Is there something I can do for you?" Claudia wanted to keep things civil. No reason not to, other than she didn't trust the woman.

Blinking and pulling her old green sweater about her like a shield, Ida stood and yawned again. "Isaiah and I came to ask if there was anything I could do to help you and your sister during these troubling times."

Claudia looked about. No one else was there but Ida. The old woman must be confusing the dream she'd been having with reality. Still, Claudia had to be careful. Ida was laying a minefield at her feet. Anything Claudia said could and probably would be used against her. Putting on an act of innocence, she replied, "Whatever do you mean, troubling times?"

"Now, dear." The old woman patted Claudia's arm. Oscar growled and crept closer. Claudia expected him to come at her, but the dog was actually focused on Ida. The old woman backed up, away from the Irish setter. Still, she continued. "You don't have to pretend with me. I heard the sheriff was going to arrest Regi for Curtis Romney's murder."

Claudia had been afraid Thomas would be forced to take such an action. Claudia summoned her best campaign face of denial. "Your information is wrong. Regi hadn't seen Romney for at least four months until yesterday morning, and he was already dead. Thomas will not arrest her."

"Oh, then you don't know about the brawl Regi and Curtis had in front of Twiggs Café the day before she killed him?"

Claudia vaguely remembered Regi had mentioned something about a disagreement between Romney and Wakanda, but she didn't answer Ida.

"See, me, Jed, and Clifford went into the café for supper that night. Everyone was talking about it. Everyone 'ceptin Stew."

Immediately, Claudia thought of that night. She had gone to the café, as well, but only for a minute and not long enough to talk with anyone.

She hadn't seen Ida there, but Claudia had been looking for someone else. She turned her attention back to Ida, who was still talking.

"Sugar, your sister has a temper like the Tasmanian Devil. They say she had Curtis on the ground and threatened to maim him for life." Ida blinked her sly eyes at Claudia, as though waiting for her reaction to the crass assumption.

Claudia had asked Regi to tell her everything. Could this be true? And if it were, why hadn't her sister told her about it? The wound of Regi's oversight stabbed deeply. But right now, Claudia was determined not to reveal her emotions to Ida. "Whoever told you that blew the situation completely out of proportion." Claudia prayed she was telling the truth and that Regi had not threatened the now deceased man.

"Sweetie, you are living in a state of denial." Ida looped Claudia's arm into the crook of hers. "Sheriff Morgan told me himself."

Claudia backed away. "He what?"

Ida shrugged. "Well, he did. At closing time tonight, he stopped by and fueled up his patrol car. I overheard him talking on the phone to Hannah, telling her everything. You know, dear, her condition grows worse every day. That disease is eatin' her brain."

Claudia's patience waned. She wanted this little old biddy to leave.

Ida continued. "Hannah must have been upset with him. Don't know why. I should have called her earlier in the day. You know I always call people who are havin' a rough time, health or otherwise. Just talkin' to someone gives them comfort. Anyway, I heard him tell her to calm down, that he wasn't leaving until morning. And that he'd take care of Regi."

How in the world had this woman come to the conclusion that the sheriff was going to arrest Regi from that small bite of conversation? Again this elderly chatterbox had put two and two together and had come up with twenty-two. The time had come for Ida to admit defeat and leave.

Claudia picked up the woman's moth-eaten, fur-trimmed coat, lying on the arm of the couch, and started for the door. "Miss Peck, it is very considerate of you to worry about my sister's well-being, but I'd prefer that you restrained yourself from ever coming here again because if Regi heard you repeat what you told me, I know she would be terribly offended."

Face flushed with indignation, Ida grabbed her coat and tugged it on. Oscar came to stand between them, little growls escaping his throat. Ida ignored the dog. "Don't you mean that she'd lose it? Regi's not one to hold back. Everyone knows it, just as everyone knows that when Regi's mad enough, well, my dear, she could kill."

That was more than even Claudia could bear. This brown wren of a woman would more than likely get on the phone as soon as one was within reach. By morning everyone in Trailhead would believe Regi was a killer and Claudia . . . Claudia would be to blame for allowing it.

She must do something, say something to stop Ida. "I wonder what Jed would think if he learned his aunt eavesdrops on his customers' private conversations. More importantly, I wonder how many people would quit doing business at the Gas-N-Grub if they found out their conversations were overheard and repeated by *you.*"

Ida stopped fussing with her coat and stood motionless, as if realizing she'd said too much. Finally, she pulled the fur collar up around her neck. "I can't help it if people speak loudly enough for me to hear."

"Maybe you can't, but—" Claudia stepped closer to Ida "—you can choose not to tell what you've heard. You can choose not to make up lies. If you've misunderstood what you heard Thomas say, you'll come out of this looking like a fool. You really should get the facts straight. You're dealing with people's lives. If I were you, I'd back off. You never know what could happen to you if you crossed the wrong person."

Ida's face flushed an angry red. She shot a murderous stare at Claudia as she stepped toward her. Oscar growled, baring his teeth; his hackles rose around his neck. Ida immediately retreated and sidestepped toward the door with Oscar following, his growls growing louder. "You and your dog don't threaten me, little missy. Isaiah and I meant no harm stopping in here. Our only concern was for you and your sister."

Claudia was confused. Again Ida was talking about her dead brother, Isaiah, as though he were here. The woman was slipping.

As if their previous conversation had never taken place, Ida continued. "So just be sure to tell Regi our thoughts and prayers are with her. There now, everything is tidy and nice." Without further hesitation or delay, the small woman escaped out the door.

Claudia gave a grateful sigh and stroked Oscar. "Good boy." Surprised by the dog's sudden protection of her, she cautiously rubbed behind his ears. He leaned into her and moaned. She'd never fully appreciated the animal until tonight, and she was surprised he had come to her aid. Maybe having Ida here made the animal grateful for Claudia.

She wondered if the old woman had truly left. Claudia dashed to the window and peered through a slit in the Levolor blind. Ida Peck hobbled to her car like a witch anxious to find her broom. Although Claudia hadn't meant for her words to sound like a threat, she was glad they had. People like Ida shouldn't get away with tarnishing the reputations of others. If what Claudia had said curbed the woman's tongue, she was relieved.

Deep in her soul, though, she knew what she'd said would not stop Ida from talking.

Samuel grabbed Regi's arm, preventing her from leaving the booth on the other side. He looked around to see if people were watching them. Hungry men rarely cared what people were talking about. Still, he lowered his voice so only she could hear. "You know darned well I didn't plant the murder weapon." He had to make this confounded woman listen to him before she ended up hurt or dead.

Regi's eyebrows rose, framing her how-dare-you-touch-me expression. He didn't let go. He needed her to stay put until he'd convinced her once and for all that he didn't kill Romney. They'd just spent the evening together, which wasn't the most pleasant evening he'd ever spent with a woman, but it was progress for them. After dinner, as they'd talked about the ranch and Clifford, Samuel could swear he saw the old Regi return, the girl he'd fallen in love with. There'd been gentleness in her gaze. He knew the girl that loved him was still under all that pent-up anger. Somehow he had to get her back. "Think about it, Reg. You and Morgan saw me at the river riding my horse. How in the world would I have time to find your vehicle at Jed's and place a knife inside?"

Regi's expression brightened as if she'd come to a realization. "By the way, until a moment ago, you shouldn't have known the murder weapon was found in my car. *And* I don't recall that it was reported in the paper, so the only way you would know that juicy tidbit is if you'd put it there yourself or Morgan told you."

Samuel cussed himself for revealing what he knew, but since Regi had caught him, there was no reason to deny it. "So what if he did? Big deal."

"Let go of my arm!" Regi demanded with grit and fire in her voice as she glanced around at the other customers.

Realizing that she was uncomfortable, plus they were drawing attention, Samuel released her.

Regi leaned near so only he would hear. "The 'big deal,' as you put it, is Morgan should not be talking to you or anyone else who isn't a cop. It's called conspiracy. Especially since *you* should be a suspect."

People thinking that Samuel was colluding with the sheriff had been exactly what Morgan had been worried about. And bless her heart, Regi had voiced her conclusion a little too loudly. Samuel had to keep this quiet and under control. He reached for her arm again. Regi glared. Realizing touching her would not be good, he stopped. "Morgan is my friend. I went to his office and asked if I could help. He refused. He's nothing but professional when it comes to his job and this investigation."

Regi appeared angry at first, and then, as though she realized Morgan was a good guy, her expression softened.

Relieved, Samuel shook his head. "Conspiracy? Leave it to you to come up with that. Morgan's worried about you. We both are." Samuel wanted to take her in his arms and calm her concerns. He hoped his sincere words eased her mind.

Regi stared at him as if she despised him. "What did you put in my car just now?"

Samuel couldn't believe she'd seen him. He'd wanted to surprise her. "The extra potatoes you left behind. Plus, I added the chocolate-covered macadamia nuts." He smiled, knowing that chocolate had always been her favorite.

Her glare softened, though she was still wary. "Thanks . . . I guess."

Maybe a little more sugar would bring a smile to her face. "Your pie looks good." He pushed the plate and fork near her. "Eat."

"I've lost my appetite." She bristled. "So a couple of days ago, when you met Romney here, was he the one wanting to buy my river property?"

Samuel regretted telling her that he had a buyer, but it was the only way he could bribe her to go out with him. And it had worked, sort of. He couldn't tell her that he'd lied. Maybe he could skirt around it. "We played a game of pool and talked was all. Guys talk."

"You never had a buyer, did you?" Regi's voice rose. She wasn't going to let this go. He tried to think of a good spin he could put on the truth.

She didn't wait for him. "And did that 'guy talk' lead to—" Regi stopped what she was going to say as she noticed a couple of cowboys in a nearby booth kind of leaning back, eavesdropping. She finished in a quieter tone. "—a disagreement?"

He rubbed his throbbing temples. Samuel moved closer to her and away from the others. "Yeah, we had a disagreement. He cheated playing pool. But I wasn't the one threatening him that day. You were." Samuel hoped his words would make her remember he wasn't the only one who had a beef with the ranger. And, in fact, Regi was in a far worse predicament than he was. But her expression didn't change, so his point had not been made as yet. "Look, pinning blame on me isn't going to work. *Claiming* you saw him on my property doesn't mean I killed him."

Regi bit at her bottom lip as though deep in thought. Samuel could see he'd thrown her a little curve. "Besides, he was found at Karen Wilson's. Using your theory that because you saw him on my property I must have killed him, does that make Karen a suspect too?"

Regi rolled her eyes. "I *claimed* I saw him because it's true. Why would I make up something like that? I don't know how he got from your property to Karen's, do you?" She glared at him as though she truly believed he should know.

Just when he thought he'd made her doubt her conclusion, she rallied. Well, he'd have to get a little rough and, though he hated to do it, Samuel knew if he could make her readjust her thinking, he might make some headway. "Maybe you killed him, took him to Karen's, and decided to lead Morgan on a wild goose chase so he'd believe you were innocent."

"Get over yourself." She folded her arms, glaring at Samuel. "Karen had hung her clothes outside earlier in the morning. Romney's body wasn't there then, and at that time I was staring at his corpse."

Okay, Samuel thought, *that didn't work. Maybe logic would be better.* "Let's say I believe you when you say you saw him at the river. How did he get from there to Karen's, which is at least two miles away? He didn't walk."

She volleyed back. "You should know. The body was on *your* land. *You* had access *and* time to transport. Just because Morgan and I saw you on your horse doesn't mean you didn't move the corpse before we arrived. We were delayed because of some nonsense about Wakanda."

Her eyes lit with new understanding as she pointed at him as if she'd found the answer to a riddle. "You were probably the one who sent us on that wild goose chase to give you time. Plus, you knew darned well I'd be fishing on a Saturday morning. I was your fishing ace-in-the-hole. Someone to blame. But . . ." She stared out the window at his Ford. "Maybe you didn't ride your horse to town; you drove your truck!" She smacked her forehead with the palm of her hand. "Of course, how foolish of me. After dropping Romney off at Karen's, you drove past your brother's gas station, saw my vehicle parked there, and had the perfect opportunity to plant the evidence."

Samuel couldn't help but admire her perseverance. That's what he loved about Regi; she'd fight with her last breath if she thought she was right. He should be upset with her for making such outlandish claims against him, but Samuel knew the woman he loved was only struggling to survive this horrible nightmare she'd landed in. And in a way, he was glad she'd focused her anger on him. She was like a cornered kitten, all hiss and spit and plenty of sharp claws, but underneath, she just wanted to be held. "Regi, how could I drop off the body, hide the knife, drive home, saddle my horse, and ride to the river, all before you got there with the sheriff? You know that's impossible."

"There was plenty of time," she grumbled and folded her arms.

Samuel was sure that she knew he was right, but no way would she admit it. This game of "who did it" had finally and hopefully played out.

Regi crossed her legs beneath the table, kicking Samuel.

"Hey, no need for violence." He smiled, knowing she hadn't meant to kick him. Samuel looked at the dessert. So she still had a hankering for chocolate cream pie with double the cream on top. Now that she'd faced the truth, maybe some playful teasing would help ease the tension between them. He grabbed the fork and took a bite. Regi's eyes followed the fork to his mouth.

"Want some?" he offered.

"No!"

He knew darned well she did. In fact, he wondered how long it would take him teasing her before she took it away. If he were a betting man, he'd guess two minutes max. He took another bite and gave a delicious sigh. "Hmm, this sure is good pie. Yep." He smacked his lips and took another bite.

Her eyes widened.

Samuel smacked his lips again, acting as though he'd never tasted anything so good.

"Sure glad you're in a sharing mood, Reg." He posed his fork for more. "When we were young, do you remember what you would do when you found out I was right and you were wrong?" He wiggled his eyebrows at her.

Regi's face turned bright red. She must have remembered that in such moments she'd give him a kiss to wiggle out of trouble. A devilish smile curled her lips. "Oh, yes. And I'm going to let you have it." She grabbed the pie and hit Samuel square in the face.

At first he was shocked. But wiping whipped cream from his eyes, he couldn't help but chuckle. He'd wanted her to blow off steam but wasn't quite prepared for pie in his face. At least now her temper had maxed out.

Maybe she'd settle down if he feigned anger. No way could he let her know he'd riled her on purpose. "What's the matter with you, woman?"

"You had that coming," Regi said. She looked about as though she suddenly realized how quiet the café had become. Everyone had stopped in midmotion, staring at them.

As if trying to undo some of the damage, she picked up the main glob of pie that had fallen to the table and put it back on the plate; then she attempted to wipe pie tailings from his cheeks. When she tried to brush it off his shirt, he grabbed her hand. "I can take it from here."

Stew tossed Samuel a towel as he approached. "Everything okay?" The smile on his face did not match his words of concern.

"Fine," Samuel said, as he used the rag to wipe cream filling and pie crust crumbs off his person. He handed the towel back to Stew, nodding his thanks. Chuckling, Stew returned to dealing with his other customers as their attention quickly went back to their own food and problems.

"Sorry, Tanner." Regi's apology was sincere.

"I had it coming." He saw a hint of gratitude shining in her eyes as she stared at a dab of whipped cream on his shirt. Wiping it up, he licked his finger. "I'm just tired of fighting with you. Aren't you tired of it, Regina?"

Her shoulders slumped as if she, too, felt the burden. She appeared to think for a moment and then said, "Let me see." Her index finger tapped her lips. "Tired of being gypped out of my husband's land and prime cattle, tired of having someone pay a pittance for a prized horse, tired of remembering the past we shared. No wait, there wasn't a past because somebody left in the middle of the night and never said a word and was too chicken to mail a stupid letter."

So she had been listening to him back at the ranch when he'd tried to tell her he'd wanted to send a letter. In a strange, upside-down way, he found this promising, even though she glared at him like a wild-eyed she-wolf. They were communicating, which meant there was hope for them yet.

"You know what, Tanner?" Her voice grew low, throaty. "I'm not tired of it. See, I know you're capable of destroying a person's heart and shattering dreams." Tears pooled in her eyes, but she continued. "Don't get me wrong. I appreciate the meal you fixed tonight and the small slice of good conversation about your nephew, but I can't help wondering if you're playing some kind of game with me like you did with Earl over his land. I could forgive your leaving me, but you lied to my husband. He worked darned hard to get the money to pay you. Then you rubbed it in his face. That, I can't forgive."

Samuel had never seen tears in her eyes before. He wanted to pull her into his arms and tell her how sorry he was, but he knew better than that. Instead he said, "I think Earl knew why I wouldn't sell. You can't tell me that your late husband didn't know there was still unfinished business between us."

Regi's brows raised in alarm. She could only glare at him as if to say *in your mind. I loved Earl.*

Samuel wished he could take back his words, but the damage was done. "Look, all I want to do is make peace, explain what really happened all those years ago, and maybe try to be friends." He wanted more than that, but he knew it was best to stop there.

Regi's demeanor changed as though she were thinking over what he'd said. Hope shot through him. Before he could say something else, Jed and his son walked into the café. Cliff stumbled over the doormat. Jed slapped him on the back of his head. "Watch where you're goin'!"

Clifford sniffled, wiping his nose on his coat sleeve. His entire hulklike frame shuddered, but a smile lit his face when he saw his uncle Samuel. Noticing a change in his son's demeanor, Jed swung around. As soon as he spied his brother, he shouted, "Ah, the man I wanted to see." His footsteps thunder clapped to the booth. Clifford tagged along behind.

"Can't find Aunt Ida," Jed said.

Samuel motioned for Jed and Clifford to sit across from him.

Before they could, Regi scooted around to the other side and got out. "Fellas, this sounds like a family matter. If you'll excuse me." She smiled at Clifford, nodded at Jed, and then—without even a sideways glance at Samuel—she left.

He watched her go, tuning out Jed as he droned on about how Ida'd left hours ago to do her goodwill visiting, but she hadn't returned home. Samuel wasn't the least bit concerned about his aunt's whereabouts. He'd learned long ago that Ida could take care of herself.

No, the woman who worried him most had just walked away.

NINE

INTENT

As Regi walked between automobiles in the parking lot to her Jeep, she worried about the conversation she'd just had with Tanner. He'd sounded like he wanted to make peace and be friends, not like a man guilty of murder. He sounded like a man with a future. But Regi couldn't think of that right now.

She dug in her pocket for the keys to the Jeep and found the note she'd stolen from Tanner's desk. Regi knew this note proved nothing, though was she overlooking something that was staring her in the face, something she couldn't see? What Tanner had said about not having time to move the body was right; however, he could have had an accomplice.

But who?

All his summer workers were gone.

And the knife issue was still unresolved. Not only did it point possible blame at Samuel but at her as well. She had to find Earl's knife to prove her innocence. She would tear the attic apart if she had to.

Regi caught sight of Mark Rankin, Stew's brother, sitting in a brand-spankin'-new white Corvette.

"Hey, nice car." She walked up beside the door and leaned over to speak with her friend. Immediately, she saw he'd lost more weight, and his complexion was a chalky gray.

"You like it?" His tired eyes glanced around the car's interior. "I think it's a bit much, but Stew insisted. I've always wanted one. He brought it home this morning. I was so excited. Just sitting behind the wheel makes me forget what's going on."

"Good for you." She eyed the car, wondering how Stew could afford such a pricey hunk of metal. And she'd given him a hundred dollars to help with expenses. Sheesh!

But she had given her money willingly. And for all she knew, maybe Stew could have taken a loan out on the café for this car. Who was she to judge? "Always had my eye on a Porsche. Kinda hard to go off-road and find good fishing holes, though, so I stay content with a Jeep. I'm driving Earl's now for a while. Older but still reliable. You doing okay?"

Mark patted her hand. "Every day that I draw breath is a bonus. Yeah, I'm doing fine."

"Well, if you need anything . . ."

He filled in her unspoken words. "Just call. I know. You're a dear friend, Reg. A rare breed is what you are."

Unable to tolerate a compliment, she said, "Best be on my way. Claud will wonder where I am. You take care."

"You too. From what Stew's been saying, you're in one sorry mess right now. If you need anything . . ."

"I know." Regi squeezed his arm and headed for her vehicle. Before jumping in the front seat, she looked in the back. Mining out the chocolate-covered macadamia nuts Tanner had given her, she crawled into the vehicle. As she selected a piece of chocolate, she wondered just what Stew had told his brother about her "sorry fix." Had Morgan told Stew everything like he had Tanner?

Probably not. Regi knew Morgan and Tanner were close friends. She looked at the Corvette.

What was Mark doing at Twiggs this time of night? Stew would work at least four more hours.

At that moment, the door of the café opened, and Stew came out carrying a to-go sack. He took it to Mark. *Ahh, he came for his dinner. Plus, he probably wanted to drive that new car.*

Regi started the old Jeep as she watched her two friends talking. Awfully nice what Stew did, buying his brother the car of his dreams. If Stew took a second mortgage on the café so he could give a dying man his last wish, more power to him.

Then she thought of Samuel's knife on the counter. Stew'd had access to the knife, but so? What did that have to do with buying his dying brother a car? What did it have to do with Romney's murder? Except . . . it put the weapon near him, and if Stew had any grudges against the man, it also gave him opportunity.

Ridiculous! Her imagination was running amuck. Regi knew it was time to go home.

As Regi drove out of the parking lot, she passed Ida Peck's rusty Plymouth station wagon. That sweet woman had probably been out helping an old friend. Oh, Regi knew Ida enjoyed spreading rumors, but she was harmless and gave comfort to those in need. Still, if Ida's good intentions led her to call Jack and Lisa and ask them what she could do to help their mother, that could be a disaster.

Regi made up her mind to call her kids, but she would wait till morning. She rehearsed the phone conversation in her mind. Lisa would be the hardest. Her breakup with Romney had been tough to get over, especially since he'd lied about the details. Lisa had sulked around the Raindancer for months, hardly eating and rarely going out with her friends.

Fortunately, Claudia had occupied Lisa with chores around the bed-and-breakfast. Sadly, Lisa had developed an unhealthy aversion for eating, but she seemed to love making fabulous fat-filled muffins as well as desserts, such as Black Forest cake, baked Alaska, and to-die-for chocolate seduction pie.

A car coming in the opposite direction passed, making the road behind very dark. Regi flipped her lights on high beam. Thinking of chocolate seduction pie, she remembered throwing the slice in Tanner's face only moments ago. Perfectly good pie gone to waste. She smiled. He'd looked surprised . . . and yet he didn't. Sure, he sounded upset, but she wondered. Tanner was a puzzle best left for another day. Instead of dwelling on him, she grabbed another chocolate and turned her thoughts to Lisa again.

Lisa never ate the desserts she made. She purposely placed temptation in her path and then turned her back on it as a way of torturing herself. Or perhaps she was growing stronger.

Regi hated the thought of telling Lisa that Romney had been murdered and her own mother was the prime suspect. Her daughter would be crushed. But what else could Regi do?

In her rearview mirror, she saw the headlights of an approaching car, but the vehicle was far away. Her mind went back to the call she'd have to make to her son, which would be a different matter from the call to Lisa. Jack was rarely surprised by his mother's actions, although hearing that Regi was suspected of murder might make him pause for a moment.

Already she could hear his patronizing drone of, "Well, Mother, that's what happens when you traipse around like a wild woman. I've got to go." And he'd be gone, busy with his own exciting college life, parties all night, and chasing girls. Talk about wild. Regi didn't know what she'd done wrong when it came to Jack. She loved her son, but he was not her favorite person. Whenever he came home for very long, an emotional tornado followed. The greeting was wonderful. Hug, hug, and all that, but within three minutes, mother and son began the cycle of out-besting each other. Jack's attitude was Earl's fault. He was an enabler, letting his son watch movies instead of helping on the ranch and giving him every computer game he wanted without working for it. Jack possessed an entitlement attitude Regi could hardly abide. But that didn't stop her from paying for his college. Weren't good parents supposed to provide a sound education for their kids?

The glaring lights of the approaching car from behind reflected off her rearview mirror and shone in Regi's eyes. "Back off."

Regi glanced down at the illuminated speedometer. The needle was around fifty-five, the maximum speed limit for night driving on this treacherous mountain road. On the right side was a cliff, and on the left side thick forest.

Jerk has no business following so closely.

She turned her mirror to keep the glare from obscuring her vision.

Blocking the tailgater out of her mind, Regi wondered how successful Claudia had been at the superintendent's. She hoped her sister had found something, anything that could help.

The lights of the tailgating car became more intense, filling the rear window of the Jeep, spotlighting it. If the person were so hot to get up the mountain, Regi would pull over and let him pass. She began to slow when the car slammed her from behind, shoving the Jeep forward.

"What the . . ."

It rammed again. The Jeep fishtailed.

The steering wheel flipped back and forth out of her hands. An ax of panic chopped through Regi. She grabbed onto the steering wheel, trying to gain control. This maniac would kill her.

Stupid drunk!

But even a drunk would let up once he bumped her the first time. This was intentional. No one else in town had a Jeep like Earl's. This person had to know Regi was driving.

All at once, things became clear. If Regi were no longer alive, she wouldn't be around to defend herself, which would make it much easier for folks to pin Romney's murder on her. But even with Regi dead, the sheriff would keep investigating, wouldn't he?

What did it matter? Whoever was in that vehicle wanted her dead and was more than likely the murderer! Regi was not going down without a fight. Somehow she had to get a glimpse of who was behind the wheel, but she'd have to survive first.

She floored the gas pedal. The Jeep sprang forward like a quarter horse cutting calves. The vehicle behind stayed with her, never falling back, never easing up. As the Jeep's speedometer slipped past eighty, a chill washed over Regi's back and limbs. She stared ahead and saw the winding curve of Neekumba Ridge. Shoshones had named it. *Neekumba* meant "kill yourself." This bend was notorious for accidents.

She gripped the wheel so hard she no longer felt her fingers. Her heartbeat became stampeding hooves.

The vehicle struck again, pushing the Jeep faster and faster, snowplowing Regi toward the edge.

After making sure the horses were in the barn and taken care of, Claudia had gone to bed. Shortly after midnight, she'd awakened, worried about Regi. Needing to assure herself that her sister had made it home and was safe, Claudia padded her way to Regi's bedroom door.

Quietly turning the knob, she gently pushed. Just as she feared, no Regi. Claudia stood for a moment in the doorway, looking over her sister's disheveled room. Regi never made her bed. Her comforter was in a wad on the middle of the mattress. Boots, socks, and jeans littered the floor. Leaning against the scarred chest of drawers was her fishing pole. The tackle box was on top of a mound of dirty clothes in the corner. Many times Claudia had hinted that her sister might pick up her room a bit. Regi joked that a clean bedroom was the sign of a nearsighted person. Claudia had laughed and asked why she thought that. Regi had replied that people who were bothered by clutter were too busy cleaning what's in front of them and missing life's sunsets.

Claudia's eyes were drawn to the painting above the bed: a sunset that Earl had painted of the Tetons with a teepee village at the base. Purples, pinks, and browns dominated the picture. Every time Claudia saw it, she wished she could find the peace the scene portrayed. Again she glanced at the empty bed and prayed Regi was safe.

Safe? Of course she was safe. Regi was just being Regi, out enjoying a good time like always. Still, would she be up to her old tricks with all the turmoil going on?

Claudia fingercombed her hair away from her face and breathed a heavy sigh as she trailed back to her room. She sat on the edge of her bed, plumping up a supportive pillow for under her knees to rest her bad back. Twisting another pillow to fit snugly under her aching neck, she lay back and tried to ignore the fear warning her that something was wrong. *No! Regi is all right,* she told herself. But the longer Claudia lay there, the more she doubted.

She flung off the covers and stormed to the bathroom for a sleeping pill. Her medicine cabinet was arranged in alphabetical order, starting with aspirin and ending with Zoloft. As she glanced at the bottles, she realized how pathetic she'd become, alphabetizing her meds. She immediately placed the ibuprofen bottle in the aspirin's place. At least that was a start toward change. Cupping water in her hands, she washed her face for the second time that night and stared at the water in the sink.

For an instant, a scene from her childhood came to mind. She had crouched on the ditch bank, trying to cup water in her hands to make mud pies, and fell in. She would have drowned if Regi hadn't been there.

Regi to the rescue. Funny how her younger sister was always there watching over her, making sure she was okay. Should have been the other way around, but it wasn't that day.

From then on, Claudia had developed a terrible fear of water and an unwavering devotion toward her sister. Now if only Claudia could return the favor and save Regi from this ordeal regarding Romney's death. But she couldn't think of what to do.

Except worry.

Claudia had that covered. She'd learned well from her years of worry over Morris and the nights he'd never come home. The thought of her late husband made her stomach ache. She glanced at the empty space where his picture sat during the day, glad she did not have to abide his eyes on her while she slept.

With all these turbulent thoughts, even sleeping pills wouldn't help her. Best to wait until Regi showed up. Claudia decided to read a book. First, though, she needed something warm in her stomach.

She made her way through the dark hallways of the Raindancer to the kitchen. As she flipped on the light, she found Wakanda sitting in the dark, staring at the back door. Oscar slept in the corner. Fine watchdog he was, letting Wakanda in without a whimper. But then again, the Irish setter knew her, and the dog had, after all, defended Claudia against Ida. He deserved the rest of the night off.

"Hello," Claudia said. "You worried too?"

The old woman nodded. No verbal reply, of course. Claudia reached for the canister where she kept the tea bags. "How about some herbal tea?" She didn't wait for an answer and began filling the old metal teapot with water.

Setting three cups on the table, Claudia squirted a dab of honey in two, one for Wakanda and one for her. The third cup was for Regi, though she would want hot chocolate when she arrived.

Waiting for the water to boil, Claudia looked at the old woman who was such a challenge to talk with. Still, she was company at lonely times.

Stone-faced, Wakanda's gaze never wavered from the back door. Determined to capture the woman's attention, Claudia grabbed a chair and pulled it close. "You know, life would be much easier for us both if we could communicate. We started off on the wrong foot."

Wakanda blinked, not looking at her.

Claudia's teeth worried her bottom lip as she tried to think of what she could say. Finally, something came to her. "When I first met you, I had just buried my husband, and my sense of cordiality was gone. I shunned you, and I'm sorry. In a way, I guess I thought of you as a threat, that perhaps you were the sister to Regi that I could never be. Anyway, now I know more about you."

Wakanda turned and looked at Claudia but only for a second; then she quickly went back to her vigil, as if staring at the door would make Regi appear.

Claudia reached to pat Wakanda but stopped when she remembered the woman did not like anyone touching her. "Don't worry. You know Regi as well as I do. She'll be home soon."

Claudia carried the empty cup to Regi's usual place. The teapot began its shrill whistle. Claudia poured water in two cups, placing a spearmint tea bag in each. Setting Wakanda's in front of her, Claudia sat down with her own cup and fiddled with the tea bag string dangling from the rim.

Wakanda didn't touch her tea. Claudia knew she probably wouldn't. That was all right. Claudia was determined to eventually win over this quiet, odd person as a friend.

The clock ticked loudly, and the night grew long as Claudia finished her tea and fell asleep with her head on the table.

Wakanda's and Regi's cups remained untouched.

The vehicle rammed the rear of the Jeep again. Panic sucked breath from Regi's lungs. Somehow, some way, she had to think of a plan.

The revolver strapped to her leg. Yes! Frantic, Regi reached down, yanked the protective strap back that held the weapon tight to her calf, and grabbed the gun. Now what? The bend of the mountain drew closer and closer. The life-threatening cliff was beyond. If she could somehow shoot at the driver, maybe he would back off. Her options were waning.

Again, the vehicle collided with hers, making Regi drop the gun to the floor. Great! The cliff was only seconds away.

"Please, Father, guide me," she prayed. Suddenly, she realized her only option was to swerve into the other lane and hope there wasn't an oncoming car on this two-lane road. With no time to think of other options, Regi firmly gripped the wheel and jerked.

TEN

TO DREAM

THE SCREAM OF SKIDDING TIRES echoed in Regi's ears as her Jeep careened across the highway. Terror-filled seconds reeled by as if in slow motion. Her vehicle hit the dirt off the side of the road and bumped into a small hill, sailing a few feet before touching down. The Jeep slowed some as trail brush battered the vehicle from beneath, but it was still going too fast.

Regi glanced up in time to see the long-reaching branches of a pine tree a moment before the Jeep rammed into it head-on.

Her forehead smacked against the steering wheel.

A high-pitched ringing clanged in her ears. She tried to hang onto consciousness, but darkness overcame her vision.

And then nothing.

Samuel drove past the Gas-N-Grub. Jed and his stupid worries. Because of his brother, Regi had slipped away before he could talk her into listening to him.

Samuel had to face the truth. Maybe he wasn't meant to be with Regi. Years had piled deep resentment toward him on her shoulders. He shouldn't have kept himself so busy ranching and pining over the woman he had loved since the first day he'd seen her. He needed to cut loose the feelings he had for Regina and find someone else.

Heck, it would be a lot less work.

Marjean Buttons or Dixie Sutherland. No, he'd already gone out with them and realized neither one was a good fit. The waitress, Julie Ann, came to mind. She was certainly gentle on the eyes and always seemed to be in a good mood. How refreshing would that be? Someone he could actually have a conversation with and not worry about getting a pie in the face or saying something that would cause the woman to go ballistic.

He sighed at the thought. As he envisioned Julie Ann, her features morphed into Regi's. Who was he kidding? He craved the verbal sparring. He liked the fire and fight and egged it on most of the time. Wondering what it would be like to live with Regi twenty-four/seven, Samuel knew life would never be boring.

As his one-ton truck rolled up the mountain highway, Samuel wondered what he could do to make amends with Regi. The mistakes of his past had cut deep scars, and now with this business over Romney, would she ever heal? Would it be worth trying to have the life he'd always dreamed of with Regi? He knew the answer.

Yes.

Regi's attitude had softened tonight: first at his place and then a little more at the café. Maybe he could send her flowers. No, Regi wasn't the flower type. Candy might have a little sway. Chocolate pie was too dangerous. But he needed something. Something spectacular.

Suddenly, on the other side of the road, he spied headlights shooting off into the timber. He pulled over and stopped. That's when he saw Regi's Jeep crunched up against a hefty ponderosa pine. Flames licked at the crumpled hood.

Pinpricks of fear dotted his skin. Filled with adrenaline, he leaped from his truck and sprinted over the ground. With each pounding step, his horror escalated. He could hardly breathe. After an eternity, he reached the wreckage.

Approaching the driver's side, he noticed the door was missing. Regi was lying over the steering wheel and wasn't moving.

"Regi . . ." He reached a shaking hand to her shoulder, touching her softly, hoping she would respond. Her hat was gone, probably blew off with the impact.

She didn't move or make a sound. The smell of gasoline grew strong. Once the gas hit the flames the entire Jeep would go up.

"Regina, answer me!" He shook her.

He had to get her out!

He fumbled with the seat belt. The earthquake he felt within made his hands tremble. Finding the release button, he pressed down, and the belt loosened. He noticed a revolver on the floor by her feet. He couldn't leave that in the Jeep. The heat from the fire could make it go off. He quickly grabbed the gun and stuffed it beneath his belt. Pulling Regi's limp body into his arms, he heard her moan, giving him hope.

She couldn't die. Not now. She couldn't die never knowing how he truly felt.

Cradling her in his arms, he hurried toward his truck. "Hang on, sweetheart! Please hang on!"

Finally reaching his Ford, he wrenched open the passenger's door. The dome light lit up the cab as he laid her on the seat. A large bump marred her forehead, but she was breathing. Earl's Jeep predated air bags. At the very least, she was going to have a whopping headache. Samuel had to take her to the hospital. Ready to strap her in, he heard her mumble, so he stopped.

"Regina." He took her hand, coaxing for more.

She blinked, and then those beautiful green eyes that reminded him of watercress in a mountain stream opened wide.

Upon seeing him, fear clouded her face, and she pushed away, trying to escape as if he were going to harm her.

"Calm down." He grabbed her, holding her tight against him.

"You tried to kill me!" she spat out as she fought for air.

"What?"

She looked at him with terror-filled eyes. "You ran me off the road."

He cradled her head to his chest. "Regina, I just got here."

She pushed against him, hitting hard, still trying to get away. "You rammed my Jeep with your truck. You tried to push me over the ridge."

He grabbed hold of her shoulders, forcing her to look at him. "Someone tried to kill you?"

"Like you don't know!"

"Regina, I swear I did not try to run you off the road. If it had been me, don't you think I would have left you for dead instead of saving you?" He stared right into those eyes that could melt his heart. He remembered the gun. Pulling it out, he handed it to her. "I found this on the floor of your car. If I'd tried to kill you, I certainly wouldn't give you a gun."

She slowly quit struggling. Regi took the weapon. "If you didn't do it, who did?" Looking around, she peered into the inky darkness as if afraid her attacker would leap out at any moment.

"Whoever it was, they're long gone now." Worried she might shoot at something, he said, "You want me to put that away?"

She pulled her pant leg up and fastened the weapon in the holster.

He noticed her gaze shift to the crumpled Jeep against the tree as she put the gun away. The flames were gaining strength. That she'd survived the crash was amazing, perhaps even a miracle, if a person believed in such things.

Suddenly, the Jeep exploded. The concussion of the blast rattled the Ford. A fire ball whooshed up the large tree the vehicle had careened into. Sparks shot into the night sky.

Samuel reached past her and grabbed the mike of his old, antiqued CB. As he radioed for help, he kept an eye on Regi. She sat still, watching the flames as if hypnotized. Tears came to her eyes, yet she fought the emotion. The Jeep was Earl's. He could well understand she still carried a love for her late husband. Samuel wondered what it would be like if it were him she loved that much. He took hold of her small, shaking hand, ending the call as quickly as he could.

He knew he should go around the truck and get into the driver's side, but he didn't want to leave her for one second. Climbing up, Samuel nudged her over; then taking her in his arms, he held her close. She leaned her head against his chest. Glancing down at her, he saw that her cheeks were wet with tears. She'd lost the battle. He heard her sniff. With no Kleenex in the truck, he pulled the wrinkly, used handkerchief from his pocket. He offered it to her. Saying nothing, she found a clean corner and wiped her cheeks and blew her nose.

"I've lost another piece of him." Her voice was soft, wistful, and without hope.

"He's always with you." Samuel didn't know if he truly believed that, but he said it because he knew it was something she would like to hear, something that might make her feel better, even though it tore him up with jealousy.

He heard sirens in the distance. One thing about Trailhead: the volunteer fire department was always quick to respond. Living in dense forest land, they had to be. Plus, the park service would send some of their folks as well.

Before too long the place was swarming with emergency workers and rangers, and even Karen Wilson came with her medical bag. As soon as she climbed out of her minivan, she marched over to check on Regi.

Karen flashed a light in Regi's eyes, as if looking for signs of a concussion. "Your pupils are a bit dilated. But I think you're all right. Have any confusion?"

"No," Regi answered softly.

Samuel nodded yes so Karen could see but Regi couldn't. Karen patted Regi's arm. Regi weakly smiled but quickly turned her attention back to the fire.

Motioning Samuel to follow her away from the cab, Karen talked to him in hushed tones. "I'd feel a whole lot better if you drove her down to Bounty Falls and had a doctor check her over."

"No problem." Samuel thanked Karen for her help. As the nurse walked away and Samuel went back to Regi, Morgan arrived with lights flashing and siren blaring.

By now the rangers and volunteers had the fire almost out. Morgan hurried over to Samuel's truck. "What happened?"

"Someone tried to kill me," Regi said in a deadpan voice that was unnatural for her. Samuel glanced at Regi; her eyes were fixed on the charred vehicle.

"Looks that way." Morgan yanked his hat from his bald head.

"A car tried to run me off Neekumba Ridge," she said in a very calm, matter-of-fact voice as she turned her gaze to the sheriff.

Morgan must have been taken aback by her demeanor because he looked at Regi then at Samuel then Regi again.

"He wanted me dead." A thread of anger laced her voice. Her fight was returning. Samuel let out a relieved breath he didn't know he'd held.

"Don't you understand?" Regi seemed convinced she'd come upon the truth. "It's so simple. If I died, everyone would label me as Romney's killer."

"Sheriff Morgan!" one of the firemen yelled.

Morgan gave him an acknowledging wave then turned back to Regi. "Relax a minute. I'm going to see what he wants, and I'll be right back." He shot Samuel a puzzled look, as if to say *is this for real?* Then he hurried to the waiting firemen and rangers.

Samuel noticed how intently Regi watched Morgan leave.

"He doesn't believe me." She stared up at Samuel. "Do you?"

"Yeah, I do." He took her hand, and she pulled away. She was withdrawing again. But she'd been through a lot this evening. She was injured and needed to go off alone and lick her wounds.

"Can you take me home?" she said softly.

"I'm sure Morgan will have more questions for you."

She glanced at Samuel, and he knew she was barely hanging on.

He wanted her to be at ease. "I'll go have a talk with Morgan first. Will you be all right for a minute?"

Regi nodded.

Samuel quickly checked with the sheriff. He was fine with getting her statement tomorrow—especially when Samuel told him Karen wanted Regi to go to Bounty Falls to be checked at the hospital.

Samuel returned to his truck and climbed into the driver's side. Starting the Ford, he turned the one-ton truck around and headed for the city.

"Wait a minute!" Regi grabbed his arm.

"What?"

"This isn't the way to the Raindancer."

"Nope. Karen gave me orders to take you to the hospital." He didn't look at her. On this he was going to stand firm, even if Regi had one of her hissy fits.

She grew unexpectedly quiet, which concerned Samuel but not enough for him to turn the truck around. Regi needed a doctor's care, and he was going to see that she got it. He'd come too close to losing her tonight to risk doing anything else.

After a couple of miles, Regi broke the silence. "On the night Earl died in that hospital, I swore I would never return. Samuel, I can't go back there. Not tonight. Not after . . ."

She'd said his first name. She hadn't done that since they were kids. He heard her sniff. Why couldn't she have accused him of murder or anything but this? She sounded beaten, no hope in her voice, only sorrow and grief. He could do nothing to help, except—

Pulling off to the side of the road, he flipped on the dome light. He turned in his seat, grabbed her chin, and tilted her head so he could check her pupils; he wanted to make sure they hadn't changed since Karen had seen them.

As he studied her, he suddenly saw much more than green luscious irises. In those eyes staring up at him, he looked past the sorrow and grief and saw something more. Something that even surprised him.

Need?

Hope?

His future?

His breathing became shallow; his heart rammed against his ribs. She was right here as he'd always dreamed—her lips but a kiss away.

"What do you see?" she whispered, her breath fanning his face.

He blinked, trying to be reasonable. She'd been through a horrible accident. Someone had tried to kill her. That desperate thought made him want to take her in his arms even more, made him want to kiss her and drink in her essence. But this was neither the time nor the place.

If he kissed her now, she would think he was taking advantage of her. Samuel wanted Regi to know that when he kissed her it was for all the right reasons.

Her pupils weren't dilated, and her coloring was coming back, except for the large bump on her forehead. Working on a ranch, he'd seen his share of forehead goose eggs. He cleared his throat. "I think you'll be all right." He reluctantly let her go and turned back to the steering wheel.

Regi closed her eyes and leaned her head on the back of the seat. Samuel wheeled the Ford around and headed for the Raindancer.

As Tanner's truck covered the miles to the bed-and-breakfast, Regi felt humbled by the events of the evening. While she'd sat watching Earl's Jeep burn, Tanner had stayed by her side, not badgering her about why she was crying or going over her story. He'd stood beside her like a sentinel, keeping her safe. He seemed to understand the torment she felt, which was not like him.

Or was it?

Another layer had peeled off Samuel Tanner that she never knew existed. And moments ago, the way he had looked into her eyes. What in the world had he been thinking? He'd stared at her for the longest time as if he were seeing inside her soul. And as she'd stared back, she'd felt those old feelings she'd thought were long dead. She'd yearned for him to hold her, kiss her, like he had when they were young. Then she remembered how earlier this evening, after they had eaten dinner, he would not tell her Morgan had been his visitor. Anger replaced her yearning. Her thoughts were as tangled as barbed wire.

This evening was one unpredictable bronc ride. Her emotions were thrown up and down, side to side, forward and backward. So many things had happened in such a short amount of time. One thing for certain: at Tanner's place, he and Morgan had talked about something important that they didn't want her to know.

What was the "good" sheriff up to? Maybe he had some type of lead that made him suspect Tanner, and that's why he'd gone to his home. But it really didn't sound like it. Could it have been something to do with Hannah? Morgan and Tanner were friends, and friends shared their worries with each other. But why did Tanner not tell Morgan she was there? Then again, Morgan would have seen Earl's Jeep parked outside, so he knew she was.

But what if what Morgan was doing had nothing to do with helping her? What if it had everything to do with convicting her?

So why did he go to Tanner and talk with him? Regi remembered watching a TV drama where one lifetime friend pinned a murder on his buddy because he needed the money for a dying loved one. Morgan was under extraordinary pressure at home, and if he'd caught Curtis Romney doing something wrong, he could have snapped.

Or if Romney had offered him money to do something illegal, he could have agreed and then thought better of it and tried to back out, but Romney wouldn't let him, so Morgan—

Could Morgan have killed Romney?

Sure, after Regi'd stumbled upon the body she had found the sheriff at the Gas-N-Grub, but if the murder had happened in the wee morning hours, he certainly would have had time to go home, change, and then act as though everything were normal, even show up at the Gas-N-Grub.

And Tanner? She stole a glance at him. From the dim glow of the dashboard, she could see his chiseled, masculine features: noble brow, Roman nose, and strong chin. For a second that thrill she'd had as a girl whenever she saw him walking her way stirred her insides. Her look drifted to his strong hands gripping the steering wheel. With those hands, had Tanner hidden the body for his friend? Morgan and Tanner had acted all surprised down at the river, but if they were covering up a murder, how else were they supposed to act? Somehow she needed to see if she could whittle more information from Samuel . . . no, Tanner. She had to keep that distance.

If *Tanner* and Morgan were working together, Regi had to be careful because if she were to simply accuse them outright, Tanner'd dismiss her as being the hot-headed person she was. Trying to sound genuinely contrite—which wasn't hard after everything she'd been through—she said, "I'm sorry for all the trouble I've been."

"What?" Tanner glanced at her, a trace of disbelief on his face.

"I'm sorry." She hoped he wouldn't make her say it again because trying to fake contrition added to the pain pressing down on her head, and she didn't think she could keep it up.

He chuckled. "You've apologized to me twice tonight. This should be in *Ripley's Believe It or Not.*"

"See, miracles do happen," she teased, hoping he would remember when they'd talked about miracles at his house. If she kept their conversation light, he wouldn't suspect she was about to pounce.

A slow country smile crossed his face. "All right. I believe you. You must be feeling better."

"Yeah, feels like a wild horse stampede tromped over my head, but I think I'll live." She was glad he'd relaxed.

"Can you give me a description of the car that ran you off the road?" He stole a quick glance away from the highway, as though checking to see if his question caused her unnecessary pain or riled her.

Regi rubbed her neck and tried to stop the shaking that instantly came over her at the thought of how close she'd come to dying. *Must be a delayed nervous reaction.* "The headlights were round and very bright."

"Oh, that's helpful." Tanner gave her a sideways look. "Morgan's going to like that description."

"Sorry. See, I said it again." Regi glanced at him, hoping he'd give her another smile. She caught sight of the grin he tried to hide by scrubbing his face with his palm.

"Heaven, give me patience." He sighed. "That's only an expression. Don't think you've converted me." Tanner leaned his left arm on the armrest of the truck's door, his other hand on the wheel. "It's a good thing you're about home. You need some sleep. Maybe by morning you'll remember more."

Regi swallowed hard and slumped back. He was right. She was tired of it all. Tired of trying to think of who could be a killer, tired of trying to prove Tanner was guilty, but mostly she was tired of hating him.

The thought of abandoning her quest for the truth, though, scared her almost as much as going over Neekumba Ridge.

Once they arrived at the Raindancer, Regi was reluctant to accept Tanner's offer to assist her inside. She needed distance from him to gain perspective. But he insisted, and she couldn't resist when he slung his arm about her waist and held her close. Oh, how she'd missed having a man's arms around her.

She glanced back at his truck, making sure there were no scrapes or dents that would implicate him as the one trying to kill her. His truck was undamaged. Shame befell her for doubting, but old habits die hard.

Entering through the back doorway, she found Oscar waiting, his body twisting in tail waggles. She wanted to pet her dog and give him a proper greeting but couldn't. Tanner guided her past Oscar. Claudia sat with her head on the table sound asleep, her hand resting beside an empty teacup.

Surprised to see Wakanda at the other end of the table, Regi remembered Claudia had asked the old woman to mind the bed-and-breakfast while they were both gone on their separate snooping expeditions. Wakanda's arms were folded. Her dark gaze took in everything, from Tanner's hold around Regi's waist, to the bump on her head.

Tanner nodded a hello to Wakanda. "Regi was almost killed tonight."

At the sound of Tanner's voice, Claudia sprang to life, standing up so abruptly that her chair toppled over. "What . . . who?" Picking up the chair, she settled her worried gaze on Regi.

Regi had hoped Claudia would be in bed so there wouldn't be the inevitable mothering and nagging that could smother a wolf, let alone a human. Trying to short circuit her sister's worry and her mothering nonsense, Regi said, "I'm fine. I was in a little accident."

Though she was feeling weak, Regi attributed it to the sickness that had threatened her the past few days, which had now settled in her sinuses, clawed at her throat, and made her achy all over. Although she knew more aches and pains from the accident would reveal themselves by morning, she tried to appear normal.

Claudia brushed Regi's bangs aside, looking at the bump on her forehead. "If you're fine, why is there a black and blue goose egg the size of a billiard ball growing on your head? And you feel feverish." Claudia cast a condemning stare toward Tanner. "Why didn't you take her to the hospital? She probably has a concussion."

Before he could answer, Claudia took Regi from him and guided her to a chair, making her sit down. Oscar immediately rested his snout on Regi's leg. Claudia pushed the animal aside. With a concerned look, the dog slunk back to his corner as if knowing he needed to stay out of the way.

Claudia disappeared into the pantry and came out with an ice bag. She began filling it with ice cubes from the freezer. "So what happened, Samuel?"

"I didn't take her to the hospital because she wouldn't go, but Karen Wilson looked her over. I think she'll be all right." He paused as if he had more to say but didn't immediately continue. Then he patted Regi's shoulder. "I'd better leave. Tell them what happened." Leaning over, he acted as if he were going to kiss her on the cheek, but instead he said softly in her ear, "Take care of yourself." He quickly retreated through the back door. Regi gave a sigh, glad but also a bit sad to see him leave.

Claudia placed the ice bag on Regi's head and sat expectantly on the edge of her seat. Before explaining, Regi first glanced to Wakanda, hopeful for a friendly smile.

No sign of one.

Taking a deep breath, Regi told her sister and her friend what had happened, starting with her evening with Tanner and ending with his rescuing her. However, she left out that Morgan had paid a visit to Tanner's and that she feared they were plotting against her. Claudia would only defend Morgan, and right now, Regi didn't think she could handle that.

A silence blanketed them.

Then Regi added, "I'm sorry I was late and worried you." She turned her attention solely to Claudia. "Tell me about your evening."

Claudia glanced at Wakanda then back to Regi. "I think I've come up with who could have killed Romney."

Regi stared at her, waiting. "Are you going to tell us?"

"Yes, poachers! The rangers are always finding poachers. They have knives, and if they cornered Romney, it's possible." Claudia folded her arms as if she'd solved the case.

Regi hated bursting her bubble, but someone had to. "When rangers go after poachers, they never go alone."

"Maybe he came upon them before he could call for help, and he had to take care of them by himself." Claudia defended her conclusion.

"Okay, we'll keep that in mind, but I really don't think that's what happened. Did you learn anything else?" Regi wished the answer to this murder was as simple as poachers, but she knew it wasn't.

Claudia shrugged. "I learned the park is planning to sell some property."

"What? Who told you that?" Regi moved the ice bag to her throbbing temple.

Claudia started at the beginning, telling how distraught Romney's widow was over his death and how on Claudia's way out she'd overheard Elliott discussing the land auction. Finished with her news, she sat back in her seat.

Wakanda gave a dismal grunt as if there had been more to Claudia's evening.

"What aren't you telling me?" Regi's pounding headache snuffed out her little patience. "If you found something, I need to know. I don't like surprises."

"Seems I've heard that somewhere before." Claudia leaned closer to Regi. "I told you that yesterday as I drew your bath." She glared.

Feeling guilty about not sharing her misgivings in regards to Morgan and Tanner working together as partners, Regi reflexively pushed the thought aside and mentally crossed her fingers. "I forgot some things. Sorry." So she'd used the one lie she'd hoped God would grant her. She'd repent later. "What's happened?"

Claudia bit her bottom lip. Then her foot began a nervous jiggling. Finally, she gave it up. "Ida Peck paid us a visit."

"Oh, is that all?" Regi pulled the ice bag from her head and plopped it on the table.

"Is that all! I know you don't think that woman is trouble, but believe me, I know her kind. She cannot be trusted." Claudia told Regi about her conversation with Ida, saying the old gossip had somehow learned of Regi's run-in with Romney at Twiggs. If Ida knew about it, the entire county knew as well. Regi didn't want to think what would happen when Ida learned of the pie incident with Tanner, let alone the accident tonight.

Regi's temples throbbed. Her blocked sinuses made her cheeks sore beneath her eyes, or did that come from the accident? Her head felt as big as a giant pumpkin. She needed her bed and soft, fluffy pillow. But mostly she needed to make all this go away for a while. "Let's go to bed and discuss this in the morning. And Ida got her wires crossed. I never said I'd maim Romney. I promised to make his life miserable, that's all. Hardly a threat."

"He doesn't need to worry about that anymore, does he?" Claudia picked up the ice bag Regi had left on the table. "Are you sure you're all right?"

Regi glared at her as if to say, *do I look all right?*

"I mean, do you need something to eat or medicine?" Claudia pointed to her head.

"I've had worse knocks tripping over my own feet. I'm just so darned tired." She smiled at Claudia, knowing her sister meant well.

Before leaving the kitchen, Regi looked at her old friend. "Wakanda, you staying the night?"

She grunted yes. The old woman never took her eyes off Regi as she left the room.

Samuel drove his truck up to the front of his house and shut off the engine. It had been a *long* night.

His mind automatically went to Regi as he glanced down at the pie stain on his shirt. Life would be so much easier if he could forget Regina. *So much easier.*

But at least now he had a glimmer of hope, remembering that moment in the truck when he'd checked the dilation of her pupils and was tempted to scoop her in his arms—tell her he loved her. But for some fool reason, he'd convinced himself that he didn't want her to think he'd acted out of pity.

Getting out of the truck, he slammed the door and stormed into the house. Flipping on the lights as he entered, he headed straight for the kitchen. After everything that had happened, he needed something to drink.

Pulling open the fridge, he found only pop, water, and milk. Long ago he'd sworn off beer and hard liquor when he found himself drinking too much. Especially when he was alone, which was most of the time. He was determined not to follow his father's path.

Grabbing the milk jug, he opened the lid and took a couple of swigs. Disappointed by the lack of taste, he leaned against the counter and glanced about the room. Gazing at the blue walls and windows, he knew in the back of his mind he'd built this place for Regi, kitchen and all.

Bluebells . . . now, as he looked at the towels and fancy curtains, he realized they didn't suit her. No, she was more the color red and straight, blunt cuts, not quite so fancy. He chuckled as he thought of the burned steaks and the blare of the smoke alarm. Little had he known that was a precursor to her nearly being burned to death in Earl's old Jeep. What if he hadn't come along and pulled her from the vehicle?

Still, even with her barely surviving a horrible accident, the evening had ended with them finding a strange peace. He wanted this peace treaty to last. Maybe he should follow the sheriff's advice and stay away from Regi until this Romney trouble blew over. Morgan had been none too happy to see that she'd been here at Samuel's place. The sheriff had stopped by to tell Samuel he was definitely going out of town tomorrow and he wanted to give his housekeeper Tanner's number in case she needed his help with Hannah. Then he'd warned Samuel not to tell Regi where he was going and why. Not telling her what Morgan had said was for her own good. What Samuel needed to do was find his stupid knife. If he could show that to Regi, he knew she would be more open with him.

He honestly couldn't remember getting it back from Stew. Samuel had been so wrapped up in bribing Regi to go out with him and then with Romney . . . There was no sense looking for it now because in the back of his mind, Samuel knew the murder weapon had been his very own knife. What he had to do was find out who had been in Twiggs and could have possibly picked it up.

Stew, Regi, Romney . . . They'd been there while Samuel was, but he supposed the knife could have been on the counter long after they'd left.

What he had to do was find out what other customers had been in the café that night.

Well, now he knew what he'd be doing tomorrow. Deciding to go to bed, he reached to turn out the kitchen light, but as he did, he gave one last look around the room. For a moment, he remembered Regi here. He added checking on her to his "to-do" list for the morning. But he wanted to do something that would show her he cared. Something more than merely saving her life by pulling her out of the Jeep before it exploded. He would have done that for anyone he came upon in an accident. He needed to do something that would push her into his arms and keep her there forever.

When they'd argued at Twiggs and she had said he'd taken advantage of her by buying Earl's cattle, the property, and even her prized horse, he knew denying her accusations would have been pointless. While Regi was right that he'd bought them all, he'd done it believing someday he and Regina would be together. He wanted to tell her of his plans, and he would.

Though not quite yet.

An idea came to him. A brilliant idea. And he could do it in the morning. This would show his willingness to bend and hopefully woo her off her feet.

Yep . . . first thing in the morning he would ignore Morgan's advice to keep his distance from Regi and head straight to the Raindancer.

Regi felt someone nudge her shoulder. Without opening her eyes, she mumbled, "Go away."

Again the nudge.

Was Oscar begging to go out? Regi'd just fallen asleep. Couldn't he hold on until morning?

Another nudge, but this time Regi didn't think it was the dog. Claudia? Unless the house was burning down, she'd better have a darned good reason for waking her. With a great deal of effort, she cracked open one eye.

Wakanda's dirt-smudged face was directly over her, and Regi noticed a most putrid smell, like rotten potatoes, though she wasn't awake enough to really identify the stench. The old woman smiled, and her yellow-stained teeth came into full focus.

Regi sat up.

Wakanda straightened, standing before her dressed in a wraparound breechcloth, a threadbare T-shirt, and holey tennis shoes. Convincing herself that she was seeing things, Regi laid back down, pulling her blankets up around her neck. She'd obviously taken too much medication, or maybe she did have a concussion. Whatever caused this hallucination, she wanted it to go away. Regi rolled over, closing her eyes.

A heavy hand pressed her shoulder. "Come."

Since when did a hallucination touch a person and talk? Wakanda was heading toward the bedroom door. She must need some kind of help, and Regi was the only person she would turn to.

Why tonight?

Regi flung off her covers and stood up. The room tilted and twirled. She grabbed her bedpost until the whirling stopped. Dressed in only thermal underwear, Regi stuffed her sockless feet into her boots. Grabbing her sheepskin coat as they left her room and headed down the stairs, she whispered at Wakanda's back, "Do you know what time it is?"

No answer.

"Where are we going?"

No answer.

At the foot of the stairs, Wakanda turned around and gave a look that said, "Be quiet!" It made no sense to argue with the determined woman.

The only way to help her was to follow.

ELEVEN
EXPECTATIONS

ONCE OUTSIDE, WAKANDA NEVER LOOKED back. Regi pulled the collar of her sheepskin coat up to her ears, trying to shield herself from the cold. Oscar followed them out of the house and raced between Wakanda and Regi, happy to see people up and about in the middle of the night. Regi patted the Irish setter's head each time the dog came to her. His arthritic hindquarters and pinned leg gave him a unique sideways gallop.

Wakanda led the way through the barn and into the bunk room. A fire burned in the Franklin stove. A large pot simmered, emitting a most foul odor, the rotten potato smell Regi'd noticed when Wakanda first awakened her. The room was amazingly hot. An old army blanket had been placed in front of the stove. A medicine pipe lay on a large flagstone next to the fireplace. Wakanda pointed for Regi to sit on the blanket and said, "First, clothes off."

"What?"

"Take off clothes."

"No way!"

Wakanda gave a disgusted sigh. "Poisons fill you."

Regi sneezed.

"Must sweat. Let them out."

"It's more likely that I'll sweat with my clothes *on*. Look, I know you only have my best interest at heart, but the very *best* thing for me right now would be to go to bed and sleep." Regi hoped she was getting through to this dear woman who was trying to help her the only way she knew how.

Regi turned to leave. Wakanda sprinted to block her path. "A death cloud hangs over you. Dark bundles are attached to your spirit. Must get rid of poison."

"Sleep will get rid of the poison, and as for the dark bundles, I'm working on that."

Wakanda shook her head. "You need help from above."

Regi was touched that her friend wanted to help her, but she had to make her understand. "Wakanda, your religion and the way you talk to the Great Spirit are very important to you. And even though you're not an Indian, you are trying the best you can to worship as they do. But . . ." Regi took hold of the old woman's arms. "As you know, I'm a member of The Church of Jesus Christ of Latter-day Saints. We believe that if you do everything you possibly can and then pray for guidance, the Lord will help you. And He will . . . tomorrow . . . after I get some sleep."

Wakanda gazed at her with no response. A thought hit Regi. Maybe now she could tell Wakanda more about the Church. "The Book of Mormon talks about the Indians. In the book they're called Lamanites."

Wakanda huffed. "I know. It says the Lamanites were evil."

Surprised that her friend had heard anything about the book, Regi went on. "The Lamanites were a mighty nation. And you're right, some of them were evil, but some weren't. And did you also know that there were evil Nephites?"

Wakanda's brows knitted together as she thought.

"It's true." Regi continued. "King Jacob was the worst, and he was a Nephite. You might want to read the book sometime. I have several copies. I'd be happy to give you one." Regi had always meant to give her friend a copy of the book that had changed her own life, but she had been holding off for the right time.

Wakanda shrugged. "Can we trade?"

"Trade what?"

Wakanda looked to the place where she wanted Regi to sit. Regi didn't want to offend her friend, but she had to make her understand. "Here's the deal. I'm not an Indian, so I don't think what you have planned will work on me."

"You have been called by celestial dwellers." Wakanda folded her arms, waiting for Regi to dispute her claim.

Curious as to what she was thinking, Regi asked, "What makes you say that?"

"Sorry trials have fallen upon you. The Great Spirit is testing you." Genuine concern creased the woman's brow.

Could that be true? Was the Lord testing Regi? Nah. From her study of the gospel, she knew God didn't work that way. She needed to place her faith in Him and listen to His promptings. It was up to her to recognize His voice and feel His guidance. The problem was, deep inside Regi didn't know if she was worthy enough to know the difference between her wishful thoughts and God's still, small voice.

Yet, as she'd told Wakanda about the Book of Mormon, Regi'd felt as though she was doing what God wanted her to do. Somehow this mystery over Romney's death would work out. And somehow the Lord would help her hang on and see it through.

She glanced at Wakanda, who was waiting. Knowing how important this was to her friend, Regi gave in. "Okay, trade. I'll go through this, and you promise to read the Book of Mormon?"

Wakanda gave a slight nod.

Before sitting down, Regi asked, "This doesn't involve my eating snakes or bugs or *rotten potatoes*, does it?"

"No." Wakanda glowered. "Just eat herbs, then sweat and pray."

"Okay. But my clothes are staying on." Regi hoped playing along with her friend would not be offensive to God. She wouldn't do anything to cross Church standards. Wakanda had good intentions, and Regi believed God understood.

Regi sat down. Oscar settled beside her. Wakanda held out her hand, motioning for Regi to take off her coat. Okay, she could give that up, but not the thermal underwear. Begrudgingly she handed her the jacket.

Wakanda hung it on the wooden post of the wagon-wheel bunk-bed frame. Next she ladled out a bowl of brown, warm liquid and handed it to Regi as she sat down. "Drink!"

Raising the bowl to her lips, Regi stopped and sniffed. Beneath the putrid smell was a hint of cinnamon and cloves. "What is in this?"

"Drink."

"But . . ."

"Drink!"

"Okay, okay." Regi took a breath and tried to put her mouth on the bowl. Her bottom lip curled to one side and then the other. She couldn't do it. Through the liquid's vapors, she spied Wakanda. The woman would not allow Regi to leave until she sipped. Finally, closing her eyes, she took a courageous swallow. Surprisingly, it tasted sweet as honey and soothed her sore, scratchy throat. This must be some wonderful herbal concoction. Regi downed the entire bowlful.

"Good." Wakanda took the empty dish.

Heat began to radiate from Regi's stomach to her limbs. The small confines of the bunk room turned stiflingly hot.

From another small pot, which rested on the coals in the fire, Wakanda poured a cup of a dark, green liquid. She handed it to Regi. "Gargle."

Regi brought the cup to her lips. "You know, this smells like something that would draw flies."

Wakanda looked down her crooked nose at her.

Regi chanced a sip and tried to gargle, but the mineral oil substance made it difficult. She spit it back into the cup. Wiping her lips, she said, "What's in that?"

"Help you."

Help or not, Regi had endured enough of Wakanda's strange concoctions. "You mentioned something about prayer?"

Regi's thermals were growing damp from perspiration. She pulled her long hair to the side.

Wakanda lit the pipe, puffing little white clouds of smoke. She handed it to Regi.

She shook her head. "Can't. It's against my religion."

Wakanda set the pipe back on the flagstone as though out of respect for Regi's belief. The old woman began chanting in the gibberish she used so often. Regi nodded with the rhythm of Wakanda's voice as she watched her friend rock back and forth like a pendulum.

Regi's eyelids grew heavy. The medication she'd taken earlier was kicking in big time. Though she really didn't want to be out here in the bunkhouse, she realized that sometimes it's best to put a friend's feelings above her own comfort. Plus, Wakanda had agreed to read the Book of Mormon. So Regi was glad she had stayed and made her friend feel as though she was doing something to help Regi in her time of need. She lay on the scratchy army blanket and fell asleep.

A beam of morning light slipped through the curtains, hitting Regi's eyes. As she moved, she found her neck ached and her right hip was sore. Her sheepskin jacket had been laid over her, and it slipped off as she sat up. Blinking several times, she forced her eyes to focus. Franklin stove, wagon-wheel bed frames. She was in the bunk room.

That's right!

Wakanda had brought her here in the middle of the night. The woman was nowhere to be seen. She must be rummaging already.

Oscar came to Regi and licked her face. She gave him a squeeze then nudged him away to find her boots. She shivered. The fire had burned out. And despite her stuffy nose, she could smell something foul. She sniffed the dog. It wasn't him, but the room reeked. From now on, Regi was enforcing a no-cooking rule in here.

She tugged on her cowboy boots and stumbled to her feet. Her throat was still scratchy, and her forehead hurt. She raised her hand to rub it and felt the bump from the accident. Too bad Wakanda's hocus pocus hadn't worked. Regi felt worse than ever.

Grabbing her coat and stuffing her arms in the sleeves, Regi started for the door. Leaving the bunk room and crossing through the barn, she heard voices from the yard. So as not to be discovered in her long johns and coat, she crept to the barn door and peeked out. The Steinfelds were leaving. They were probably looking forward to another day of sightseeing in the park. Once their car pulled away and disappeared, Regi stepped outside.

The air was crisp and cold, twice as cold as she thought it should be. She hurried, not wanting Claudia to catch her. Regi had no desire to explain Wakanda's doctoring to her sister, especially since she didn't understand it herself. Starting up the slope of snowy grass, she heard the honk of a horn.

Now what!

With her luck, it would be Ida Peck.

Regi turned to find Tanner pulling in with a horse trailer in tow. He smiled and waved hi. Here she stood in all her glory: long red thermal underwear, sheepskin coat, and cowboy boots. How Regi wished the ground would open and swallow her. A great start to what looked like another dismal day.

Samuel chuckled at the sight before him. Despite her strange getup, Regi looked magnificent. Her long golden-brown hair—seasoned with strands of striking white—was usually pulled into a braid or a ponytail, but now it hung loose about her shoulders down to her waist.

Though he was happy to see her, Regi seemed none too pleased to see him. He hoped what he had in the trailer would bring a smile to her pouting lips and a sparkle to her green eyes.

He stomped on the brakes, turned off the engine, and climbed out of the truck. "You're up early. No aches and pains from the accident?"

She didn't reply, only stood there staring.

He was nervous. "Guess not. Got up this morning and thought, 'Regi is right.'" He noticed her face gentle with surprise. She folded her arms and still said nothing.

So far, so good. Maybe Samuel hadn't imagined it, and something had changed between them. Her patiently waiting to hear what he had to say was a good sign. A few days ago she would have told him to load his sorry caboose back in his truck and leave. He felt more confident. "So I loaded up the trailer and came over."

Still, Regi stood there staring at him. This was unusual for her. Maybe after the accident last night, she had started thinking about what they had discussed at Twiggs; maybe she, too, wanted a better relationship.

Encouraged, Samuel went to the rear of the trailer, unlocked the latch, and swung open the gate. He stepped up in the trailer and squeezed past the pinto to untie her. The filly innocently blinked at him. For some reason, Samuel thought about wild horses, how gentle and calm they appeared seconds before going berserk. Gypsy was not a wild horse.

Samuel poked his head out of the window, checking on Regi. Her arms were no longer folded as she waited. There stood the wild horse in Samuel's life, though last night she'd seemed tamed not only by the accident but also by the kindness Samuel had shown her. He wished he were a religious man because he would pray that the Almighty would help him make this peace offering.

Leading Gypsy out of the trailer, he guided the pinto to Regi. A smile came to her lips as she gazed upon her prized horse. As he neared, he noticed the large bruise on Regi's forehead from the accident. He pointed to the mark. "Looks worse this morning."

"Thanks. Just what I wanted to hear." Her voice sounded scratchy, her nose stuffed up. Her smile disappeared. She touched the bruise and winced. "What's this all about?" She motioned to Gypsy.

"A gift." He tried to hand her the reins.

Regi cautiously reached out and took them. "Huh?"

Standing close to her, he detected an odor. "What's that smell?"

"Smell?" She sniffed a couple of times. "Oh, great." She tried to hand back the reins. "It's me. Keep your distance. See, I caught a cold and because of that and the accident, Wakanda had me drink some medicinal concoction that reeks."

He refused to take the reins. "The smell doesn't bother me, and I have a strong immune system."

"Samuel! I . . ." She glanced at the horse, who took a step toward her. Regi's fingers nervously fiddled with the reins as her eyes drank in the sight of the animal she loved so much. With a trembling hand, she stroked the filly's forehead then threw her arms around the horse's neck and hugged it for the longest time.

Standing there feeling all sorts of awkward, Samuel realized Regi had said his first name. She'd also called him Samuel once last night when her guard had been down and she'd relaxed. Maybe, just maybe, everything would work out like he'd planned.

Finally, she let go of the horse and gazed at him. "This was very thoughtful, but I can't accept her." Again she tried to hand the reins to him.

"Says who?" He would not let Regi mess up this moment with some cockeyed notion.

"It's too much. You bought her fair and square."

"You didn't think so last night when you were telling me off at Twiggs."

"You did this because of what I said?"

He nodded.

Regi dropped the reins and started for the house. "You *have* to take her back."

"Why?" Samuel grabbed Regi and turned her about to face him. "Sure, I brought the horse to you because of what you said, but Regi, the entire time I've never really thought of Gypsy as mine."

Regi was so close he could see dark flecks in her malachite eyes that now puddled with tears. He'd seen her cry last night as she'd watched her late husband's Jeep burn. That was understandable, but now?

Why would she cry now? She must still be weak from the accident. Worried that he'd done something wrong, he said, "I . . . I want to help you." Again the odor, but he wasn't going to risk mentioning it.

She stared up at him. A shudder racked her body, and her bottom lip trembled. "I don't want your help."

Her words conflicted with the tender expression on her face and the emotion reflecting in her watery gaze. He had to make her understand.

"Doesn't that God of yours frown on a prideful heart?" Samuel's arms ached for her. "Let your guard down. Let go. You're what's important to me, not the horse or the cattle or the river land. Since we were young, it's always been you." Finally, he could stand it no longer. He leaned over, only a breath between their lips. "Always you."

And then he kissed her. Her lips were sweet and soft and luscious. At first she did not respond, but finally one cautious arm rested on his. Her other arm reached to his neck, then both were there, hugging him tight. He returned her embrace, savoring the moment. He could finally hold the heaven he'd sought for so very long. Combing his fingers through her wild hair, he cradled her head in his hands and deepened the kiss.

Somewhere in the distance, Samuel heard the gears of a truck shift. Someone was coming.

Reluctantly, he straightened. Regi must have heard, too, because she pulled away, collected herself, and stepped back as Jed's pickup pulled off the main highway.

What did *he* want? And how in the world had he trailed Samuel to Regi's? Samuel cleared his throat and glanced at her. She left his side, grabbing hold of Gypsy's reins. He hoped she wasn't going to force him to take back the horse in front of Jed. This was unfinished private business, and he wanted it kept that way.

Jed pulled to a stop and got out of his beat-up truck with the Gas-N-Grub logo on the doors. In his arms was a grocery bag. He smiled from one Dumbo ear to the other. The man was tickled about something. Of course, seeing Samuel and Regi together this early in the morning, with her in her long johns and coat, would give him considerable pleasure and fodder to laugh over with his customers who stopped at the Gas-N-Grub every morning.

"What do you want, Jed?" Samuel asked.

"I didn't come to see you, but since you're here, I do have a question." The way Jed stared at him, Samuel knew his brother was angling for a fight. "On the night Curtis Romney was murdered, Stew told me that you had words with him."

"Why would he tell you that unless you were prying into my business?" Samuel sensed Regi immediately tense. Leave it to Jed to rain all over his progress with the woman he loved.

"Clifford and I went to Twiggs for dinner that night. Stew mentioned you and Romney had been playing pool and that you'd had some disagreement, but by the time he could check it out, you were both gone. He was worried about you, is all."

Samuel heaved a deep sigh. "Yeah, so what? A lot of people talked with Romney the day before he died."

Jed chuckled, then shaking his head, he turned serious. "You dirty rotten . . . you were trying to get inside information on the sale, weren't you?"

Samuel didn't know what his brother was talking about, but by the worried and condemning expression on Regi's face, she'd jumped to the conclusion that Jed was talking about the river land Samuel'd promised not to sell. He had to say something quick. "As always, you're talking crazy, Jed." Though he spoke to his brother, Samuel kept an eye on Regi. Gone was the warmth in her eyes, replaced with instant mistrust. Back to square one.

"I've got your number, brother. Have since the day you turned tail and left me alone with the old man." Jed gritted his teeth. A blood vessel bulged in the middle of his forehead. "You'll stop at nothing to get what you want. Maybe even kill?"

Samuel's right hand fisted.

"Must be close to the truth, huh?" Jed stepped near and jutted out his chin as if daring Samuel to take a swing.

Samuel held back.

Jed snickered. "I can tell I've hit a nerve. What happened out there on the river? You try and finish what you started with Romney at Twiggs?"

Samuel stole a glance at Regi; he noticed she appeared to be in shell shock. Worse, she looked as though she believed every word. She was slipping back to her old misgivings. Did last night and this morning mean nothing? Feeling as though he'd lost the battle, Samuel had to get away.

He strode to his truck, not looking back, afraid if he did, he'd do something he'd regret. He leaped into his vehicle, slammed the door, and drove off. Glancing into his side mirror, Samuel saw his brother and Regi standing next to each other watching him drive away. He wanted to turn around and go back, but the damage was done.

And Samuel had no idea how he would ever repair it.

Regi watched as Tanner's Ford and horse trailer disappeared from view. Jed's words had awakened her again to the nightmare of Romney's death.

"Is there something else you need, Jed?" she said over her shoulder as she guided Gypsy to the barn.

"I'm sorry you had to witness that." He seemed sincere. "Sam and I have never gotten along, and I probably shouldn't have said half of what I did. When I see him, crazy words come out of my mouth."

"Believe me, I understand." She'd reached the barn doors, with him following. Regi really wanted Jed to go away. "Why are you here when you should be at the Gas-N-Grub?"

"Oh, Aunt Ida." He glanced inside the bag he held then back to Regi. "She feels bad about her visit here last night. Guess she and Claudia had some heated words, and your sister told her to never come back. Anyway, Aunt Ida felt so bad that she sent you some of her chicken and dumpling soup."

"Oh, she shouldn't have. Claudia overreacted. After dealing with politicians, my sister is suspicious of everyone. I know your aunt meant well." Regi took the goodwill token from him.

He sniffed the air.

Knowing he'd picked up on her bad scent, she quickly stepped away. "Tell Ida thanks. Sending this soup was very thoughtful of her." Jed would probably hurry back to his aunt and tell her about finding Samuel at Regi's. She wondered if this bit of news would become tangled up with the murder gossip. Even if it did, she could do nothing about what people would say on their own private phones . . . or anywhere else, for that matter.

Thinking about telephones, Regi remembered she'd intended to call the twins today. So much to do. She hoped Jed would leave now that he'd delivered the soup. Still, he stood there with a quizzical look on his face. "Is there something else I can do for you, Jed?"

"Don't want to trouble you none. I know your plate's pretty full and all, but I was wondering, has the sheriff been out here this morning?"

Regi was taken aback. That was the last question she expected. "No, why? He always stops at your place in the morning."

"That's what has me worried. He didn't."

"Maybe he had someplace else to go." *Or a murder to solve. Or cover up.* She hated thinking like that, but after overhearing him tell Tanner to keep secrets from her, she couldn't help it. That man was up to something, and it had her plain scared.

"Well, been sixteen years he's been stopping, and in sixteen years he's never missed a morning. I'm a mite worried about the guy. You haven't seen him, huh?"

"No. Did you call Hannah? Maybe he's sick."

"Hannah doesn't know if *she's* there half the time. Aunt Ida said on her last visit out to their place the poor woman sat in her rocker, rocking and rocking. Wouldn't even talk to her."

Though people thought Hannah didn't know what she was doing, Regi believed her friend knew her mind was on instant replay, so many times she didn't say anything to visitors. Life was safer that way. And maybe she just didn't want to talk. At this moment, Regi didn't want to talk with Jed, either. She had to get rid of him. "I'm sure Morgan's okay. Thank your aunt for me. Tell her not to worry. I'm fine."

"Oh, she put medicine in there too. She noticed you were starting with a cold the other day when you came into the Gas-N-Grub all wet. I swear that woman's close to a saint the way she frets over people."

"Yeah, well," she wanted to push Jed along. "Be seeing you."

Jed started to his truck but stopped midway. "Regi, I know you're in an awful pickle over Curtis Romney. I want you to know, I don't believe you murdered him."

Comforted by his belief in her innocence, Regi held the bag he'd given her tightly. "Thanks, Jed." He was once again taking up the supportive role he had shown her after Tanner had disappeared. Jed had been there for Regi when his brother had left. Seemed he was always helping her in her times of crisis.

Jed waved and climbed into his pickup.

As the man drove off, Regi wondered about him accusing his own brother of murdering Romney. No brotherly love between those two. Something was odd about the entire scene.

Wait a minute. Jed had said Samuel and Romney were arguing at Twiggs. What was the deal there? And what was the deal about a sale? Had her first intuition been right and Tanner had been talking to Romney about selling her river property to him? Tanner had denied it last night, and he'd been so nice and all, rescuing her from the Jeep and giving her Gypsy.

If she had heard Jed spout off such accusations yesterday, she would have gone along. Now, though . . . For a moment, she remembered the feel of Samuel's lips on hers, how he had made her skin tingly as if a soft Chinook wind breathed over her. An old sizzle she'd had for him as a girl had been awakened, and maybe she was foolish, but she believed Samuel.

Wow! What a difference a day had made. She sat on the hay bale next to the door as she savored the memory of the kiss and how she had resisted at first, but then she couldn't help herself—she'd kissed him back. In all the years that they'd been apart and all the disagreements they'd had, she never thought she'd find herself in his arms again . . . nor that she would want to be there.

No, he didn't murder Romney, but that's not to say he didn't know who did. Before questioning him again, she was going to have to talk with Stew and get the facts about that argument he'd overheard between Tanner and Romney.

She remembered Sheriff Morgan visiting Tanner while she was in his den. This fueled the theory that Morgan could be the killer and Tanner had helped him. Was she so desperate that she didn't trust anyone?

Sheesh, she couldn't tell who the snake in the grass was. But she wanted to. She wanted to think the best of her friends and of the man she was falling for all over again. *And* she would think the best of him, as soon as she figured this all out. Still, what was the deal with Morgan not showing up for his coffee?

One thing was certain: she had to get to the bottom of all this once and for all.

Guiding Gypsy inside the barn, she took care of the horse then hurried to the house with the bag Jed had given her. She needed to speak with Claudia and get her opinion.

Entering the kitchen, she was surprised not to find Claudia madly fixing breakfast for the Mattiases, who had stayed behind. The kitchen was empty and nothing was cooking. As Regi glanced about the room, she found a note on the table.

> *Dear Regi,*
> *I have an idea to help you, but I need to go to Monticello to see if I'm right. I probably won't be back until late afternoon. Sorry about ducking out on you.*
>
> *Love,*
> *Claudia*

Regi felt paralyzed. How could her sister go off, especially after everything that had happened?

"Is anyone here?" A voice came from the dining room. The Mattiases were expecting breakfast, and Regi was the only one here to cook it.

TWELVE
BLEAK

CLAUDIA SAT IN HER CADILLAC Eldorado at the curb of Fifth and Main in Monticello. She stared at the old Tudor-styled building that had been such a part of her life only six months ago. Ivy trellised up the walls and around the entryway.

She gazed at the second-story window where her husband's office had been. Congressman Morris Osborne. She yearned to walk in there, see him behind his desk, and have her old world back the way it had been before. Her husband had spent much of their married life in this building when he was in the state. In DC, his office wasn't nearly so impressive, but those people weren't voting for him. This office had determined Morris's fate and had made him the man he was.

Or wasn't. She didn't want to play this game of *was* and *wasn't*. Not now.

Trying to summon more courage than she felt, Claudia didn't know if she could go inside and find what she needed. She wouldn't for herself, but with God's help, she could for Regi. Had her sister's beliefs rubbed off on her? Maybe.

After Regi was nearly killed last night and Claudia had lain in bed unable to sleep, she'd marveled that Samuel had come along and saved her sister's life. Claudia knew in her heart his being there at the right time was more than mere coincidence, especially since there had been so much contention between them before.

Thinking about Samuel and Regi's spats over property, Claudia had remembered a map of the park that she'd found while she was in Morris's old office packing his things. Willard Goodard, Morris's interim replacement until the next election, had snatched the map from her hands, telling her it shouldn't have been included in her husband's belongings. The map belonged to the government, and Willard needed to keep it.

Claudia had thought his actions a bit odd, but at the time she'd been in a cocoon of grief and in no condition to find out what the map was about. However, if memory served her well, the map showed the federal land boundaries of the park. Claudia remembered that certain sections were highlighted with an asterisk. At the bottom it explained that the asterisk meant "auction."

When Claudia had stopped to give condolences to Romney's widow and overheard Superintendent Elliott's conversation, she had wondered what the deal was with the land they were talking about. Something wasn't right, and she wanted another look at the map.

With any luck, Willard, who was now hot on the campaign trail to fill Morris's seat, would be out drumming up support. If Amy Townsend was still the secretary, Claudia stood a good chance of getting her hands on a copy. But there were a lot of ifs involved. And the only way Claudia would find out would be to fasten some of Regi's fearlessness to her backbone and go inside.

Grabbing the car's door handle, Claudia summoned the determination to see this through and climbed out of the car. She hurried up the steps into the building, as though she were afraid her cowardice would catch her.

Walking toward the secretary's sleek chrome desk, Claudia brushed a hair from her designer jeans. She should have dressed up. In the past, she would never have visited Morris's office in such laid-back attire, but in the last six months, Claudia had done many things she never would have before. Though she'd always known that titles and clothes really didn't make the person, she had become especially aware of it living with Regi. What a person wore didn't make them important or good or bad. Such a determination had to do with something deep inside, hidden from the naked eye. Something that she now realized only God knew for certain. Claudia hoped He'd help her make sound judgments for her sister, especially today.

Approaching the desk, Claudia didn't recognize the woman sitting at the computer. Her back was toward Claudia. Thick, straight black hair hung to her elbows. Amy kept her red hair cropped short.

Claudia stood beside the desk, waiting for the woman to turn around. Surely she'd heard her approach and knew someone was there. Finally, Claudia cleared her throat. The woman whirled about.

"Can I help you?" Her lips were slathered with burgundy-colored lipstick; her eyebrows were severe black arches. While she spoke, she glanced at the computer screen. She was playing hearts and obviously did not want to waste time with an intruder.

The woman didn't see ordinary people. Her attention was saved for those of position. Claudia couldn't help but think that this gal was the typical, self-serving pariah that hung around congressmen, hopeful to get a glimpse of power. Claudia's stomach twisted. Nausea stirred. Did she look like the woman who had turned Claudia's world on its head? She wasn't sure. Not wanting to dwell on the haunting images of her past, Claudia cut to the chase. "Does Miss Townsend still work here?"

The question did not deter the woman's concentration on her game. "Yes."

"Would you please direct me to her office?" Claudia waited patiently.

"This is it." The woman still did not look at Claudia but pushed a computer key. A card turned over on the screen. The receptionist smiled to herself.

Claudia's patience waned. "Will she be in today?"

"Not sure," she said, studying the screen.

In a sterner tone, Claudia asked, "Would you please find out?"

Finally, the woman pried herself away from her game long enough to glare directly at Claudia. "Lady, I'm doing a favor for Willard by answering his phones today. Other than that, I don't know anything."

Claudia bit her tongue so as not to agree. Finally, she trusted herself enough to speak again. "Could I speak with Mr. Goodard?"

The put-out woman gave a long-winded sigh. "Told me he didn't want to see anyone." A fake smile graced her burgundy lips. "Have a good day." She turned to her computer.

Claudia was not about to be dismissed by this lazy, inefficient shrew. "I know I'm taxing your finely tuned secretarial skills, with which I'm duly impressed, but would it be too much to ask if you'd tell Willard that Claudia Osborne is here to see him."

The surly woman whipped around in disbelief. "*You're* Claudia Osborne? Widow of Congressman Osborne?"

Claudia smiled and nodded, wondering if this woman was the one.

The woman's face paled, then she nervously fumbled around the desk, not looking up at Claudia, as if ashamed. "I'm so sorry. I had no idea. You should have told me who you were . . . are . . ."

"If you're searching for the intercom button, it's on the phone." Claudia weakly smiled, all the while watching her with a critical eye.

"Of course, where is my head?" She jerked the phone to her ear and pushed the button.

Within seconds Willard opened his door. As always, he looked as though he'd stepped off the cover of *GQ*: dimpled smile, hair in place, and not a wrinkle in his tailor-made suit. "To what do I owe this honor?" He stepped aside, gesturing for her to enter his office.

Claudia turned her attention to him. "I was in town and thought I'd stop by and see how your campaign is doing. I'm surprised to find you here this close to the election." Claudia went in, wondering what she'd say next and how she could possibly get her hands on the map.

She sat in a leather wingback chair in front of Willard's desk. "Who's the new receptionist?"

"My wife's niece. Amy has sick children. I was desperate. That aside, what can I do for you?"

Claudia straightened. "Merely came to wish you luck. I know how tough running for office can be."

"I'm sure you do." He folded his arms and leaned against his ornate mahogany desk, which had replaced Morris's walnut Levenger. "I truly miss Morris. He campaigned so effortlessly and didn't allow the pressure to get to him. Your husband was a good example. The people loved him."

Morris's smile came to Claudia's mind. Oh, how she'd loved that man, and despite all the locked-up hurt and feelings of betrayal, she still did love him.

The intercom buzzed. Claudia was surprised the woman could find it two times in a row. Willard excused himself and picked up the phone. After talking briefly, he replaced it. "I'm sorry to cut our visit short, but I'm late for an appointment downtown. I'm hoping to gain a big contribution today."

Claudia stood. "I understand. Take care of yourself, and say hello to your wife."

"We're expecting our fourth child." He smiled.

For a brief moment, Claudia was jealous. His wife had everything Claudia thought she'd always wanted. That is, until she'd learned the truth. She pushed aside the distasteful green monster. "Congratulations. Tell her to take care."

He walked her to the door. "I will." He gave Claudia a reserved hug. "Don't be a stranger."

As she walked down the tiled hallway to the exit, a dismal feeling of failure overcame her. Claudia saw the "Restroom" sign and dodged in. She needed to regroup and think things through. Surely she could still get ahold of that map. She was so close.

Washing her hands, she glanced out the window. Willard Goodard and his niece were walking to his car. As he helped her into the vehicle, he leaned over and it looked like he was telling her something, but then

Claudia realized he had nuzzled her ear. No. He wouldn't do such a thing out in the open. Claudia's mind was playing tricks on her because of Morris's betrayal. Willard was just telling her something, that was all. But if he were having an affair, that would explain why he'd put up with the girl's inefficiencies as a secretary.

Anger flared within Claudia. Disgust for Willard followed as she thought of his naive, expectant wife. After everything Claudia had been through with her own husband, she thought nothing would surprise her . . . and yet it did.

Yanking a paper towel out of the dispenser, she realized that with both of them gone, it meant no one was in the office. Claudia's mood suddenly brightened. And she still possessed her own set of keys. She'd meant to return them, but Willard had never asked, and she'd never thought of them until now. If she were lucky, he wouldn't have changed the locks.

Almost giddy with her turn of good fortune, Claudia left the restroom and came face to face with Amy Townsend.

"Amy!" Claudia liked her. She was the woman every mother wanted her son to marry. She smelled of soap and had a toothpaste smile and a caring look in her eyes.

"Claudia, what are you doing here?" Amy gave her a warm, friendly hug. "I've thought of you often and wondered how you're doing. Been so long."

"Willard said your children are ill."

"They are, but my husband came home for lunch. I needed to take care of some fliers I promised I'd mail last night. What brings you to town?"

Claudia knew she could trust her friend. Amy was a godsend. "I need some help."

"What can I do?"

"Morris had this map . . ."

Regi stood with her arms elbow deep in suds, glad breakfast was over. Once she'd made her apologies to the guests, she'd dashed to her room, changed, and hightailed it back to the kitchen to make the Mattiases the breakfast they were expecting. Their faces had turned downright grim, though, when she'd served them burnt scrambled eggs smothered with ketchup. The fact that they hadn't eaten much and quickly left to go hiking reflected poorly on her cooking skills and would not help maintain the Raindancer's five-star rating.

As Regi rinsed the last dish, her mind tripped back to the beginnings of this cursed day. Waking up in the barn's bunk room should have been a tip off that only bad things would follow. Tanner bringing Gypsy home was an unexpected plus—as well as his kiss. But Jed's arrival had burst her momentary balloon of happiness, solidly grounding her to the trouble she was in, especially when he'd accused Tanner of killing Romney. He'd also said something about a land sale.

Suddenly, what Claudia had overheard while at the superintendent's house popped into her mind. The park was going to sell some land. Regi thought of Jed's accusation. At first she'd thought he was referring to Tanner selling Romney her river property, but what if it was something else? What if Romney had gone to Tanner about the park's land sale? She remembered the memo she'd stolen from Tanner's desk. Romney'd asked him to meet him at Twiggs because he had information he needed to know. This was bigger than she'd thought. Ordinarily this would have added the missing link to convict Tanner in her mind, but not any more.

Tanner had been right. Things had changed between them. He had saved her life last night, and this morning his kiss—the memory of it made her insides quiver—well, she just knew Tanner didn't kill Romney.

Still, she had to give the note to Morgan. She had to! It was the right thing to do. Regi pulled the plug, letting the dirty water drain from the sink. Thinking about this would drive her nuts. What she needed to do was talk with Morgan, lay her cards on the table. She picked up a dish towel, madly wiping the Corning cookware. Before she could speak with the sheriff, she would have to find him. Where could he be? He was such a creature of habit.

Stopping the menial task, Regi grabbed her coat from the wall hook and started for the door. She was determined to find him and ask him in no uncertain terms what was going on and why he'd been at Tanner's last night. She reached in her pocket for her keys and suddenly realized she was without wheels. Morgan still had her Jeep, and Earl's had been demolished in the crash.

Snatching the phone off the hook, she called Newt Birch's garage. He ran a car shop out of his home a couple of miles down the road. More junk cars were in Newt's south pasture than working cars in the whole community of Trailhead. He might have something she could drive at a good price.

Newt answered. "Yeah." A man of few words.

"This is Regina Bernard."

"Need wheels?"

"How did you know?"

"Samuel Tanner called."

"Tanner?"

"Yeah."

"When?"

"Earlier."

Regi knew prying information from Newt was like pulling tree roots from granite. She was wasting time. "Do you have something I could drive for a while?"

"Got an old Chevy truck. Runs good. Looks bad."

"How much?" It really didn't matter, though, because at this moment, she'd pay any price.

"Paid for."

"What?"

"Samuel said you'd call wanting something to drive and that I was to send the bill to him."

Regi didn't know what to think. Thoughts of a wooden horse arriving at the gates of Troy came to mind. "Newt, send the bill to me."

"Can't."

The Neanderthal man was driving her crazy. "Why?"

"He already paid for it."

"Why did you tell me you were going to send the bill to him?" Talking with Newt was downright frustrating and very similar to pounding a nail into a knot.

"That's what he told me to do. But then he showed up wanting to know if anyone had come by wanting body work on their car. While he was here, he checked the truck over and paid for it."

"Okay, then. I'll be right there." Regi stomped out of the bed-and-breakfast on her way to Newt's. She needed a good walk. She thought about Tanner asking Newt if anyone wanted their car worked on. That could mean he was looking for the person who'd run Regi off the road. It made her feel as though he were watching her back. Nice. She would keep that in mind as she snooped around today.

Regi had a lot to do. First, she had to find the sheriff. Jed said he hadn't stopped at the Gas-N-Grub as usual, and surely he'd checked the sheriff's office. She'd start by going where people had last seen him, and that meant going to Morgan's home.

The road to the sheriff's place meandered west past Bridger's Lake. Hundreds of beautiful quaking aspens lining the highway had shed their golden leaves on the first snow of the season. Five miles out of town, Regi came to the turnoff to Morgan's small ranch. She struggled to gear down the ornery stick shift of the old Chevy. Quickly using both hands, she finally jammed it into low. The old heap of rust and bolts moaned a little, stuttered, and then continued as if nothing had happened.

And this was Newt's best vehicle?

As Regi pulled into Morgan's driveway and parked, Hannah's pack of dogs sent up a ruckus of welcoming barks. They had been lying on the front porch beside the gentle woman's feet while she swung in the porch swing. She waved at Regi.

Regi plowed through the dogs. The canines trampled over each other to greet her. A black Labrador, a golden retriever, a brown spaniel, a basset hound, a schnauzer, a Yorkshire terrier, and a small yappy Chihuahua made up the motley crew.

"Hi, guys." Regi petted them, showing no favorites.

They followed her as she walked up the porch steps. "Hannah, how are you?" Regi's friend wore a light sweater over her sundress. She wore only flip-flops on her reddened feet that looked painfully cold. The skin on her legs was also red.

"Freezing." She rubbed her arms. "Don't tell Effie. She'd only gloat that she was right and that I should have put on a coat." She stared at Regi's bruised forehead as though wondering if she should say something, and then deciding not to, she got up and walked into the house. "Come in," she said over her shoulder. "I believe Effie has finished cleaning the parlor."

Hannah was a tall, thin, willowy woman. Her long caramel-brown hair hung nearly to her knees. Her eyes were big and copper colored and always looked sad, even when she smiled. She shut the door behind Regi, banning the animals to the outside.

The parlor was spotless. A grandfather clock stood near a large wall where giant, blown-up pictures of a young Hannah were hung. Morgan toyed with photography in his spare time.

In the room were two beige, modular sofas that were parallel to each other and adjacent to the old brick fireplace. The couch pillows were rich colors of forest green. A glass-topped coffee table sat in front of the couches.

"Have a seat." Hannah pointed to the sofa opposite the one she stood in front of, waiting for her guest to be seated first. "Effie always leaves a room smelling like lemons. I suppose it's the furniture polish."

Regi knew Effie Mcquire was more than a maid for the Morgans. She cooked and cared for Hannah as well. She was family more than family was.

"I hate to bother you, but did Morgan mention where he'd be working today?" Regi wanted to inquire about Hannah's health. But she also knew Hannah hated discussing her illness. The woman chose to ignore it the best she could and wanted her friends to do the same.

Hannah stared into the cold fireplace. "Do you like sparrows?"

Not an answer to the question. Regi cleared her throat. "Sure."

"They're pretty birds, sadly overlooked, don't you think?" Hannah didn't wait for a reply. "One flew down the chimney today. Just like that. Flew right into the room. I thought Effie would have kittens trying to chase it out. Made a mess. Soot all over the walls and everywhere that little thing lit. Effie cleaned it up. She always leaves a room smelling like lemons." Hannah smiled at Regi.

Her friend's condition had vastly deteriorated since Regi's last visit. She made a mental note to visit more often. "Smells nice. Did Morgan say where he was going today?"

Looking straight at Regi, Hannah said, "It's not natural for a wild bird to be in a house, is it?"

"No, it's not."

"He flew around and around. I finally caught him. Held him in my bare hands. His little body trembled so."

Regi once again tried to pry answers from Hannah. "Did Morgan mention where he would work today?"

At that moment, Effie walked in. She was an "Aunt Bea" type, who cooked pot roast and mashed potatoes and was always concerned about others. But that's where the similarity ended. Though Effie was in her seventies, she was slender and wore jeans and a plaid flannel shirt. Her white hair was braided and twisted into a knot on top of her head. She abruptly stopped when she saw they had a visitor. "I didn't know we had company." She came over to greet Regi and gasped when she saw her forehead. "Ida Peck phoned and told me you were sick and had been in an accident, but she didn't say you had a bruise the size of Trailhead Park."

Regi should have known Ida would call Effie. The two probably wasted more hours on the phone than should be legal. Add Thelma Watts, the sheriff's dispatcher, to the gossip link and the trio made a formidable force for spreading rumors. The odds were very high that Thelma had learned of the accident through Morgan; therefore, all of Trailhead would know. Maybe Regi's next stop should be at Thelma's place. She should know where Morgan was—that is, if she hadn't been dealing with the mail when he radioed in.

Embarrassed by the bruise, Regi tried to fluff her bangs. "It's nothing, really."

"Does it hurt?" The elderly woman winced as she stared at Regi.

"Only when I think about it." *Or when somebody else says something.* She didn't want to waste time talking about her injury, and she sure as the world didn't want to tell Effie the details of the accident. Time would be wasted. Time Regi needed.

"You should be more careful, hon. Runnin' off the road like that. On top of being sick and all you're going through, you must be miserable, Reg. Can I get you anything? Tea, coffee?" She stopped a moment. "You don't drink those anymore since you joined that church of yours. Well, how about a compress?"

"I wouldn't care for anything right now. And I'm not sick." At that inopportune moment, Regi sneezed. Her body worked against her. She wanted to cuss for the untimely sniffle. Trying to deflect the obvious contradiction, she said, "Effie, did Morgan say where he was going this morning?"

The woman swiped her hand over the fireplace mantle on the hunt of escaped dust. "Up and gone before I got up. Let me get you some hot cider, hon. It will help your cold."

"But—" Regi watched the flannel-clad woman disappear down the hallway. She called after her, "I'm not sick." Then she sniffed, and, dang, but her throat burned.

Returning her attention to Hannah, Regi found her friend staring at the empty fireplace.

Thinking of a different tack, Regi asked, "Hannah, were you up when Morgan left this morning?"

"That sparrow flew right in here, right into the walls. Little thing was so scared. Went from wall, to wall, to wall."

Regi's eyes threatened to tear up, watching her friend struggle. She wanted to take Hannah in her arms and hold her until her mind settled. Poor Morgan! Every day and night he watched the woman he loved deteriorate. Must be eating him up something awful. He'd probably do anything to help her.

Anything?

Even murder?

What was the matter with her, thinking this way about the sheriff? Sheesh! Still, her mind wouldn't let it go. What could possibly be his motive? Maybe Romney somehow bribed Morgan to turn a blind eye to some sort of shady business to do with the park's land. She needed to talk with someone and get her thinking straight. With Morgan AWOL and with no help from Hannah, and not wanting to ask Effie and set off the gossip chain, Regi didn't know who to talk to about this.

Tanner? Could he possibly tell her what she wanted to know if she pressed him hard enough? Even though Jed's visit this morning had set her to doubting Tanner again, he could very well have the answers. On her way to his place, she'd stop at home and check in to see if Claudia was back. *And* call Thelma to see if Morgan had mentioned where he was going. But Thelma could start to wonder what was going on and possibly call Effie. Nope. Regi couldn't risk that. Regi stood. "Please tell Effie I'm sorry I didn't stay for the cider, but I think I'd best get going. Claud will be wondering where I am."

Hannah rose and followed her to the door. Before Regi stepped over the threshold, Hannah grabbed her arm. "Thomas is upset about the land. That ranger caused trouble."

Regi's blood turned ice cold. Had her wild idea about Morgan been right? Was Hannah reaching out, trying to warn Regi? Worried that she may have heard Hannah wrong, she calmly patted her friend on the arm. Coaxing her for information, Regi said, "What land?"

Hannah sucked air between her teeth as if worried she couldn't remember then whispered, "Not supposed to tell."

Regi hugged her. "It's all right. You can tell me."

"Oh, no! Can't tell you. Especially not you." Hannah pulled away from Regi. She bit at her thumbnail, her sad eyes glancing about the room as if afraid someone had overheard them.

Feeling like a bully, Regi knew she had to press her to say more. "Hannah, it's okay. No one is here, and I won't tell Morgan you said anything."

That brought an instant sigh of relief. "You'll come again?" Hannah's pleading eyes searched Regi's face.

"Of course." Regi hugged her friend and gave her a kiss on the cheek. She didn't have the stomach to push for more. "You take care." Regi waded through the dogs, hopped into the sorry excuse for a truck, and waved good-bye to Hannah, who stood in the doorway looking like a thin, lost waif.

As Regi sped down the aspen-lined road, the trees now looked bleak and forlorn with most of their leaves fallen. She thought of Hannah . . . bleak and forlorn with most of her memories gone.

And Regi couldn't help but wonder about her friend's parting words. *Thomas is upset about the land. That ranger caused trouble.*

THIRTEEN
BLACKMAIL

"WHERE HAVE YOU BEEN?" CLAUDIA was kneading dough as Regi entered through the back door. "I returned to find no one here minding the place. We could have had paying customers stop by then leave because no one was here!" Her sister glared at her.

On the burner simmered Claudia's famous pizza sauce. Pizza! Regi's favorite meal. So Claudia couldn't be too awfully upset. Itching to share what she'd learned about Tanner and Morgan . . . and the land, she gauged her sister's mood more closely. Nope, Claudia did not appear to be in the frame of mind to hear about Regi's conspiracy theory regarding Morgan—and possibly Tanner—right now. She'd have to play nice for a while. Teasing usually helped tame Claudia's gnarly moods.

"Wait a minute." Regi pretended to stand her ground, even though she was in the wrong. "That's my question. Who took off this morning and left me with everything to do?" She smiled, hoping her sister would see the irony, since taking off was Regi's trick.

"Have I ever left you in a lurch before?" Her sister stopped what she was doing and stared at Regi, daring her to answer with anything but the truth.

Regi noticed an odd sadness about her sister's face. "Well, no, but . . ."

Claudia avoided Regi's gaze and dusted the pizza dough with flour. "And how many times have you taken off? Make sure to count this afternoon."

Something big ate at Claudia. Regi had to let her sister vent until she was ready to really face what it was.

"Okay. You've got me. I skip out, and you don't. Where did you go?" Regi took a spoon from the drawer and tasted the simmering pizza sauce. Delicious.

"First, you tell me what was so important that you left the Raindancer with no one here." Claudia kneaded dough with the heel of her hand.

"Jed Tanner came by and said Morgan hadn't stopped in for his coffee." Regi dropped the spoon in the sink.

"Oh, Thomas didn't have his morning coffee. Did you call the paper and let them know?" Claudia punched the dough as if she were a prizefighter.

Since Claudia and Morgan had been sweethearts in high school, Regi had expected more concern from her. Whatever was bothering Claudia was big. Why couldn't she just come out with it? But Claudia usually festered for a bit before saying what was really on her mind, kind of like Regi.

Regi defended herself. "Morgan always has his coffee at Jed's. It's not like him to disappear. I'm telling you, something's not right." She sat, noticing that the counter she'd left cluttered with drying dishes was now cleared and spit-polish clean.

"Did anyone think to call Hannah?" Claudia slapped the dough.

"I went out to their place."

"On foot?"

Claudia was beginning to get on Regi's nerves. "Sure, I hoofed across the county." Trying to play nice was a lot of work. "Newt had a truck. What is with you?"

"Nothing. So when you drove out to their place, did Hannah know where he was?" Claudia paused. "How is she anyway?"

"No, she didn't know. And she's not good. She knew who I was and all, but her concentration isn't what it used to be." Nervous about Claudia's building storm, Regi got up and stirred the pizza sauce with the spoon she'd licked then stopped.

She thought of something she could tell her sister that might put her in a better frame of mind. "I remember about five years back, before Earl died, Hannah took me fishing. She knew I'd been tending to him day in and day out and that I needed to get away whether I thought so or not.

"Morgan stayed with Earl while we went. In the middle of a hot July day, the fish weren't biting, but walking under the pines and feeling the breeze on my cheeks renewed me and kissed my soul with peace. We knew Earl was going to die, and that little fishing expedition gave me the strength to get through his passing."

A silence hung in the air like a misty cloud. The remembrance of being in the woods fed her soul even now. Then Regi thought of her friend. "Hannah loved going to the river. It tears me up to see her mind deteriorate. I don't know how Morgan can stand it."

For a moment, it seemed to Regi that Claudia's inner turmoil turned to compassion as she paused from kneading. With flour clinging to her finger, she pointed to Regi. "When this murder case is solved, you need to take Hannah fishing."

Regi had already planned the trip.

Claudia placed a dish towel over the pizza dough bowl and set it on the counter in the sun. She washed off her hands and dried them on a paper towel.

"Hannah was very confused today," Regi thought aloud. "Talked about a bird most of the time. Effie Mcquire didn't know much. Guess Morgan left quite early this morning. Don't know what to make of his disappearing. Hannah did say something about Morgan being upset over a land deal and that some ranger had caused trouble. Plus . . ." She hesitated telling her sister about Tanner's visit this morning, but without that piece of knowledge there was no way they'd put this puzzle together. "Tanner came by this morning. Jed did, as well. He said something to Tanner about selling some land and then accused him of killing Romney. I thought at first he was talking about Tanner selling the land he promised me, but when I coupled that with some of Hannah's mumblings over land and trouble with the ranger . . . well, I'm coming to believe something big is about to happen with the park."

Claudia sat on the edge of a chair. "Oh, my stars," she said under her breath,

"That's what I thought." Regi had expected her to say how puzzling this was, but she didn't. "Wait a minute, what did you say?"

"Come with me." Claudia led Regi into the dining room. Spread out on the table was a map of Trailhead Park. Large sections around the perimeter were colored and an asterisk placed in each. Reading at the bottom, Regi realized the colored parts were for auction.

"Where did you get this?" Regi glanced at her sister then back at the map. The map was amazing, showing not only the park, but the surrounding ranches and grazing lands. Nearly all of the colored sections were next to privately owned property. Regi noticed Claudia hadn't answered her. She turned to her sister. "Come on, tell me where you got this."

"From Morris's office. I remembered it late last night and thought it might help you. That's why I left so early this morning, to look for it." Claudia eased down on a dining room chair, her shoulders slumped.

"Are you kidding me? Yeah, it will help. Look at this." Regi pointed to the word *auction*.

Claudia nodded but made no attempt to look where Regi pointed next. She couldn't believe her sister's lack of reaction. This was a major find. Regi stared at the map. "Do you know what this means? Do you know what would happen if some of the ranchers around here got hold of this? A modern range war is what it would mean. People still fight over property boundaries, you know.

"Earl told me that years ago the government claimed prime grazing ground as part of the national park, and people remember things like that. Those people are going to want their land back. Tanner must have known about this all along." Regi glanced at her sister. Claudia wasn't looking at her but was staring at the floor.

Exasperated, Regi plopped down on a chair. Then a new idea came. She smacked her forehead and winced—she'd hit the bruise. Still excited though, she asked, "Do you realize you may have found why Romney was killed? If the land were to be sold in a silent auction, he probably told a few ranchers that if they paid him enough money under the table he'd make sure their bids won."

Claudia finally looked at her sister, still not uttering a word. Regi scooted her chair closer to her. "And what if Romney got greedy? What if he decided he wanted more money and told that to the ranchers? Cattlemen will put up with an awful lot, but if they feel as though they are being cheated, well, it's no wonder Romney ended up dead."

Again the memo from Romney to Tanner came to mind. Twenty-four hours ago Regi would have been elated about this news, but now . . . though the noose around her neck had loosened, she actually feared it had tightened for Tanner. Especially since it was very likely that the murder weapon was his. She glanced at her sister.

A deep sadness filled Claudia's eyes. It tore at Regi's heart to see her this way. "Is there something you're not telling me?"

Slowly, Claudia pulled a letter from her back pocket. "You need to read this, then we'll talk."

Perplexed, Regi took the letter. On the front was written Claudia's name in Morris's handwriting. Regi glanced up at her sister, concerned that this was too private.

Claudia nodded for her to go ahead and read.

Regi pushed up the envelope flap and pulled out the letter.

Dearest Claudia,

By now you know I'm dead. Everyone will think I suffered a heart attack. Digitalis is a wonder drug and when used to excess leaves no conclusive evidence. I tell you the truth now because I worry for your life. But I've made a mess of things, and I'm sorry I'm such a coward that I can't be with you to face the results. Hopefully my death will stop the blackmailer and keep you safe.

For too many nights you've slept alone and have not known why. Sweetheart, it was not your fault. I don't know how else to tell you, other than just saying it. Honey, I've been unfaithful. I've kept it a secret. Unfortunately, someone else found out and threatened to go public unless I backed a land bill I don't believe in. This I can't do, but mostly, I can't face you with the truth.

Always remember I love you,
Morris

Shock rocked Regi, churned her stomach, and took her breath away. Willing herself not to overreact and make things worse, she glanced up and met Claudia's gaze.

Her sister had grown pale. "I don't know what to say. Did you just find this?" Regi asked.

"No. I found it a week after the funeral when I was cleaning out his things. He'd put it in his underwear drawer," Claudia softly answered.

Regi rubbed Claudia's arm. "Why didn't you tell me sooner?"

"I was trying to adjust to it myself. At first I felt so betrayed. How could I be such a fool not to know he was cheating on me? Then I felt like a failure that my husband chose death over coming to me and discussing his problems. Did he think I was so fragile that I couldn't deal with his infidelity and that it would be so much easier for me to deal with his death? What kind of idiotic logic is that?" Claudia sniffed and turned away as though ashamed of her feelings.

Regi caressed Claudia's shoulders. "Don't blame yourself for his death."

Claudia's red-rimmed eyes narrowed, her face pinched. "I'm not. I'm mad at him. How could he do such a thing, Regi? He was everything to me. At the beginning of every day, my thoughts were, 'What do I need to do to help Morris? What kind of breakfast would he like? Are his suits pressed? Have I done enough networking, called enough people to help him pass a bill or stop one?' I lived and breathed that man. I thought we were a team. And all along he was living this separate life." She inhaled deeply as if to try to hold back threatening tears, but a tear trickled down her cheek anyway.

Regi hugged her then rubbed her hand over Claudia's back. She expected her sister to break down and sob, but Claudia released her breath slowly, in control, which perplexed Regi. If her sister had kept this secret for the last six months, she'd become a master at penning up emotions.

Regi pulled back to look directly at Claudia. "Ever think Morris told you this so you'd accept his death and not blame yourself?"

Claudia stood, crossing the room to the picture window, looking out on the ranch. She stared at the corrals where the horses grazed. "When I packed up his clothes to send to the Salvation Army, I found a letter from the blackmailer. And there was a DVD too."

Overcome with empathy, Regi went to stand near Claudia. Her sister's courage was amazing. "Don't torture yourself with this."

They stood gazing out the window, not really taking in the scene. Claudia leaned her head on Regi's shoulder. "I don't want to, but I have to."

Regi didn't move. She knew Claudia needed to talk and that whatever she had to say was too difficult to be said with eye contact.

"The blackmailer's letter was short and to the point. 'Do what I asked, or this will go online.' The DVD was of Morris and his lover. I remember sitting in my living room, watching my husband make love to another woman, and I thought, *who could be so evil as to record this and use it against him*? Suddenly, there was a voice-over demanding money from Morris."

Regi nervously looked at Claudia. "That had to be tough."

"Yes, it was. I became sick to my stomach."

"Did you recognize the voice?"

Claudia stared at Regi for a long time, saying nothing, as if weighing her words.

Finally, she spoke. "Not at first. Not until I came here."

"Here?"

Claudia nodded. "I'm positive it was Curtis Romney."

FOURTEEN
ORDEAL

SHOCKED, REGI STEPPED BACK. "CURTIS Romney? Are you sure?"

Claudia nodded, biting her fingernail. Regi knew her sister was an expert at recognizing voices. She had an ear for such things. A talent.

Suddenly, anger and compassion warred within Regi, both directed at Claudia. Questions stampeded her. Questions that needed answers. She nervously paced between the table and the dining room window then stopped in front of her sister. "You've known about him all this time and said nothing?" She didn't wait for an answer. "You didn't tell me that my daughter had been in love with a man who was . . . who had . . ." Regi couldn't complete the sentence. She willed herself to get a grip.

Glimpses of Lisa crying on her bed and her tearstained face flashed through her mind. And then Regi remembered how she'd been unable to soothe Lisa. Claudia had stepped in and put Lisa to work in the kitchen, keeping her busy.

Trying to give her sister the benefit of a doubt, Regi let out a sigh. "I don't get it. I just don't get it."

Claudia's forehead furrowed with worry as she walked to the dining room. She pulled out a chair as if to sit down but instead just stood behind it. "Are you ready to listen?"

Regi folded her arms, waiting.

Standing behind the chair, Claudia grasped the back as though to brace herself. "If you remember right, when I moved here, Lisa and Curtis had recently broken up. I didn't even meet him until well after he had married Melissa Elliott. And I had no name to go with the voice on the DVD." She nervously rubbed the wood of the chair and studied a nick in the smooth surface.

Placing her hand over the flaw, she looked up. "Then just before Lisa left for college, she and I ran into him and Melissa at the grocery store. I can't tell you what it did to me to hear that voice again and then to come face to face with the man who had blackmailed my husband and pushed him to suicide. I wanted to tear him apart with my bare hands, but you know me. I stood there dazed. My only saving grace was that he didn't know I knew who he was. All in all, that was the strangest experience I've ever had in my life." Her voice caught.

Claudia shook her head as if she could shake away memories along with emotion then continued. "Out of courtesy, Lisa introduced him to me. When he shook my hand, I almost retched right there in aisle three. In fact, I made my apologies and left. Lisa helped me to the car. She thought I was faking illness to get her out of an uncomfortable situation. Sweet thing, she didn't know how unsettling the entire ordeal had been." Claudia rubbed the side of her face. A strand of blonde hair fell over her cheek. "I had planned to face Curtis Romney. Even asked him to meet me at Twiggs on the night he was killed." She looked up at Regi.

Surprised by this revelation, Regi didn't know what to say.

"I went there. Waited for a while but then chickened out and came home." She nervously brushed her hair back with her hand. "Morris took his life to prevent the public from learning his secret. I had to keep it, Reg. Somehow I felt as though I owed it to him. So I left. Came home and burned the DVD but kept Morris's letter." She gazed down, and the irritating lock of hair fell into her face again.

"Oh, Claud." Regi could hardly bear to watch her sister's torment.

"It dawned on me that the DVD I'd destroyed was probably a copy. No blackmailer would send the original." Claudia looped her distracting hair behind her ear. "I debated over and over what I should do, and then all this happened. I should have gone to Morgan and told him, but I had destroyed the proof, and all this stuff with you was going on. I didn't want to add to it. Hoped it would go away. Then I thought about Lisa."

Claudia clasped her hands together. "Lisa almost married Curtis Romney. But at least he was out of her life. He couldn't hurt her anymore. She was at college, away from his reach. She was safe. Then I thought I should tell Melissa, his wife. The poor creature had been married to such a vile man. When I went to her home to console her over his death, I couldn't tell her." Claudia's bottom lip trembled. "Seeing her grieve and remembering what I'd gone through . . . I couldn't destroy her memory of him." Her knuckles turned white as she pressed her hands together.

Claudia didn't go on. She'd reached the end of her horrible story. She had been through so much. Regi parted Claudia's hands, placing her arm in the crook of her sister's. "This is what you tried to tell me when we found the knife in my Jeep, isn't it?"

Claudia nodded.

Regi could go on and on about how Claudia should have informed not only her but Morgan as well. Yet, going over what her sister should have done would not fix the sorry mess they were in now. Life was not a rewind. Better to think about what they could do to fix the situation. And the good thing was, she'd told her now. Claudia had done her best in a difficult situation. Regi had to let her know things were all right between them. "You know what?"

Claudia stared blankly at her.

"I have sorely misjudged you." Regi squeezed her sister's arm. "I always thought you were weak. I know you like things in order, and sometimes you take on too much responsibility, but I thought you were sheltered from the awful things of this world, and here you've weathered this horrible storm. It would have flattened me. You did it all by yourself. Mom would be proud. So would Dad."

Claudia chuckled. "They thought Morris was perfect. And strange as this may sound—" She drew a deep breath as if to fight an onslaught of tears. "I want to leave it that way. It would only upset them to know the truth."

Regi kissed Claudia's forehead. Her sister was always trying to make everyone happy, never wanting to cause them pain or worry. Claudia couldn't bear to put a worm on a hook, let alone cause needless pain to those she loved. "Are you going to be okay?"

"Yes." Claudia sighed. "I'm sorry I didn't tell you sooner, but I'd planned never to tell anyone, and then I thought of that—" She pointed to the map on the table. "—and knew I had to tell you."

Regi walked over to study it. "I think we can keep Morris's secret safe and solve the crime. Somehow the land is connected to Romney's murder. Let's go over what we think could have happened." She stared at the map and the property lines where several ranches bordered the parcels marked for auction. Even Twiggs Café and the Gas-N-Grub bordered some of the land, but neither Stew nor Jed would want it badly enough to commit murder.

Would they?

Jed might want the land to vindicate his grandfather and irritate Samuel. And Stew? He bought that new car for his brother so buying land wouldn't appeal to him. He wouldn't have murdered Romney . . . unless Stew was blackmailing Romney because he'd found out what the twerp was up to and that was why Stew had money for the car. Hmmm. Interesting thought. She looked at the other properties.

"Any one of these guys—" Regi pointed to the different ranches. "—could have killed him." Another realization hit. "Claud, someone had to have put Romney up to blackmailing Morris. He wasn't bright enough to think of that himself. Someone higher up on the ranger food chain."

"Superintendent Elliott?" Claudia nodded as if she, too, had thought of him as the one manipulating everything.

"You said he was mighty upset you happened to overhear him talking to another ranger. Could all the rangers be in on it?"

Claudia scratched her forehead. "That doesn't make sense. Why would the rangers want a bill passed to free up park property? Less land means fewer jobs."

"You have a point." Regi tapped her chin. "But what if—okay now, hear me out. What if they were pooling their money to buy the land? Once they purchased it, they wouldn't have to share it with the public. No more cars driving through polluting the air, no more tourists to contend with. Think about it."

"No," Claudia said. "All those people couldn't keep a secret like that. *And* blackmail my husband. Plus, the rangers count on tourists to visit the park. It's what keeps them working."

"You might be right." Regi had thought for sure she was on to something, though she wasn't ready to give up yet. "We're back to the superintendent. Elliott hates the tourists and fakes being a fanatical environmentalist. Plus, Romney married his daughter, which he was none too happy about. Maybe once Romney lived out his usefulness, Elliott offed him."

Claudia folded her arms. "That's too easy. I think we should explore other options as well."

Disappointed, Regi started over. "Okay, we're back to the ranchers. Oh, and I forgot to tell you something big." Regi proceeded to tell Claudia about Morgan's mysterious visit to Tanner's house last night and how, even though she didn't want to think it, she believed there was a possibility they could have been the ones who'd run her off the road, though Tanner had saved her life and even returned her revolver.

"You took a gun with you?" Claudia looked horrified.

"Hey, someone's out to get me, and I'm not going to be defenseless."

Regi knew her sister was scared of guns and had never handled one. She wanted guns banned, even outlawed. But Regi believed if guns were outlawed, *only* the criminals would have them.

"The revolver didn't stop someone from running you off the road. Promise me you won't take your gun anymore." Claudia's brows pinched together.

"You're kidding, right?" Regi had no intention of making such a promise.

"Regi, please. I've lost too much. The thought of something happening to you . . . I just can't stand it. You have to promise me you won't take your gun." Claudia bit her bottom lip.

"Okay." To not agree would only torture her sister more. But if push came to shove, Regi knew she'd break that promise. Once home last night, she'd locked the gun in the safe in her room. She knew where it was if and when she needed it.

Trying to sort out her jumbled thoughts, Regi paced and pondered out loud, "Back to Tanner and Morgan. Is it ridiculous to think they could be working together?"

"Sounds a bit far-fetched." Claudia gave Regi a slight smile.

Regi said nothing.

Claudia continued. "Wait a minute. Just yesterday you thought Samuel had killed Romney, and suddenly you've dropped that conclusion and now think Morgan could be the killer. What changed?"

Regi couldn't look at her. "Well, Samuel actually bought the truck for me from Newt."

Claudia's eyebrows raised.

"And Newt said Tanner wanted to know if anyone had come by wanting their front bumper fixed." Regi stopped.

"This is important because . . ."

"Well, it looks to me like Tanner was trying to find out who could have run me off the road, so it doesn't stand to reason that he killed Romney if he's trying to find out who wanted to kill me, does it?" Saying her reasoning out loud made Regi doubt herself.

"Now I'm worried because I'm beginning to follow your logic. Does make him less likely." Claudia tapped her chin. "However, I think there's something more."

The way Claudia appraised Regi made her nervous that her sister was onto the truth. She didn't want her to know that Samuel had kissed her this morning. Then all of Claud's objectivity would be almost as cloudy as hers, and she might overlook something important about the case. Something that might still point to Tanner's involvement.

Claudia continued. "You had dinner with Samuel, and he rescued you last night." Her eyes opened wider. "Admit it, you have feelings for Samuel again."

Regi had hoped to keep her newly awakened emotions to herself. Talking about them would only make them real.

"And it frightens you?" Claudia added.

Regi stared up at the ceiling, shuddered, and started for the kitchen. "Yeah. Okay. Drop it."

Claudia followed. "What you need is more information. You have to return to Samuel's and ask him point-blank what's the deal with him and Morgan. That way you can see if what you're feeling is genuine."

Regi took a deep breath and let it out slowly. "Well, I'll go, not because of this imaginary feeling but because I need more information. While I'm there, I think you need to go back to Elliott's."

Claudia had passed her but stopped in front of Regi near the counter. "Go back to Elliott's?"

Regi stepped around her sister. "If the DVD of Morris's affair is a duplicate—like you think—the original's either saved on Romney's laptop or filed away in his DVD library or on a flash drive. Melissa probably has it and doesn't even know. That is, if Elliott doesn't have it. He's probably the one who put Romney up to blackmailing Morris. And if that's the case, that helps build motive for him to kill his son-in-law." Regi paused a moment. "Though, maybe you shouldn't go alone. Or you should at least take my gun."

"Are you serious?" Claudia folded her arms. "I'll be careful. I'm not afraid of Melissa. And Elliott wouldn't do anything to me in front of his daughter."

"You're probably right, but be careful, okay?" Regi was very worried for her sister. "Especially driving home."

As if by second nature, Claudia checked the pizza dough but kept her mind on the conversation. "I'm always careful. Too careful. If Melissa suspected Romney was double-dealing her father, she might have killed her own husband. I know how it feels to be betrayed. Stranger things have happened." Wiping her hands on the dish towel, Claudia added, "Before we head out, you need to call Lisa and Jack to let them know what kind of sorry fix we're in."

"I hate to do that. Don't you think it can wait one more day?"

Claudia shrugged. "Do you want to take the chance that someone else tells them?"

"No." Regi had put this off for far too long, but how was a mother supposed to tell her children she was a murder suspect? Such news should be delivered in person, not over the phone, but in her heart she knew she had to do it. Regi grabbed the phone and dialed Lisa's cell number. On the fourth ring a girl answered. "Lisa?"

"Nope. She left her phone at my place. She's at the library. Can I give her a message?"

"Yes, thank you. Please have her call her mother." Regi said good-bye and hung up, relieved yet anxious. Before her courage waned, she called Jack. No answer. Not a big surprise. He usually kept his phone off unless he had to use it. She left a voice mail asking him to call as soon as he could.

Regi was glad she couldn't reach either one of them but knew this was only postponing the inevitable.

Claudia grabbed her pink parka from the coat rack. "At least you tried."

"Yeah. If we're lucky, we could have this solved before either one calls back. What about the guests and the pizza dough?" Regi snagged her sheepskin jacket.

Claudia paused a moment, looking at Regi as though remembering how she'd told her off for leaving without anyone here. She shrugged. "This is an emergency. With any luck, we'll be back before anyone misses us and before the dough rises too high."

FIFTEEN
UNEXPECTED

AFTER SAMUEL STOPPED AT NEWT Birch's garage and asked if anyone had come in needing their front bumper repaired, he checked over the only running truck he could buy for Regi. While paying, Samuel received a call from Ranger Knutson that someone had reported a poacher bagging a deer in the park and dragging the animal across the boundary. The ranger knew Morgan usually deputized Samuel to help this time of year and since he couldn't get ahold of the sheriff, Knutson hoped Samuel could help them out. The rangers were swamped. The incident had taken place near Coffee Pot Rapids.

Knowing Morgan was in Bounty Falls, Samuel decided to see what the deal was. He drove to the area and found a cold, empty campsite. He hiked around and discovered where someone had cleaned a deer. Disgusted that they'd left such a mess so close to a camping area, Samuel buried it. But he decided he'd better report his findings to Morgan. Plus, he wanted to talk to him with regards to Jed's accusations this morning. The look on Regi's face when his brother had accused Samuel of killing Romney haunted him.

Samuel wondered if Morgan could possibly be home by now. He'd take a chance. He drove by the sheriff's office and the Gas-N-Grub to make sure he hadn't missed Morgan, but there was no sign of his patrol car.

As he pulled up to Morgan's home, Samuel expected to meet the pack of dogs his friend kept around for Hannah's sake. They weren't in sight, which struck him as odd. Even when he climbed out of the truck, they didn't appear.

Leaping up the front steps, Samuel rang the bell and listened intently, hopeful to hear someone stir within. If Morgan had taken Hannah into the city, Effie Mcquire should still be here and so should the dogs. As he was about to head around back to check, he heard footfalls scurrying toward the door.

Effie wrenched it opened, and right away Samuel knew something was wrong. The warm, friendly smile that ordinarily graced her elderly face was replaced with total fear.

"Thank goodness you're here. Tried to call you, but no one was home. Did you see her?" She wrung her blue-veined hands together. Hair had escaped the braided bun atop her head and swirled about her neck.

"Who?"

"Hannah, of course." She opened the screen door and walked out on the porch. As she frantically glanced around, she rolled up the sleeves of her flannel shirt. Samuel noticed her breaths came in panicked huffs. Effie was one tough broad, but even she could be ripe for a heart attack. Perspiration dampened her face as though she'd been in a steam room. "I made her lie down for a nap. She was so upset after Regi left."

"Regi was here?"

She ignored his question as she swooshed into the house all aflutter like a worried killdeer protecting her chick. Samuel followed.

Effie was shaking, and if she didn't calm down, he knew he'd have to call the county nurse. Bewilderment and panic pooled in her darting eyes. She couldn't seem to focus. "I thought she was sleeping. But when I went out to hang up the wash, the dogs didn't come." She stopped and stared at Samuel. "They always come, you know. A person can't step outside this house without the entire pack swarming around."

Samuel hated to think it, but had Hannah taken off on foot with the dogs following? He turned about, heading for the door. "Call Morgan and tell him Hannah is missing," he said over his shoulder.

"I know I should, but with him in Bounty Falls, what could he do a hundred miles away?" Effie's face flushed. She pushed a hair up to the white braid on her head. "He'd only worry." She paused, placing a quivering hand on her chest, and took a cleansing breath. "He had to take some things regarding Regina to the city. Told me not to tell her in case she came snooping around. He doesn't want her worrying about the case, and if she knew where he was, she'd come up with all sorts of wild stories. He wants her to stay put at the Raindancer.

"She came by, you know. Has a cold and with all the hullabaloo about Curtis Romney . . ." Effie bit her bottom lip as if to keep a swell of emotions from overtaking her. "Hannah's missing! We've got to do something."

"I plan to. Don't worry, Effie. I'll find her." Samuel pushed open the screen, but before letting it shut, he turned around. "Stay close to the phone, in case Morgan calls."

He bounded off the porch and hurried to his truck. Samuel had a hunch. Many times Morgan had taken Hannah to the river because the rushing water calmed her. Regi's visit may have upset her, so she'd gone to the river where she could find peace. A long shot at best but possible. And with her thoughts so muddled, Hannah's life could be in danger. The problem was Samuel didn't know exactly which place Morgan had taken her: down by the bridge, down by the rapids. Regi's favorite fishing spot came to mind. Maybe Hannah went there . . . or was drawn there. That place seemed to pull people to it.

Samuel couldn't have driven faster if his winter hay had been on fire. He broke all sorts of speed limits but finally came to the turnoff from the main highway that led to the river. The washboard, graveled road soon turned to dirt, which was now mud because of the light snow that had fallen. Deep ruts and large rocks bucked his truck back and forth, but Samuel never let up. The road turned sharply, and his truck fishtailed. He gripped hard on the steering wheel and kept going.

Finally, the road ended, and he slammed on the brakes. The truck slid in the mud and came to a stop. Looking to the hill above the river, he saw her.

Something was wrong.

Hannah was bent as if to slip through the fence he'd put up to keep his cattle on his land—and also to annoy Regi—but Hannah wasn't moving. The dogs were fussing, running between fence posts, sniffing the ground.

She must be caught in the barbed wire. Tiny barbs would slice her skin to shreds.

Samuel jerked open the door, drawing the dogs' attention. They ran to him, the black lab leading the way. Samuel leaped out of his vehicle and, ignoring the anxious canine herd that looked to him as a savior, hurried to Hannah. She was crying and pulling at her knee-length hair caught on the wire. Her legs were tangled in it too. She had deep gashes in her bare calves. Blood trickled down to her reddened feet clad in muddy flip-flops. Her eyes held bewilderment and confusion. She wore only a thin dress and shivered in the cold breeze.

"Hannah, dear. Calm down. It's all right." He quickly removed his Levi jacket and placed it over her shoulders, being careful not to pull her hair caught in the fencing. Thankful he always carried his Leatherman tool with him, he slipped it from his hip pocket. The device was multifunctional and had wire cutters that could bite through near anything. Every rancher worth his salt kept one on his person.

"I know she's down there." Hannah stared at the river as if someone were calling her name. The coursing water seemed to mesmerize her. "Regi loves to fish."

Her skin was ice cold. Holding her leg still so she couldn't move and make matters worse, he quickly set to work and cut the rusty wire away from her skin.

"Thomas warned me not to tell her." Her blue lips trembled. "But I did."

Believing she was delirious, Samuel ignored what she said and studied Hannah's beautiful hair tangled in the upper wire. It was so tightly wound that it would take hours to undo. She'd been exposed to the cold too long, especially dressed as she was. Hating to do it but knowing he must, Samuel cut her hair. He then guided her out of the wire toward the truck.

"That ranger died down there, didn't he?" she said in a monotone voice, never taking her eyes off the river.

Samuel stopped and looked at her, wondering if she were more aware than he'd first thought. "Did Regi tell you that?"

"No, you did." Hannah turned her sad, copper-colored eyes on him. "You knew the ranger was trouble."

He realized she now thought he was Morgan. Trying to calm her, he said in a soothing voice, "He's not causing trouble now." Samuel gently placed his arm about her waist.

Reaching the truck, he quickly settled her in the passenger seat, buckling her in. He closed the door and hurried to the rear, pulling down the tailgate so the dogs could ride. He helped the smaller ones in. Once they were loaded, he slammed the gate shut and looked back at the river.

He thought he heard a voice . . . or was it a whisper?

Staring at the stand of willows where Regi had claimed the body had been, he knew no one was there. A shudder caught him, and he cursed. While Curtis Romney was alive, the man had brought pain to so many people. Samuel knew the man's death would bring even more, especially for the woman Samuel loved.

Regi rang Samuel's doorbell at least five times, and still no answer. She tried the doorknob. Locked. Where was the man? Whirling about, she headed to her horse trailer, thinking she might as well unload Gypsy. As much as it pained her, she had decided to return his "gift." That stubborn pride of hers wouldn't let her complicate things even more by accepting such an expensive present.

Opening the trailer, she gazed at the pinto she loved so much and wondered if she could give her up again. She had to. It wasn't right to accept such a present. As she untied the filly and guided her from the trailer, Regi thought about what Tanner had said when he'd returned the horse. He'd claimed he purchased the filly to help her and never thought of Gypsy as his.

Regi's steps slowed as she and the horse reached the barn. The pinto nuzzled her arm, pushing her. Gritting her teeth, she opened the heavy planked doors.

Regi glanced about. Stalls lined both sides of the barn. A roan gelding came to a stall gate. Regi recognized him as the horse Tanner had ridden the other day down by the river. The equine gazed in her direction, ears erect, expecting something or someone else.

"It's all right, fella, just bringing Gypsy back to the fold." Seeing an empty stall next to the gelding's, Regi led her pinto to it, opened the gate, and sent the filly in. Once inside the stall, the horse turned about and returned to Regi. She stroked Gypsy's forehead and tugged off the hackamore. "It will be all right." Regret once again bit at her. Forcing the feeling away, Regi secured the latch on the gate and turned around.

Where could Tanner be? She had psyched herself up for a talk, and now that he wasn't here, she didn't know what to do. If Tanner were on the range, hours could go by before he returned home, but his horse was here, so that was unlikely. If he'd caught up with Morgan, wherever that man was hiding, it could also mean hours of waiting. She might as well store Gypsy's hackamore in the tack room.

Seeing only one door in the interior wall, she knew that's where he kept the tack. As Regi stepped in, the whiff of well-polished leather escaped the very organized room.

She and Tanner had more in common than Regi'd thought. He obviously liked an orderly tack. Sitting on top of wooden sawhorses were saddles: a full double-rigged, a center-fire, and a slick fork. Bridles, bits, and hackamores hung from wall pegs. Bat-wing, shotgun, and wooly chaps were displayed as well. A wooden crate contained old horseshoes, some with nails still in them.

For a second, Regi thought she heard something. She held very still as she strained to hear more. Nothing. Gypsy was probably stirring around, wanting Regi to come back and give her something to eat. Regi relaxed and hung the hackamore next to the others.

She could tell a lot about a rancher by how well he kept his tack. Tanner was a very organized and clean man. But that she already knew from having dinner with him and seeing how orderly his house was. A table against another wall held a box of sugar cubes, currycombs, brushes, and some bottles of animal medicine.

She left the tack room and wandered through the barn. Maybe she should come back later. Wanting to give her horse one last good-bye, Regi pushed open the gate and went inside. Gypsy came to her, lipping at her hand for a treat. "Sorry, I don't have anything." She stroked her sweet filly's backside.

And then she saw someone standing in the doorway. For a second she didn't recognize who it was. But then she knew. Tanner stood in the barn's doorway, looking every inch the cowboy from his hat down to his boots. He must have been watching her for a while.

"Regi, what do you think you're doing?" Anger rode his voice.

"Returning your present." Why was he so upset?

Samuel walked into the barn right up to Gypsy's stall. His chocolate eyes squinted in anger. "Haven't you caused enough trouble for one day?"

"What are you talking about?" She couldn't imagine why her being in his barn would make him act this way. "I'm merely returning something that isn't mine; that's not causing trouble."

"You might not be causing trouble here, but you did at Morgan's. I found Hannah down by the river cut and bruised from barbed wire." Anger and frustration filled his words. "Your visit upset her."

Regi couldn't think what she had said that would have made Hannah go to the river. "I visited her, but she was fine when I left."

"She's not fine now," he said, clenching his teeth. "She went looking for you and got herself all tangled up."

"You mean, on the fence *you* put up to keep *me* out?" she fired back.

He slowly nodded. "I didn't do it to keep you out. I did it to keep my cattle in, but, yeah, that's the one." Tanner's anger still simmered. "What did you tell her that made her go off like that?"

"I only asked where Morgan was," she replied, grateful that the stall stood between them. "Hannah's my friend. I wouldn't do anything to hurt her." A rush of emotion threatened to bring tears to her eyes. Regi sniffed and tried to remain composed. She had no idea her questions had upset Hannah so. "Will she be all right?"

"Yeah. Effie cleaned and dressed the wounds, said she didn't need stitches." Tanner's angry expression softened.

"Thank goodness." That Hannah had been hurt looking for her tore at Regi's heart. She sniffed again and swore she felt a tear roll down the side of her face but decided to ignore it. *Please, Lord, bless my friend and don't let me cry in front of Tanner. Please.*

He opened the gate and stepped inside the stall, standing next to her. He brushed the tear from her cheek. Without thinking, she leaned into him. He hugged her.

"She's resting." He didn't let go, and Regi couldn't pull away, didn't want to pull away. She gazed up at his eyes, then at his lips, remembering the kiss they'd shared this morning.

Only this morning he had held her to him.

Only this morning she had felt this same magnetic pull vanquish her temper and misgivings and hypnotize her.

He pulled her more tightly to him, against his warm body. Then, as he had only a few hours ago, he kissed her. An unexpected brush fire flamed her insides and raced over her skin.

Reason soon whispered her name, reminding her why she'd come. She pulled free and backed away from his embrace.

"Samuel, I have to know something." She had to say it and quick. "And I'm praying you'll tell me the truth."

"Praying?" He tugged off his hat and drove his fingers through his thick gray hair, looking down at the ground. Then he glanced up. "Since when does praying help? It didn't save Hannah from losing her mind. Didn't stop my old man from . . ." Hurt and doubt filled his voice.

Regi almost reached out to him but held back. "Your father hurt you badly when you were young, didn't he?"

Samuel didn't reply, only stood gazing at her with a clenched jaw.

She continued. "You can't blame the Lord. For all you know, He protected you from something much worse."

A mocking smile flickered to his lips. "Worse than having my father quote Psalms while he whipped me? 'But he, being full of compassion, forgave their iniquity and destroyed them not; yea, many a time turned he his anger away, and did not stir up all his wrath.' Want to see what religion did for me?" He didn't wait for her to answer but tugged off his shirt and turned his back to her. Large, ugly scars riddled his skin.

Horrified, Regi prayed silently that she could say something to ease his pain. "But you got away. How do you suppose that happened?"

Samuel pulled his shirt back on. "My legs. I crept away in the night. No God opened the door. No Lord lit my path. Did it all on my own."

"No, you didn't." Regi desperately wanted him to understand. "God was with you every step, watching over you, keeping you safe. You were meant to escape."

"Oh, and I suppose the Lord meant for us to be separated, for your husband to die, and for Romney to get murdered?"

Instinctively, Regi was ready to argue. She realized that was what Samuel wanted her to do. He wanted her to lose her temper to stop her from talking about God. As much as she hated to admit it, in the last few days, she'd felt that God had abandoned her, but deep down she knew He hadn't. She didn't know quite how to explain her faith. Still, she had to give it a try. "Look, believing in a higher power is tough. The Lord works in mysterious ways that we humans can't comprehend. Who knows, maybe we were separated for you to get your head on straight. I was hurt for many years after you left, but I found Earl and had my beautiful children."

"Children we should have had." His gaze locked with hers.

"Maybe, maybe not. We'll never know." Could she tell him what was in her heart? What did she have to lose? "All I know is I loved Earl dearly."

Samuel still stared at her, not turning away as she had expected him to.

"His death has been very hard for me to get over. A miracle happened when the Mormon missionaries knocked on my door and explained the plan of salvation and that families could be together forever. The gospel gives me comfort."

"I don't believe in miracles, but good for you. Guess that tells me where I belong." Samuel was about to turn away.

"Do you think Earl—let me rephrase that—do you think God wants me to be alone the rest of my life?" Regi could hardly believe that she was stating the case that she and Samuel may still have a life together. And until this very moment, she hadn't really thought about having a future with Samuel. Leaning on a sudden prompting, she continued. "I don't think so."

Samuel's expression softened with hope.

"Look, I don't have all the answers." Her shoulders slumped. As much as she wanted to dwell on these new feelings, there was no time to get into their relationship right now. The clock was ticking, surrounding Regi with the need to solve Romney's murder. "For instance, I don't know why Romney was killed, but I know his death was not something manipulated by God. *Someone* made a very wrong choice." She didn't know if she could ask what was on the tip of her tongue, but she had to. "I know you didn't kill him, but do you know who did?"

Samuel tugged his hat on, took her hands in his, and solemnly answered, "No, I don't."

Relief erupted through her, stronger than a geyser. Still, she had more questions she needed answers to. "Why did Morgan come to your house last night?" If Samuel answered this truthfully, she'd press him with more about the sheriff and whether their mutual friend had any motive to kill Romney.

Samuel drew away. "He asked me not to tell you. He didn't want you to worry about what he had to do today."

"I'm a big girl. You can tell me. What has he been doing?" Regi hated people deciding what was best for her.

"His job." The stony look that overcame Tanner's face let her know he was not going to break a confidence and give her details.

Regi was back to square one.

SIXTEEN

WARRANT

No cars were parked at Superintendent Elliott's. No lights were on in the house. Claudia knocked on the door, hoping someone might be there, in a back room or something.

The sun was setting, and there was still so much to do. Again, she knocked, pounding a bit harder than before. A distant thud came from within the house. Someone was inside. Claudia needed to be patient and wait.

No one came.

She hurried down the concrete steps of the old gray-stone building and walked around back. Again she heard a noise from within the house, as if someone were pounding on a wall. She stood still, straining to hear. The noise stopped. She hurried up the wooden steps to the back porch and knocked. As she did, the door swung open as though it hadn't been latched. Eerie.

For a moment, Claudia stood frozen. This felt like a setup, something she'd seen in a Hitchcock film, not in real life. She'd heard a strange noise. Now that the door was open, she knew she had to go in. Someone could be hurt, pounding on a wall in a last desperate plea for help. Claudia was the only chance for that person to be rescued.

Feeling a bit melodramatic, she resisted entering. Instead, she poked her head in and called, "Hello. Is anybody home?"

Silence answered.

Another scenario—someone could have broken into the house, and Claudia was now catching burglars in the act of robbing the place. Absurd. Again, she yelled, "Anybody home?"

A loud bang chased her words, as if something heavy had fallen on the floor. The sound came from upstairs. Without further thought of her safety, Claudia raced inside. She scanned each room as she passed through the house. No one was in the kitchen, dining room, living room, or den. That left the upstairs. Claudia scaled the steps two at a time. She checked the bedrooms and bathroom as she progressed down the hall. No one, nothing out of the ordinary, until she came to the last door.

Claudia opened it to find Melissa lying on the hardwood floor, a rope tied around her neck. At the other end of the rope was the ceiling light that lay beside her. In an instant, Claudia saw a vision of her husband, Morris, lying dead on the living room carpet. Shaking her head and blinking her eyes, she focused on the reality before her and the girl on the floor.

"Melissa!" She quickly ran to her. With shaking hands, Claudia untied the rope and felt the girl's wrist. "Please, God, don't let her die. Please!" She couldn't feel a pulse.

Frantic, Claudia examined Melissa's throat. A brilliant red mark traced around her neck. Placing her fingers along the side of the girl's windpipe, Claudia frantically waited. Relief flushed over her as she finally felt the beat of the girl's pulse. Melissa was still alive. The fall must have knocked her out. Claudia stroked the young woman's head, feeling a large bump. "Melissa, honey, wake up."

The young woman groaned as her eyes opened. "Where did you come from?"

"I stopped by to visit. When I heard you fall, I let myself in." Claudia smoothed a lock of hair away from the young woman's face. "Melissa, hon, were you trying to kill yourself?"

The girl didn't answer but started to get up and staggered.

Claudia grabbed her arm to steady her. "Maybe you should just lie there a while and make sure you're all right."

Melissa ignored her, trying to get to her feet.

"Let me help you." Claudia guided her to the bed.

"You wouldn't understand, Ms. Osborne." Melissa's shoulders shuddered as an onslaught of tears overtook her. She lay down. "I don't want to live without Curtis. He's the only man who ever really cared for me. I'd never been on a date until I met him. And he was so nice. I don't want to go on." Big sloppy tears streamed down her cheeks, dropping onto the pillow.

Claudia knew how she felt. After Morris had died, there were times when Claudia didn't want to go on—that was, until she'd found his letter and realized what a fool she'd been. "Melissa—" Claudia sat on the edge of the bed. "Taking your life isn't the answer." For a second, Claudia wished she had converted to the church Regi had found. Maybe then she'd know what to say. She did remember that Regi had told her everyone, no matter their faith, had the light of Christ to guide them. Claudia needed His guidance right now.

Morris's suicide and then his betrayal had scarred her. On one hand, Claudia felt the act of killing oneself the most selfish thing a person could do, but gazing at Melissa and seeing the pain on her face, Claudia realized Morris must have had tremendous mental torment. So much so that in his mind he'd made the ultimate sacrifice for her. Perhaps Melissa felt she was making the ultimate sacrifice for her husband.

"Melissa, I don't think Curtis would want you to kill yourself over his death. And I know one thing for sure, and that is that suicide solves nothing. It may stop your pain, but what about your father? What would he do without you? His grief would be insurmountable."

All at once, a swell of emotion overcame Melissa. She turned away from Claudia and sobbed uncontrollably. Claudia didn't know quite what to do or say. She rubbed Melissa's arm then smoothed a lock of hair away from the young woman's face. Tears covered her upper lip and cheeks. Claudia grabbed a tissue from the box on the nightstand beside the bed and handed it to her. Melissa took it as her crying calmed a little.

"You're wrong," Melissa said. "My father has the park and the rangers. He wouldn't miss me." She wiped her tear-washed cheek.

"You're his flesh and blood. He loves you. Your death would break his heart."

Melissa quit crying as she began to comprehend what Claudia was saying. "My father was relieved that I'd finally married. He was afraid he was going to be saddled with me all his life."

"Oh, hon, I know you're wrong." Claudia wasn't sure how Cameron Elliott felt about his daughter, but at this moment, this girl needed to hear that her father loved her. "I've heard the love your father has for you in his voice. Parents worry that after they're dead their children who haven't married will be alone. If he seemed relieved, that was probably why. If you had succeeded and committed suicide, he would have been devastated."

Melissa sniffed. "I don't want to hurt my father. But I can't stand being without Curtis."

Claudia patted her arm. "I know. But your pain will ease with time. You have your father, and I'm here with you now. You have friends who care about you." Claudia's words echoed in her mind as her thoughts turned to Morris.

He had needed someone, and she'd failed him. The feeling of guilt was overwhelming, but so was the knowledge that guilt had taken over her life too often in the past year. How many times had Claudia been over this? She would have helped Morris. She *would* have. But she hadn't known his pain. Looking at Melissa's brown lock of hair that had once again fallen back into her eyes, Claudia knew she could help her. This sweet girl was willing to give her life for Romney. She was yet another one of his victims. Claudia hated that man.

She quickly grabbed another tissue and dabbed the young woman's cheeks. "No man is worth dying for. Even if he was the sweetest, noblest, most extraordinary person you've ever known. Your life is your most precious gift." Claudia looked directly into her eyes. "No one else can be you. No one else can make a difference like you can." Flashes of Morris dead on the floor wanted Claudia's attention, but she would not dwell on them. This girl before her needed her more than Morris ever had. A shudder racked Melissa's body. "I wish I could believe you."

"It's true. Last spring my husband died. I know how you're feeling."

Melissa gazed at Claudia with appreciation. "Curtis was always kind," Melissa said. Clearly, the young woman idealized him and had no clue to his true character. Claudia could understand such blindness. She had lived with blinders on too. She realized this situation was too similar to her own pain for her to help Melissa properly.

"I know someone who is much more qualified to help you through your grief than I am. Do you know Karen Wilson, the county nurse?"

"Kinda."

"I'm going to call her. She'll come over and help you through this, but you have to promise to tell her everything that's worrying you." Claudia spied the phone near a laptop on the desk by the window. She patted the girl's arm and started across the room to the phone, skirting around the ceiling light that lay in pieces on the floor. Claudia made a mental note to clean the mess up before she left.

"My father didn't understand Curtis."

Claudia had picked up the phone to dial, but she put it back. "Your father?"

"A few weeks ago, he came home so mad at Curtis. He and Curtis went to Daddy's den, and they were yelling at each other. I couldn't stand to hear such foul language, so I came up here and surfed the web on Curtis's laptop."

Claudia looked at the computer on the desk. "This laptop?" She pointed.

The girl nodded.

Claudia cautiously made her way back to Melissa. "Do you remember what they were saying?"

Melissa cleared her throat. "I only heard bits and pieces."

"Bits and pieces?" Claudia held her breath.

Melissa squinted, as if doing so helped her memory. "Yeah. A sentence here and there. My father told Curtis he was a devious . . . I don't want to say what he said. That's when I left. I refused to take sides. I love my father and my husband. Before that day, my dad and Curtis seemed to get along, but after that argument, Daddy's whole attitude toward Curtis changed."

"Changed?"

"Daddy wouldn't talk with him at home. He assigned Curtis the late shift and had him work in the office on weekends. If only Curtis had confided in me what had happened maybe I could have smoothed things over. And now, my father's so upset and worried, and it's all my fault. If I would have insisted the two of them make peace, then Curtis wouldn't have been working so late, and maybe he'd still be alive."

"What?" It took Claudia a minute to react because she was still absorbing everything Melissa had said about the argument between Elliott and Romney. "You can't blame yourself."

Melissa turned away.

Claudia took both of her hands. "Look at me."

The young woman shuddered and then turned her gaze to Claudia. "Curtis's death is not your fault! Your dying would not make things better for your father. It would make it far worse. Believe me, I know."

Melissa's bottom lip trembled.

"Don't cry." Claudia had to say something that would comfort her. But what? "You're all your father has left in this world. He'd do anything for you."

"I'm not the son he always wanted."

"No, but you'll always be his little girl." Claudia placed her palm to Melissa's cheek. "And I know he loves you very much."

The worry lines on Melissa's brow softened as a slight smile crossed her lips. "Thanks."

Relieved that Melissa was feeling a little better, Claudia thought about the argument between Romney and Elliott. She was certain Elliott must have stumbled upon something about Romney that was shady.

Had Elliott been so upset by what he'd found that he'd killed his own son-in-law? Or—this thought made her even more anxious to find the truth—had Elliott found the DVD of Morris and his mistress and recognized Curtis's voice as she had? A definite possibility.

Gazing at Melissa, she realized she needed to call Karen. After asking the nurse to come as soon as she could, Claudia hung up. "Well, what shall we do until she gets here?"

"You don't need to wait. I've already taken up too much of your time." Melissa seemed genuine in her concern.

"I have all the time in the world." Claudia started to pick up the broken glass on the floor and put it in the wastebasket.

"I'll do that." Melissa began to get up but staggered.

Claudia immediately went to her. "I think you'd better lie still for a while. Do you have a TV to watch?" She glanced around the room.

"Sometimes Curtis and I would watch movies on his laptop."

Claudia quickly retrieved it from the desk, handing it to Melissa.

The young woman turned it on. It took a minute for the screen to come up. Melissa clicked on an icon and a welcome sign popped into view. Two accounts showed.

"Is that your e-mail?"

"No, it's Curtis's."

Right away Claudia wondered if there could be a clue to his death in his email. "Don't you think you'd better check and see if someone has been trying to get in touch with him?"

Melissa clicked on his icon. His files had been wiped clean. "Daddy must have checked it." Melissa then clicked on the movie program.

"What movie would you like to watch?" Claudia quickly searched the desk for DVDs as she pulled open one drawer after another looking for a copy of the DVD of Morris and his mistress. She finally found a box of DVD disks.

"Those are Curtis's personal files. He doesn't like anyone looking at them." Melissa stared at Claudia as if expecting her to stop. And out of respect for Melissa she wanted to, but knowing Romney was a liar and cheat, she couldn't. She pulled out first one and then another, reading the labels written on them.

"He may have put a movie in here." Claudia justified her snooping.

"The movies are over there." Melissa pointed to a bookshelf as Claudia read the last one. All appeared to be park business. But would he actually label it "Osborne Blackmail"? What had she been thinking?

She walked to the bookcase that held the DVDs. "Which one do you want?"

"What are you doing here?" The voice was male and very upset.

Claudia spun around to find Cameron Elliott walking into his daughter's room. His gaze went to the broken ceiling light on the floor, to the rope, and then to his daughter lying on the bed. Worry framed his eyes, and for a moment, Claudia forgot that he could be Romney's killer. No, for a second he was a father concerned for his daughter. "What's happened?"

Melissa started crying uncontrollably. Claudia went to her, letting her cry on her shoulder. She looked up at Elliott. "I stopped by to visit and heard Melissa fall." She hoped he wouldn't make her tell him everything. What Melissa had done should come from her, not Claudia.

He glanced back to the rope and then as though a tidal wave washed over him, realization set in. He gently pushed Claudia aside and drew his daughter into his arms, rocking her. Claudia felt out of place and very much an intruder. She grabbed the laptop off the bed and set it back on the desk.

"I hope you don't mind, but I called Karen Wilson. She's on her way." Claudia picked up more glass from the floor.

"I'll take care of that." True gratitude graced Elliott's concerned face.

Claudia put the bits in the garbage. "Well, I'll let myself out."

He nodded, not looking up.

Claudia quietly slipped away. Heading toward her car, she realized she should have questioned Elliott about the land sale, but she just couldn't. Melissa's needs came first. However, this meant she would have to visit the Elliotts again. In a way, she was glad. She wanted to make sure Melissa was on the road to recovery. Claudia's thoughts turned to Romney. He had ruined so many lives. Again the scene of Morris dead on the living room floor flashed before her. She couldn't help it, but she was glad Romney was dead. Too bad his demise hadn't happened sooner.

What would Regi say if she learned her sister could be so heartless? Regi's new religion had taught her to forgive. Claudia wished she could, but in her heart, she knew no religion could relieve her pain or save her now.

Regi shut off the old truck's engine and gazed at the neon sign that read "Twiggs." Only Stew's classic '63 Chevy II was in the parking lot.

She had left Samuel alone in his barn. No reason to stay if he wasn't going to explain what Morgan was up to. She'd stopped at the Gas-N-Grub to call

Claudia. No answer, which was just as well, since Ida seemed to hover. With no sign of Jed, whom she had wanted to quiz more, Regi had bought some gum and left. She had to get back to the Raindancer, but she also had to talk with Stew to cross him off her suspect list. Claudia would hopefully beat her home.

As she climbed out of the pickup and trudged into the café, she realized there were no customers. Stew rarely kept waitresses on slow nights, and tonight was no exception. He waved her over to the counter.

"Ooh, what happened there?" He pointed to her forehead as she sat across from him.

Her hand automatically reached to cover the bruise she'd forgotten. "Ran into something."

"Wait a minute. Newt Birch came in, mumbling something about you running into a tree." He reached over, moved her hand, and gave her a sympathetic wince. "Looks like it hurts."

"It did but not anymore." She didn't want to talk about the accident. In fact, she wished she could forget it had ever happened. The last few days would be good to delete as well, but she was stuck with every second of every day.

"What brings you out tonight?" Stew poured her a glass of water and set it in front of her.

"Needed to see a friend."

"Came to the right place. Want a burger? Fries?" He wiped off the counter with a towel.

Though she knew Claudia had pizza in mind for dinner tonight, Regi was hungry now. "Why not?"

Stew immediately reached down to the small fridge below the counter, grabbed a hamburger patty, and threw it on the grill. The meat instantly sizzled. He pulled golden fries out of the deep fryer with a wire scoop and dumped them onto a plate, sprinkling salt over them. "Put these in for me, but I'll share."

He gave her the plate and a bottle of ketchup. Regi sprinkled more salt on before she tasted them. Stew frowned. "Don't you know that's rude? Never put salt on your food in front of the chef."

"Sorry. But you know me." Regi dipped a hot string of potato into the red sauce and chomped down. Stew made the best fries in Idaho, especially after she added salt. "Yum."

He went back to the grill and flipped over her burger. "Stew." Regi hated bringing up the subject, but this was the real purpose of her visit.

He swung around as if to give her his full attention. "Yeah?"

"You've heard about Curtis Romney, haven't you?"

"Small town, Reg, what do you think?" He buttered a hamburger bun, turned to the grill, and put the bread on it to toast.

She kept talking, even though his back was to her. "Well, I know you've heard that he's dead."

Stew nodded.

"And that I'm the one everyone suspects killed him."

Again, he nodded.

"I was wondering about the other day. Do you remember if Samuel picked up the knife he left on your counter?"

"Must have because it disappeared."

That wasn't very conclusive. If it just vanished from the counter without Stew knowing who picked it up, anyone could have taken it—if someone really did. What if Stew . . . ? She had to think of motive. What motive would Stew have to kill Romney?

"Have you heard that Romney knew about the park selling off land parcels and was trying to profit from it?"

He froze but didn't turn around to face her. "News to me. What makes you think the park's selling some land?"

"I've seen the map showing the upcoming sale. It not only borders a lot of ranches, but get this—" She was afraid to say it, yet had to. "It borders your property too." Regi watched Stew closely. He turned around, not looking at her. He'd built a mental fence between them.

Stew took the bottom bun, placed the meat on it, then added the top bun, and set it on her plate. He garnished her dinner with a lettuce leaf, tomato slice, red onion slice, and dill pickle. Setting her meal in front of her with a bottle of mustard, he finally looked at her. "What does park land matter to me?"

"Well, probably nothing. I was just wondering if you knew, that's all." Regi tried to maintain eye contact, but he busied himself wiping the already clean counter.

"Just because my property borders the park, doesn't mean I'd want more land," he finally said. Stew began scraping the grill.

Regi knew he was upset and that she shouldn't push him, but she did anyway. "Stew, if you added onto the café and built a motel, the tourists would flock here."

"I'd have to change sheets, make beds. Not my thing." He stopped and stared at her. "Get to the point, Reg. What does land and Romney's death have to do with me? You have some strange notion now that I killed him?"

She gulped. Regi hadn't expected this and felt foolish. "Of course not. I merely wondered if maybe Curtis approached you about the land is all."

"Well, he didn't," Stew said flatly.

Regi pushed the hamburger away. Her appetite had vanished, replaced with the concern that she'd offended a good friend.

Stew slung his dishcloth over his shoulder. "On the day he was killed, I know he played a billiard game with Tanner. They had a few harsh words with each other. And after Tanner left, Romney met with Morgan. Don't know if that helps."

Regi perked up. Now she was getting somewhere. "Did you overhear what they were discussing?"

"Who, Tanner and Romney or Morgan and Romney?"

"I want to know what you know." She smiled.

"Well, I only overheard his conversation with Tanner because they were shouting at each other. Romney was trying to cheat, and Tanner called him on it. Oh, and Romney brought up his argument with you. Said something about not letting a little old woman get the draw on him again." Stew poured himself a glass of water.

"Oh." Regi frowned. "Was he referring to me or Wakanda?"

"You. I can't imagine Wakanda standing over him threatening to make his life miserable."

"He called *me* a little old woman?" She didn't know which was more upsetting, the fact that Romney thought she was old or that he thought she was little. Looking at Stew, she realized something much more disturbing. "So you heard about the misunderstanding I had with Romney?" Regi automatically picked up a fry to eat it, but before putting it in her mouth, she put it back. She felt as though cell doors were closing on her.

"Like I said, it's a small town. Want some cocoa?"

"No, thanks. I need to get going." Regi realized she'd stayed too long, and she still didn't know where Morgan was. "By the way, have you seen Morgan today?"

"Nope."

"How much do I owe you for the hamburger?" Regi dug in her pants pocket, pulling out her wallet.

"The hamburger you didn't touch?" Stew shook his head. "Keep your money. I'll eat it and the salty fries as well."

"Thanks, Stew." Regi started for the door.

"Reg, I think you should know something." Stew's face turned serious and thoughtful.

She walked back to the counter. "What?"

"One night about a week ago, Romney and some of the rangers came in here pretty late. When I gave them their order, he was bragging about giving 'the what for' to a certain congressman."

Regi's stomach nosedived. She felt blood drain from her head. Claudia would be devastated if word got out about Morris. Regi blinked to focus on Stew and whatever else he was about to say.

"Anyway, I thought you should know. Claudia came in here looking for Romney the night he died." Stew gave her a look of concern.

"I know. She told me Romney never showed up."

"Really?" Stew looked confused. "I could swear he came in."

Regi's heart sank.

As if realizing he'd upset her, Stew continued. "I'm probably mistaken. But just the same, Reg, I think you ought to watch your back."

Somehow Regi made her legs move. She now stood outside her truck, fumbling with the keys, unable to find the right one.

Claudia, older, stronger, wiser sister, Claudia. Surely there was a reasonable explanation. Regi knew she had to give her sister the benefit of the doubt. Determined not to cast judgment until she'd spoken with her, Regi finally found the right key, climbed in, and started the truck.

Heading down the road, she glanced at the gas gauge. The needle slipped past *E*. This beat-up pile of bolts had been half full when she'd left the Raindancer. Of course, pulling a horse trailer around didn't give good mileage, but this was ridiculous. When life settled down, she would have to drive to civilization and buy a new—no, make that a "gently used"—vehicle. No money for new anything.

She pulled into the Gas-N-Grub to fill up. When the tank was full, Regi headed inside to pay and grab a candy bar. A Snickers would tide her over until she reached home.

Entering, she saw Jed and Clifford in the back stacking supplies. She was glad she wouldn't have to speak with them. The only hurdle Regi had to leap over was Ida, which wouldn't be too bad. Claudia may have thought the woman a meddling snoop, but Regi kind of felt sorry for her. Besides, she genuinely cared about people. But deciding to put off the inevitable questions Ida would ask, Regi ducked into the restroom. After using the facilities and washing her hands, she took a deep breath and decided the time had come to pay for her gas and leave.

Stepping out of the restroom, Regi was surprised to find Jed waiting for her.

"Regi, you've got to get out of here. Superintendent Elliott and Ranger Knutson are up front. They're looking for you. Elliott has a warrant in his hand. I think you'd better go out the back while I distract them."

"They have a warrant?"

Jed glanced over his shoulder then back to Regi. "Yes. They are here to arrest you."

"They have no authority outside the park. Morgan is the law in this town." Her words could not deflect the sonic wave of fear rippling through her. Obviously Elliott and Knutson were up to no good. Maybe they had been in cahoots and had killed Romney and now they were trying to kill her. One of them had probably tried to run her off the road last night.

Jed shrugged. "All I know is they are after you. Maybe because the crime happened to a fellow ranger, that gives them authority. Now, I personally don't believe you killed Romney. I saw you the morning you found him. You were as surprised as anyone else. No one guilty could have acted like you did."

Regi was relieved to have an ally. "Thanks, Jed." She realized he seemed to always deliver bad news. He'd been the one who'd told her about Samuel running off. He'd been there to help her through that heartbreak until she'd met Earl. Regi had not given Jed near enough credit for being a nice guy.

"We can't stand here talking. Elliott will head out to the Raindancer as soon as he leaves here. You'd better hide at my father's old place. No one's lived there for ten years. Go in the back way. The door's never locked. I'll call Claudia, Samuel, and Morgan and tell them what's going on as soon as Elliott and Knutson leave."

Regi was overwhelmed by the man's generosity. "Thanks, Jed. I owe you."

"No problem. What are friends for? You'd do the same for me." He winked at her.

She slipped out of the store and made a mad dash to the old truck. Jamming the key into the ignition, she coaxed the engine to fire up. If she hurried, she'd be long gone before Elliott could stop her.

SEVENTEEN
TRUST

CLAUDIA GLANCED UP AT THE clock for the hundredth time. Eight o'clock. Regi was supposed to be home hours ago. Claudia wrapped the leftover pizza and placed it in the fridge. Oscar wagged his tail, hitting the cupboard. Since the run-in with Ida, the dog had taken a liking to Claudia. "You want pizza?"

The setter licked his lips. She took out a slice and gave it to him. By the time she'd put the rest away, the animal was finished and wanted more. Patting the setter on the head, Claudia once again glanced up at the clock. Two minutes had passed. She stared down at the dog. "Regi was late last night because someone tried to kill her."

Fear grabbed Claudia. She called Tanner's place, hoping her sister was still there. No answer. Then she called Morgan's. Effie answered. The sheriff wasn't home yet, and Regi wasn't there, either. Effie told Claudia about Hannah getting tangled up in wire, so Claudia couldn't very well hurry her through the conversation. Finally, after ten minutes, she was able to hang up. By then Claudia feared Regi could have been in another accident. She shouldn't leave without telling their guests, but right now Regi was more important than paying customers. Claudia snagged her coat and keys and headed out the door with Oscar close on her heels.

Grateful for the company and thinking she might very well need the dog to track her sister, Claudia put Oscar in the back seat of her Caddy. As she pulled out of the barn, the car's headlights found Wakanda standing in the middle of the pasture, her arms outstretched to the stars above.

Claudia slammed on the brakes. When they'd eaten supper, they hadn't been worried over Regi as yet. Wakanda had taken her slices of pizza and disappeared into the barn. That was hours ago. Maybe Regi had mentioned going somewhere other than Samuel's to her friend. Claudia jumped out of the car, climbed over the jack fence, and sprinted the distance to Wakanda. "Did Regi tell you where she was going?"

The woman turned her back to Claudia, keeping her gaze glued on the night sky. Dressed in ragged jeans, a sweatshirt, and what looked like a large, animal-skin coat draped over her shoulders, Wakanda paid Claudia no mind. "No paint in the sky. No help from the warriors."

Tired of being treated like a castoff and enraged that this person was talking jibberish in a time of crisis, Claudia whipped around in front of her again.

"The sky doesn't matter right now. Listen to me, you old, dried-up buffalo."

Wakanda let her arms down and stared at Claudia with surprise and then anger.

For a second, Claudia was a little scared, but desperate to find answers and help her sister, she said, "Yes, I dared call you a buffalo. Had to gain your attention some way. Remember the accident Regi was in last night? Well, she's not home. She may be out there somewhere and needs our help."

Wakanda gazed up at the sky. "Too many dark bundles. No good."

Dark bundles?

"Are you coming with me or not?" Claudia didn't know if she'd need the woman's help, but Wakanda cast a foreboding presence wherever she went. She could come in handy.

Wakanda finally nodded.

They made their way to the car and got in. Claudia glanced at her passenger then at the back seat where the Irish setter wagged his tail. The three of them made an odd rescue team.

Claudia started the car and pulled out onto the main highway. "We'll check the usual places first. I wish cell phones worked here."

She pressed the gas pedal to the floor. "Keep a lookout for that old beat up truck Regi's driving, just in case."

Wakanda nodded. And for the first time ever, Claudia was glad the woman was with her.

As they passed the parking lot at the Gas-N-Grub, she couldn't see Regi's truck, and the place looked closed, which was odd since it was only eight-thirty. Claudia glanced at the second floor where Jed, Ida, and Clifford lived. No lights. Ida's car was there, but Jed's truck was missing. "Great! I was going to stop and see if they'd seen her. Of course, they're always there when you don't need them, but tonight—" She didn't finish her sentence.

She drove on to Twiggs. As they cruised past, only Stew's car and some new fancy sports car was there. "Where in the world could Regi be?"

Wakanda merely stared out the window.

"We have to go to the sheriff. He might be home by now." Staying on the highway, Claudia headed for Thomas Morgan's.

"Black moon found the sheriff too," Wakanda said.

"What?" Claudia was always surprised when Wakanda spoke and frustrated that she spoke in circles.

"Same black moon." Wakanda sounded scared.

Claudia quickly glanced at her. "What are you talking about?"

"Death."

"Death?"

"Death follows the sheriff. Don't go there." The light from the dashboard reflected off the old woman's worried eyes and cast a bluish glow over the interior of the car.

Claudia had to be rational. "You know, when you say things like that, people think you're either drunk or crazy." She quickly checked the road then looked back at Wakanda. Her serious expression was unchanged.

"I know you're not drunk," Claudia said. "And you might be a little mixed up at times, but you're not crazy. So why would you say death follows the sheriff?"

"Whenever I hear his name or see him, darkness clouds my vision." Wakanda bit her lips together as though she'd just shared something very personal.

Claudia knew the woman had exposed a tender side of herself. "I don't know why you see darkness." Claudia sensed the old woman withdrawing. "Or . . . maybe the Lord has given you a special gift."

Wakanda's forehead smoothed, as though she were grateful. "The Great Spirit watches over us."

"We surely need Him. Okay, if we don't go to the sheriff's, where do we go to look for Regi?" Claudia saw the turnoff to Morgan's coming up. Did she go where she knew help waited, or did she wait for Wakanda to answer?

She glanced at the woman, who had not taken her eyes off Claudia. Oscar whined.

Claudia had to make the right choice; her sister's life could be hanging in the balance.

Samuel stood looking at Gypsy. The pinto munched on the oats in her trough. Poor horse probably wondered what in tarnation those silly humans were doing, lugging her all over the countryside from one stall to another and tussling with each other. The filly raised her head, gazing around. One ear turned as she listened intently.

"She left," Samuel told the horse because he knew the animal was looking for Regi. "I would have asked her to stay, but you know when that woman gets something stuck in her craw, nothing can budge it. Believe me, I've tried."

He thought about how angry he'd been at Regi for going to Morgan's and upsetting Hannah. He could still see Hannah tangled in the fence and disoriented. She was Morgan's world, and for him to watch that vibrant woman deteriorating mentally had to be hell. If she'd reached the river today, there was no telling what would have happened to her. As Samuel thought, he realized the anger he'd first directed toward Regi really had nothing to do with Hannah.

As he'd seen Regi standing in the stall with her horse, he was angry at himself for the wasted years of not being with the woman he loved. They'd been tangled in a type of mental fencing that had kept them apart. Standing there looking at the purple bruise on her forehead had made him realize how close he'd come to losing her. As he'd told Regi about Hannah, he'd seen how her face had changed and how concerned she was for her dear friend.

In that instant, remorse overtook him as he'd watched her eyes grow cloudy, and when a tear had escaped, he'd almost come undone. He blamed himself for not keeping Regi from her accident. He blamed himself for putting up the fence that had hurt Hannah. And he blamed himself for time lost.

Rufus stuck his head over the stall's gate. Samuel needed to pay attention to his spoiled gelding. He pulled a sugar cube from his pocket and gave it to the animal. While the roan chewed, Samuel rubbed the horse's cheek, then massaged its ear, but his mind automatically went back to Regi.

When she'd asked why Morgan had visited him last night, he should have told her the sheriff was going out of town to hand deliver the evidence and hopefully get some answers right away. But Morgan had not wanted Regi to know, afraid she'd read too much into it. Samuel could have lied, made up some story. But in the end, Regi would have found out.

Gypsy whinnied and tossed her head. Samuel went to the pinto and gave her the last sugar cube in his pocket. His thoughts returned to Regi. Could she be home yet? He hated leaving things the way they were between them. He wanted to call and explain. He didn't want to screw up the progress he'd made. Today she'd allowed him to kiss her, not once but twice. Odd how things happened—as if a higher power were throwing them together for strength during a difficult time.

This startling thought surprised Samuel. He almost wished he had Regi's faith in God. He shouldn't have become so upset when she'd mentioned prayer. If prayer helped Regi through the day, who was he to criticize? Samuel hoped Regi's God was watching over her tonight, wherever she was.

Rufus hoofed the ground. "All right. I'll get you one more sugar cube, but that's it." Samuel went in his tack room where he stored the treats on the work table against the wall. Taking one for Rufus and another for Gypsy, he turned to leave but stopped. If he remembered right, he sometimes kept his pocketknife in the table's drawer. Maybe he'd put it there and had forgotten. Hopeful, he pulled the drawer open. Clippers, hoof files, and various other supplies. No knife. It had been a long shot at best. If he'd only picked it up off the counter at Stew's café, this nightmare would not be happening.

Anyone who had been in the café on the night Romney had died was suspect. But who hated Romney enough to have killed him?

Samuel heard a vehicle drive into the barnyard. Maybe Regi'd returned. As he left the building, the sun was setting and the last fading rays hit the shiny chrome on Morgan's patrol car. Samuel was disappointed at first, but maybe Morgan had good news.

As the sun set, Regi turned off the main highway and followed the winding road for nearly a mile before she came upon Isaiah Tanner's lonely Victorian ranch house. The headlights of her truck shone on the white, two-story ghostly home resting on a small hill. The shutters hung askew, the dark windows looking like giant hollow eyes pleading for help.

As she pulled behind the house, her headlights illuminated dry, brittle thistles standing courageously tall against the threat of winter, with the light dusting of snow that had fallen on them. Old farm implements lay rusting on the ground: a tiller, a hay bailer, a broken shovel. All discarded relics of a once-working ranch.

Although Regi'd spent most of her life in Trailhead, she'd only come here once—on the morning she'd found out Samuel had left. What had gone on in that house? Isaiah's wife had died shortly after giving birth to Jed. Ida Peck, Isaiah's sister, had helped raise Jed and Samuel.

Regi thought about what Samuel had told her, how his father had quoted scriptures while beating him. He must have lived through misery with that man. When Regi was young, she'd never really thought about how tough Samuel's home life was. And after he'd left, she'd purposely tried not to think of him at all.

Shaking memories away, Regi turned off the vehicle. She slowly got out and walked up the small path to the back door. Turning the doorknob, she found it unlocked like Jed had said it would be. The foul, musty smell of dead mice pervaded the room. Flipping on the light switch, Regi was not surprised to find no electricity. With the sun down, the house was bear-cave dark.

Standing still for a moment, Regi waited for her eyes to adjust. Finally, shadowy silhouettes of kitchen chairs, a refrigerator, and a stove became visible. She felt her way to the cupboards and opened the drawers, searching for matches, or candles, or hopefully a flashlight.

Pulling out drawer after drawer, she finally found a half-used book of matches and a pack of cigarettes.

She quickly lit a match. Ants and small beetles skittered across the counter. She frantically searched the cupboards. No candles, no flashlights, nothing to help.

The flame burned down to her fingertips. She lit a new one and shook out the dying flame. Giving up on the kitchen, she made her way to the living room. Here, she was lucky. She found a few sticks of kindling and a log in the wood bin, plus old newspapers. Someone might see the smoke, but it was nighttime so it wouldn't be as visible as during the day. And she was cold, and as much as she hated to admit it, she was scared. A fire would give her comfort. She'd risk it to get warm and give her much-needed light. By the time Regi set up the paper and wood for the fire in the wrought-iron stove, she was down to only one match. Fortunately, that was all she needed. Once the fire took hold on the newspapers, Regi gazed around the room.

The carpet was threadbare. Wallpaper on the stained walls was torn in places. An old armchair with the form of a man's backside permanently pressed into the Naugahyde cushions sat in front of an empty television stand, both coated with dust. An ashtray rested on the arm of the chair, cold forgotten ashes still in it. A couch with faded images of sailboats seemed to lean against the wall.

She was surprised Samuel hadn't cleaned out the place, but maybe these walls held too many painful memories. It struck her as odd that Jed had told her to come here. The house belonged to Samuel, not Jed. However, he was right that this would be the last place Superintendent Elliott would look for her.

Regi thought about Claudia. Even though Jed had said he'd call, her sister would be worried. Regi hoped Jed would keep his word. She looked around. Photos thumbtacked to the wall by the armchair showed pictures of a pretty woman with Samuel's smiling eyes and Jed's prominent cheekbones. It tugged at Regi's heart that Isaiah Tanner had them on his wall. He must have loved her very much.

Regi glanced down the darkened hallway. Curious, she made her way to the first door. She couldn't see much, but the room appeared to be empty, stripped down to nothing. She continued her exploration to the next room. Shadows fell on an unmade bed. Clothes cluttered the floor. Dresser drawers gaped open, as well as the closet doors. The disarray seemed recent, but she couldn't tell for the lack of light.

Was someone living here?

Could it be a place Wakanda crashed every once in a while? Maybe this room was Isaiah's and his boys wanted nothing to do with his things and had never cleaned it up. She backed away.

She found two more doors at the end of the hall, but darkness squelched her desire to snoop. She made her way back to the living room and planted herself on the floor in front of the crackling fire.

She didn't have time to worry about Isaiah Tanner and his misguided life. *Her* life was in a big enough mess without poking around in someone else's problems. She needed to think about her situation and try to find an answer. Coming here probably wasn't the smartest thing she'd ever done, but where else could she have gone?

No answer came to mind. Didn't matter. She was here now. She might as well make the best of it and try to figure out what her next move should be. To do that, she needed to think about more possible suspects who wanted Romney dead.

Regi knew Curtis Romney was probably on the take, promising large parcels of the park's land to the highest bidder. Once again, she thought about the ranchers whose land had been confiscated by the park years ago. Why wasn't the park giving them first crack at it? Maybe that was the plan. But an auction wouldn't do that. Regi certainly didn't understand the workings of the federal government, and no amount of trying to figure them out would solve her immediate problem.

"Okay, what else?" She questioned aloud and felt foolish as her voice echoed through the empty house. So she reasoned in her mind, as she once again mulled over her most plausible conclusion. Morgan could have killed Romney, and Samuel was helping him cover it up. Good friends help each other, right? Making this theory plausible was Morgan's meeting with Samuel while Regi was in the den. And today Morgan had obviously gone out of town for some reason. Add that to his taking so long to show up when Regi had nearly been run off the road. Things weren't adding up when it came to Morgan. A new sinister thought crept alive: maybe he'd been delayed arriving because he had been the one trying to kill her and he didn't want to show up too soon.

Regi should have questioned Samuel about what he'd seen when he'd first found her. She thought of the murder weapon. Morgan had been at Twiggs on the night Romney was killed. Could he have picked it up? No. Anyone there could have picked it up, even Stew.

He'd acted mighty strange when she'd stopped at the café. And the other night when she'd left Twiggs and found his brother, Mark, sitting in a new car—what was the deal with that? She thought Stew was struggling financially; that's why she'd given him a hundred dollars, money she needed. What if Stew and his brother were blackmailing Romney because they'd learned that the creep was taking bribes for the land sale? Romney decided not to pay, and Stew ended up killing him. *And* maybe Mark had tried to run Regi off the road. He had been at the café last night. Regi had left before he did. No. Regi didn't want to think that a man dying of cancer would want to kill someone over a stupid car or money. Had to be someone else.

Superintendent Cameron Elliott. He very well could have been behind Romney's blackmailing Morris to pass the legislation. But if he weren't and Elliott found out Romney had taken such actions on his own, endangering everything Elliott had worked for, that might have been an interesting conversation. And if Elliott had found that his son-in-law was trying to make some extra cash by promising ranchers that he'd make certain they won the auction, would that be motivation for Elliott to kill Romney? But the auction couldn't be a sure thing. However, what if it were? Sprinkle in the fact that Elliott didn't like Romney, and that made this theory more interesting and worth pondering.

Again, her thoughts turned to Morgan. He, too, could very well have come upon Romney's scheme and blackmailed him. Morgan had been missing all day. Hannah's illness was worse. Their medical bills must be piling up, what with the prescriptions Hannah was taking and having to hire Effie full time. Morgan didn't make a lot of money. At some point, he was going to have to place Hannah in a home. That could possibly cost thirty or forty thousand a year. The man probably had some type of insurance, but still, the amount of money he'd need could be staggering.

Regi thought of her visit with Hannah earlier in the day. Beautiful Hannah with her long flowing hair. Regi wondered what she would do in Morgan's situation. Earl's illness had only lasted a matter of months, and then he was gone. What would Regi have done to prolong her husband's life? Anything and everything possible. She would have stolen, she would have cheated, and maybe, if pressed between Earl's living and someone else dying, she would have . . . No! She knew she could never take someone's life. But that didn't mean that Morgan wouldn't.

With striking clarity, she realized Morgan could have planted that knife in her Jeep. He was the one who had found it. A wave of gooseflesh sprinted up her spine.

What if he had?

What if he'd made himself scarce today because he knew the rangers were going to arrest her? And Hannah had said, "That ranger caused trouble." Regi wished she could talk with Claudia about some of these concerns.

She thought of the meeting Stew said Claudia had had with Romney. Her sister had also been in Twiggs that night, so she'd had access to the knife. Although, what if the knife used wasn't Samuel's? What if it were Earl's knife? Claudia had been awfully quick identifying the weapon in Regi's Jeep as his. Clearly, she was directing blame on Regi. Was her sister capable of such deviousness?

Regi drew in a deep breath, summoning reason. Claudia was not the type to allow her sister to take the rap for something she'd done. No, Claudia would step up and take the blame. Except, why hadn't she been truthful about meeting Romney? Why had she said she'd left before he'd gotten there?

A powerful fear grabbed ahold of Regi, leaving her feeling exposed and alone. Her throat was raw, and her muscles ached. Regi dug the decongestant pills out of her pocket and swallowed a couple. It would have been nice to have had a glass of water to wash them down, but she figured that if there wasn't electricity, there wouldn't be water, either, and she didn't feel like stumbling around in the dark to test the theory.

Sitting in front of the fire, she gathered her knees under her chin and wrapped her arms around her legs. Her mind went back to her sister. What if the one person who knew Regi better than anyone else . . . *what if Claudia was the killer?*

EIGHTEEN

HUNCHES

"Have you been home?" Samuel asked as he opened the passenger door of Morgan's patrol car.

"Briefly." His friend nodded, his tired eyes reflecting worry, concern, and gratitude all at the same time. "I was on my way to Regi's and thought I'd stop by and thank you for finding Hannah. I don't know what Effie would have done if you hadn't shown up when you did."

The sheriff swiped his hand over his bald head and gave a deep sigh. "What the blue blazes was Regi doing at my place, anyway? I told her to stay home."

"Regi was looking for you." Samuel stepped into the car.

Morgan cussed under his breath. "Doesn't listen, does she? You would think after her accident last night that she'd wise up and lay low."

"I know." Samuel stuck a wooden match in his mouth. "There's something else I have to tell you."

Morgan stared at him.

"I'm fairly certain the knife was mine. Can't find it here, and I can't remember picking it up when I left Twiggs."

The sheriff exhaled heavily. "And it gets better and better."

"Was the lab in Bounty Falls able to lift any prints?"

"Ended up having to drive to the Monticello lab. Luckily they were able to get some fingerprints. They were too large to be Regi's. So that's one thing in her favor. Something in your favor is that the prints didn't match yours, either. I thought as much, but the genius at the lab confirmed it. He's going to search their data banks, see if they can find a match. Takes the computer a while to run through them, and I was itching to get home, so I didn't wait. Once I knew my two friends were off the hook, I hauled on out of there."

Morgan leaned against his seat and looked straight at Samuel. "However, since I was in Monticello, I decided to check on a hunch. I stopped at Willard Goodard's office."

"The fill-in congressman? What for?"

"When I was at Superintendent Elliott's, I heard something about a new land bill that's coming up for a vote in Congress."

"What does that have to do with Romney's murder?" Samuel couldn't connect the dots.

"Not sure it does, but I've learned over the years to follow my hunches. If Elliott's pushing this bill, you can be darned sure Romney knew about it. I was curious whether one of them had visited Osborne before the congressman died last spring. Unfortunately, his replacement was clueless, and the regular receptionist wasn't in."

"Don't congressmen hire new help when they take charge?" Samuel thought that was standard procedure.

"Usually, but since Osborne died before his term was up, this new guy, Goodard, kept the receptionist. He didn't know much about the bill, only that Osborne was trying to block it."

"So you found nothing there?"

"I didn't say that. Seems Claudia stopped by earlier, which I find more than a little curious. Goodard said she wanted to know how things were going with his campaign."

"Maybe she did."

"Why would she drive all that way to find out how Goodard's election bid was coming along when her sister might be facing murder charges?" Morgan's fingers drilled on the steering wheel. "And I learned from Cameron Elliott only moments ago that she'd been to his place too. Seems Claudia called Karen Wilson because Melissa was having troubles."

Samuel didn't like where this was going. "Something's wrong."

"Yep. Want to come with me to the Raindancer? Think I'd better have a talk with Regi and Claudia. Trying to take care of those two is like herding squirrels."

"Sure." Samuel didn't know where this investigation was heading, but he wanted to be there in case Regi needed him.

The sheriff started the car. "On the way, I want to stop and talk with Jed. Elliott also said that your brother had called him to see if the superintendent was going to stand by the deal Romney had made."

"What deal?"

"That's what I want to know." Morgan pressed his foot down on the gas, and they peeled out.

Regi woke up with a jolt. The decongestant must have made her drowsy. She'd fallen asleep with her knees under her chin and her arms locked around her legs. Her hands tingled, fighting numbness. The fire had dwindled. She needed to find more wood.

Stumbling out the back door where she expected to see the woodpile, she found it wasn't there. The barn was her next guess. Logically that would give good shelter to keep the wood dry. The moon was exceptionally bright tonight and lit her path. A silvery sheen shone over the dust of snow on the ground. Crisp air made her hug her sheepskin jacket to her body.

Reaching the barn, Regi found it an object of wonder that the building still stood. The roof was swaybacked, with much of the wall structure missing.

Regi pushed the door. Groaning hinges gave way and allowed her entrance. A cat burst out in front of her, scaring Regi so that she jumped against the door. Her heart thrummed hard against her rib cage. She stole several deep breaths, trying to stay her panic.

Once she settled down, Regi focused on what was inside the old barn's ruins.

In the shadows, she made out warped stalls and a few scattered bales of hay by the door. Next to them was a jumbled pile of firewood. Grateful for this good fortune, Regi bundled the logs into her arms. Her load quickly became heavy, and deciding she had enough to last the night, she turned to leave.

Something fluttered in the wind near the end of the stacked firewood, bringing her to a halt. A paper of some kind. She stepped around the chopping block and drew closer.

A grocery sack. Didn't appear old and weatherbeaten. Looked fairly new.

Regi set her load on the ground. Feeling like a snoop, she looked around and realized how silly her actions were. She was the only one here. She grabbed the bag and stepped out into the moonlight to have a better view. Inside were clothes. She pulled them out. A man's shirt and jeans. They were big in the shoulders and long in the legs. As Regi turned them over, she saw that they were covered with stains.

At first she couldn't tell what kind of stains they were, but her nerves became jittery as realization kicked in.

Blood!

Trying to remain calm, she rationalized that in the country there were many valid reasons for clothes to have blood on them: injuries sustained while working or taking care of animals. But no rancher would stash bloody clothes in the barn. They'd either wash them or burn them. They wouldn't try to hide them in the firewood at an old abandoned ranch house.

These clothes were the murderer's.

But why leave them stashed here? She supposed the person could have been afraid, stored them here until he could come back and safely dispose of them. Regi stared at the shirt and pants.

Men's clothes.

Could be Samuel's? This was his father's place.

Or Morgan's?

Jed's? But Jed was the one who had sent her here to hide. He wouldn't send her here knowing he'd stashed evidence in the firewood, unless . . . he was trying to frame his brother. After all, Samuel owned the place.

On the night she'd burned his dinner, Samuel had said he was returning from his father's. He'd been here recently. Again, she thought of the note she'd found on Samuel's desk and the knife.

A bitter chill streaked down her back. Her head throbbed. She needed to go inside and think. With trembling hands, she quickly returned the clothes to the bag and put them back where she had found them. She gathered up the wood and dashed to the house.

Carefully making her way through the kitchen to the living room, she laid the supply of wood on the hearth. She thought about how Jed had told her Elliott had a warrant for her arrest. Was Elliott really at the Gas-N-Grub? She hadn't seen him. What if Jed had sent her out here to get her alone? He knew an awful lot about things: the history between Regi and Samuel, the sale of park land—plus he'd been quick to blame his brother.

With striking clarity, she knew she had to get out of there and find Samuel. His ranch was next to his father's, though her sense of direction was turned around since she'd only been here once many years ago. She tried to think which way to go. Time was critical.

Regi started running back through the kitchen while pulling her keys from her pants pocket.

Headlights flashed in the kitchen window.

She automatically ducked. Slowly, standing to peek out, she froze as she saw Jed's pickup. Her heart kicked to her throat as she watched Jed, Clifford, and Ida climb out.

Ida? Good. She could help get to the bottom of all of this.

Then Regi noticed Jed held something in his hands.

A shotgun!

They walked with purpose in their steps and were headed for the house.

Leave! Leave now!

Terror blanketed Regi. Frantic, she retraced her steps out of the kitchen and raced through the living room. She was so rattled that she bumped into Isaiah's easy chair, ramming her shin into the television stand. Pain needled her leg. Ignoring the hurt, she hobbled to the front entrance. Undoing the locks, she yanked the door back. The threshold was draped with cobwebs.

She heard a noise from the kitchen.

They were in.

Without further delay, Regi plunged into the cold, dark night.

NINETEEN

PERFECT PATSY

CLAUDIA TOOK THE TURNOFF TO the sheriff's but only to see if Regi's truck was parked there. As the headlights of Claudia's Caddy panned the parking area, she couldn't see any cars in front of the house, not Regi's truck, not Thomas's patrol car. He should be home at this time of night.

"Not here," Wakanda stated the obvious.

"Nope." Claudia swung the car around, heading back to the main highway. "Where could she be?"

Oscar whined from the backseat.

"Listening to whispers." Wakanda stared ahead.

"Again, you're not making sense." Claudia pulled off to the side of the road, where she put on the brake. "We need a plan."

Wakanda stared directly at Claudia. "The river whispers to her. She is there."

"No. She wouldn't go this time of night." Claudia knew Regi went to the river to gain strength, but that was during the day. But if Regi felt trapped, if she were in trouble . . . "You're right." Claudia moved the gear stick to "drive" and sped down the road. "Do you know where the turnoff is?" Claudia had only gone to the river once, and she hadn't paid much attention. All she remembered was a graveled road.

"There," Wakanda yelled as they passed a turn.

Claudia stomped the brakes. Tires squealed. Oscar flew against the back of the front seats. "Hang on, old dog," Claudia called to him as she flipped a U-turn and followed Wakanda's directions.

The Cadillac shimmied and shuddered, but Claudia kept her foot on the gas. The large car felt like a boat in water as it struggled over the washboard road. As Claudia cornered curves and switchbacks, the trees lining the way stood as formidable as concrete walls. Ruts and holes the size of boulders jerked and rocked the car. Claudia had never driven so recklessly in her life, but she knew this time she had to.

Without warning, the road sharply dipped, and the car slammed to a halt. Immediately air bags burst open. The abrasive material swallowed Claudia's face. For an instant, she couldn't breathe. Pain jackknifed her neck. And then the world around her fell silent.

Samuel and the sheriff stopped at the Gas-N-Grub, which was closed. Jed never closed this early. To make matters worse, Jed, Ida, and Clifford weren't home.

Morgan shrugged it off, saying their main interest was Claudia and Regi anyway. As Morgan drove to the Raindancer, he passed Samuel's father's old place. Out of habit, Samuel looked in the direction of his childhood home. The house was set off from the road about a mile. Samuel thought he saw headlights in the barnyard, but they blinked out. No one would be there. His eyes were playing tricks on him. In fact, in the next few days he was going to gut the place so he could bulldoze it.

When they arrived at the Raindancer, they found the guests had been on their own much of the night. Samuel's concern heightened. No Regi, no Claudia, no Wakanda, and no Oscar. Where was everybody?

As they climbed back into the patrol car, Morgan looked worried. "Something is very wrong. Regi might leave guests on their own but not Claudia. I know her. Where do you suppose they went?"

"If Regi's driving, it could be anywhere." Samuel tried to think where they could have possibly gone. They weren't at Twiggs or the Gas-N-Grub. He remembered the flash of light he thought he had seen at his father's, but they had no reason to go there. No reason at all, yet the notion tugged at him, demanding attention. "Let's drive out to my dad's."

"Claudia would never go there."

"I know, it doesn't make sense, but I think I'm having one of those hunches you talk about."

Morgan didn't question further, only started the car.

Samuel's gut churned. His father's home was haunted with abuse and heartache. Years ago he'd run away, hoping to keep Regi away from the place and safe from his father. The thought of harm befalling Regi or her sister was unthinkable, but he somehow knew he'd find them at that place he had tried so hard to protect them from or at least close by.

Bolting across the open pasture toward the seclusion of the trees, Regi fought the frigid night as icy air stung her face and lungs. Pain knifed her sides. But she pressed on, hurdling fences and racing over rough ground.

Once she reached the stand of trees, she stopped and gazed around. Giant lodgepole pines and alder trees loomed overhead like swaying watchtowers. The wind blew hard, throwing branches and dead leaves over the snow-licked ground. Maybe it was the cold wind and her freezing hands and feet, but all at once she thought how crazy it was that she ran away from Jed. It only made sense that he'd come out to his father's ranch to check on her.

But he had that gun, and the way he and Ida and Clifford had walked toward the house . . . she knew something wasn't right. A fear had washed over Regi like a tsunami, and she had known she had to run.

But could Jed really be the killer? And if he were, why were Ida and Clifford with him? Were they in on it? Nothing made sense. Yet, she had this foreboding feeling that she had to get away from them.

Jed had to be on her trail by now. Once he'd found the fire burning in the fireplace, he'd have known she'd left recently. Her tracks in the snow would lead him right to her. At least the darkness of night would give her cover.

Remembering Samuel had walked from his father's, she knew his place couldn't be far. She had to make her way to him. But she had no idea how. Then she realized the river would guide her because it ran toward Samuel's home.

Straining to see some recognizable landmarks, she decided to head south, reasoning that water ran downhill. As she sprinted over the ground, she tugged the sleeves of her sheepskin jacket over her bare hands. Regi only had herself to blame for the sorry fix she was in. She had trusted Jed—he'd always been so thoughtful of her. Or was it that he just *seemed* thoughtful of her?

Just this morning he'd stopped by with soup and cold medication that Ida'd had him deliver. Then Regi remembered how Jed and Samuel had argued. Jed thought Romney had given Samuel information about a sale, and then Jed brought up that Samuel was the last one with Romney on the night he was killed. Brothers may fight with one another, but to try to deliberately blame your brother of murder was something else. No one would do that unless they were trying to cover up something, unless they were trying to deflect suspicion from themselves. Realization pulsed through Regi. Jed wanted her to believe Samuel had killed Romney. He, better than anyone, knew how Samuel had hurt her. He, better than anyone, knew that Regi would believe the worst of his brother. But there was one thing Jed didn't realize: Regi loved Samuel. For a moment, she was surprised by the thought. After years of contention and hurt, the truth had surfaced as if it had always been there. Yes, she loved him, always had and always would. She trusted Samuel, and now she had to go to him.

Once Regi reached Samuel's, she'd call Morgan and tell him everything that had happened. She knew that the story Claudia wanted to keep a secret would surely come out, and Regi would try her best to steer the investigation away from Morris Osborne, but it wasn't going to be easy.

How could she have thought her sister would have been the murderer? Stew must have been confused about her meeting Romney. Needless torment would not help Regi now. She had to get to the river and then to Samuel's.

The night was suddenly rent with the heart-stopping sound of gunshot. Regi dropped to the ground, hugging the cold, wet earth. Snow froze her cheek. Her breath came in cold puffs. The echo of the shot made it impossible to tell where it had come from. But she knew Jed was shooting at her. This proved that her gut reaction at the ranch house to run was right. Jed had to be the one who had killed Romney, and now he had to get rid of her. She could hardly fathom that Jed was the murderer, but that shot was real. And it was meant for her. And there wasn't anyone else out here with a gun.

Feeling defenseless, she wished she had looked for a weapon while in the ranch house. If only she'd kept her gun with her instead of locking it in the safe at home. Thinking of things she should have done would not save her now. Jed was bent on killing her. Like it or not, she couldn't lie here. She had to keep running to stay alive.

Making up her mind, Regi jumped to her feet. Running as fast as she could, she dodged tree branches that hung low and scraped her. She stumbled over ruts that seemed determined to trip her. Breathing like a winded horse, she stopped a second to listen. Rushing water?

The river.

Forging on, Regi came to Samuel's barbed-wire fence. Recognizing the slope of the hill that led to the river, she knew she must be near the place where she'd found Romney dead. She didn't know how she'd wound up here, but to get out of this nightmare, she needed to cross the river to reach Samuel's.

Stepping on the bottom wire, she tried to slip through, but her jacket caught on a barb, ripping a good sized hole in the material.

For a second, Regi thought of Hannah caught in this fence earlier today. Probably not in the same place but near. Poor Hannah had come this far on foot. Regi hated that she'd upset her friend so. Thankfully, Samuel had saved Hannah. Regi prayed he would rescue her as well. She had to go to him.

Sliding down the riverbank to the water's edge, she realized she couldn't cross in this spot. As she raced through tall river grasses and cattails, her boot slipped into the water every few steps. Finally, she came upon her favorite fishing hole.

Earl's fishing hole.

The night became eerily still, with only the sound of the river echoing up to the silent sky. Regi listened for the river voices Earl had told her about, hoping that in this frenzied moment they would guide her. She barely dared to breathe, she wanted to hear them so badly, but the only sound was rushing water.

Regi had to press on.

Footfalls behind drew her attention. Someone was coming. Suddenly, a light burst through the rushes, and Clifford sprang out as big as a burly bear.

They'd caught her.

Panicked, she leaped into the bone-chilling river. The frigid water quickly filled her boots and swallowed her pant legs. The river beat against her body, threatening to sweep her downstream to the deadly main current. Still, she forged on. She had to get to the other side. Had to get to Samuel. But her feet slipped and slid over moss-coated rocks.

A loud splash came from behind. Large masculine hands grabbed ahold of Regi's arm, wrenching her backward. Clifford had followed her in. He held her tight against him. Icy water coursed around legs that were as sturdy as a grizzly's. She tried to fight him, but her efforts were useless against his iron muscles. He trudged through the current, up the riverbank in the exact spot where only days ago Regi had found Curtis Romney dead.

Death haunted the ground. Frantic, Regi kicked and clawed at Clifford. His grip loosened. Regi bolted from him.

Running out of the willows, she started up the hill. Water sloughed off her from the waist down. Her legs were jittery, spongy, and numb. But she forced them to work. She glanced behind in time to see Clifford leap, tackling her. She landed on the ground with an abrupt thud.

Digging her hands in the earth, she threw snow and mud at him. He raised up and in that second, she scrambled to her feet. A light flashed in her face, nearly blinding her.

Shielding her eyes, she saw Ida on top of the rise, holding a gun and shining a flashlight down on them. "There's been an accident. We need your help, Regi. I sent Cliffy after you."

What the . . .

Bewildered, Regi gazed up at the woman. Clifford raced past Regi to his waiting aunt. What was going on? Were they just setting her up? What kind of accident? Did Ida really need help? With Clifford's mental inabilities, maybe he might not have known how to ask Regi for help, and instead of explaining, he'd just grabbed her.

When they'd arrived at the ranch, Regi had just found the bloody clothes. Her hyperimagination could have deluded her into thinking Jed and Ida meant her harm. *And that gunshot?* It was all so confusing. But since Clifford had left her as soon as he had seen his aunt, it was plain that he had been following orders.

With great trepidation, she climbed the hill. Drawing nearer to Ida, she saw Jed lying face down. Clifford had already dropped to his knees beside his father. The flashlight in Ida's hand glanced over the man's back. There was a spray of bullet holes from a shotgun between Jed's shoulder blades. It was amazing that a single shot could cause such damage. Regi had always heard how deadly shotguns were, and now she could see it with her own eyes.

Shot in the back? Who did it?

Clifford turned his father over. Light illuminated Jed's face. His eyes were open, glassy. No life. The front of his jacket was soaked with blood, the body limp with dead weight.

Clifford tenderly cupped his father's face in his hands. "Pa?" He patted his cheek. No reaction. Clifford hugged his father.

The old woman set the flashlight down and stroked the top of Clifford's head. "Child, let him rest. Isaiah and I can finish this." Clifford's bear-sized arms scooped his father to his chest. Holding Jed, he rocked back and forth, humming.

Isaiah? He had died long ago. Still, Regi glanced around. No one else was with them. The flashlight Ida had set on the ground caught the double barrel of the shotgun as she reloaded.

Why was she talking about her brother—Jed and Samuel's father—as though he were alive, and why was she putting more ammunition in the gun? Had she shot Jed? The sure and steady way she handled the weapon showed that the woman knew how to use it. But why shoot her nephew?

Desperately needing answers, Regi ignored the shivers racking her body and asked, "Ida, what happened?"

The old woman snapped the gun shut and slung it in the cradle of her arm, like an experienced hunter. "Isaiah told me to do it. Jed was damaged."

"What?" It was obvious now that Ida suffered from a psychotic disorder. Regi had read about this shortly after losing Earl because there were times when she could swear she saw her late husband. She'd learned that brief psychotic breaks happened during intense stress.

Ida glared at Regi as though she were an irritating child. Then she turned a little, as though listening to someone speak. Regi peered through the darkness but could see no one. She remembered on the morning she had found Romney dead in the willows that she had seen Ida do this while standing at the till of the Gas-N-Grub. When had Ida's break occurred?

Ida nodded her head, as though agreeing with the imaginary Isaiah, then turned her full attention to Regi while speaking over her shoulder. "I'll kill her, don't worry."

Kill? Regi was the only "her" here besides Ida. Panic jerked Regi backward, ready to run.

"No sense running." Ida aimed the gun at her. "Isaiah's a good shot, but so am I."

Regi stopped. Terror tore at her heart. Why hadn't she done what Morgan had asked her and let him solve this case? Why did she think she had to get involved? She didn't want to know that people she'd loved and cared for all her life were behind it. But she was part of it—right in the middle of it—and her only option to survive it now was to keep Ida talking. That might give her enough time to think of a way out of this nightmare that grew more surreal by the minute.

Ida relaxed a little, though she kept the gun on Regi. "You look like a scared little girl, just like me."

"You're right, I'm just like you, Ida." Regi didn't know what she was saying. She frantically glanced behind the woman, hopeful to see something that might help. Only darkness and land.

Land!

"The government stole your father's land, didn't they? Were you afraid of the government?" Maybe Ida had killed Romney over that old squabble.

"I used to walk amongst those trees." She pointed to the pines and aspens that were now part of Trailhead Park and bordered Samuel's property. "They

were my friends. Never really had friends. You think I have a lot 'cause I talk
to everyone. But I don't."

"I'm your friend, Ida." Regi tried to calm her. She needed to somehow
ease the gun away. She stepped a little closer.

"You're no friend of mine. Tried to give you a fair chance. Just like
I tried to be fair with Jed. I heard him planning to meet Romney down
here. When he took Clifford with him, I knew he was up to no good. Jed
always had Cliffy do his dirty work. Sweeping the floors and cleaning up.
Just like my daddy did with me."

Ida walked over to Clifford. He leaned his head against his aunt's leg,
still cradling his dead father to his chest.

"What happened to Romney?" Regi asked.

Ida stopped as though listening again. Then she shouted, "I'll do it,
Isaiah. Said I would."

The urge to run nearly made Regi scream, but she held her tongue, waiting.

The elderly woman raised the gun.

"Ida, did you kill Romney?" If Regi was going to die, she wanted to
know the truth first.

Ida lowered the weapon. "No. What made you come up with that fool
notion?"

Regi grasped for something to say. "Did Isaiah?"

"You really don't have the brain of a chicken, do you?" Ida pointed the
gun at Jed. "He did it. Left Cliffy and me in the car—told us to stay—but
I followed and saw Jed stick that knife in the ranger's neck. That's when
Isaiah came to help us."

Ida's psychotic break must have happened when she'd witnessed the
horrific act.

"Just like he's here now to help me clean up this mess. Took care of
Jed when he gave me the gun to hold for him. Now it's your turn." Again
she raised the weapon.

"But why did Jed kill Romney?" Regi had to keep her talking.

"Dumb as a sack of hammers, aren't you? Both you and that sister of
yours."

Regi wanted to defend Claudia but didn't want to press the issue since
Ida held a gun on her with her finger on the trigger. "Ida, you're one of the
smartest women I know. Explain it to me."

"Romney said his father-in-law suspected he was accepting money
under the table to force the auction for the land Jed's way, so the deal he'd

made with Jed was off. If the ranger would have stopped there, things would have been all right. But Romney—that weasel—got greedy and turned the tables, just like the government did on my father and like Samuel did on Jed. Romney said that unless Jed paid him ten thousand dollars, he'd tell Superintendent Elliott that Jed had tried to bribe him. His word against Jed's. Jed had a knife. One thing led to another, and he stabbed Romney good."

Regi glanced at Jed in Clifford's arms. The boy seemed oblivious to their conversation as he rocked his father. "Ida, you should have gone to Morgan with all this. He would have helped you."

"Isaiah told me how to clean up Jed's mess right after you showed up at the Gas-N-Grub wet as a beaver. He knew you'd found the body. He set my mind straight and explained the whole thing."

The poor woman was dealing with what had happened the best she could by hallucinating her brother as her guide through it all.

Ida continued to talk. "And if Jed had done what his father had wanted him to do, it still would have worked out. The day you found the body, you were leading the sheriff right where Isaiah said you would, but Jed . . . isn't very smart. He panicked, disguised his voice, and called Thelma with that cock-n-bull story about that friend of yours walking down Highway 89 naked and shooting a gun. While the sheriff was investigating that, Jed and Clifford went and got the body."

Ida chuckled a little. "Funny thing was, when Jed stopped at our place to talk to me about what to do next, Cliffy took Romney to Karen Wilson's, hoping she could fix him."

"How did the knife end up in my Jeep?" Regi couldn't help but ask.

"Fell out of the corpse in Jed's truck. When he found it, he put it in your Jeep. See, Regi, you became the perfect patsy and a way for Jed to even the score with his brother. Oh, he was tickled pink to see Samuel out at your place the other morning."

"How could framing me for the murder get even with Samuel?" Regi was fighting to understand.

"Samuel loves you. Always has. Jed knew hurting you would hurt his brother."

Maybe it was the slight lift of Ida's voice or the way the night wind started blowing again, but another chill rippled over Regi's already cold skin. Ida was obviously temporarily insane, but Jed had had all his faculties. He'd deliberately killed Romney and framed his brother and Regi. What had happened to the man? He'd been so kind and thoughtful when they were young. How could he have changed so much? Gazing at his body in Clifford's arms, then looking at Ida and realizing she'd shot her own nephew in the back, Regi felt panic nearly buckle her knees. But she hung on. She didn't know why Ida was offering so much information, but as long as she was willing, Regi was going to get everything she could out of her. She knew Ida was probably telling her everything because she was going to kill her, but in a way, Regi felt better knowing she could solve the mystery and ease her mind about what had happened, even in all this madness. A new realization hit Regi. "You were the one who tried to run me off the road, weren't you?"

Ida chuckled. "Me and Isaiah. We'd been at your place. You know your sister has a lot to learn about being a gracious host. When I got to the car and told Isaiah how she treated me, well, he was as upset as I was. So when we saw your Jeep pulling out of Twiggs, I told Isaiah if you were dead, we could blame you for Romney's death; plus, it would serve your snotty sister right. We could force you over Neekumba Ridge, and everyone would think you committed suicide because of your guilt over murdering the ranger. Samuel would be heartbroken. And Jed, Clifford, and I would live happily ever after. Didn't expect for you to swerve like that."

Regi gulped.

"Tonight when you stopped by for gas, Isaiah knew we needed to act and told me what to do. Superintendent Elliott wasn't even there. You lapped up everything Jed said, falling right into our trap. We could have had this all over with by now, except for those lollygagging customers at the store. Then things got all messed up when Jed sent Clifford after you."

Regi had a feeling the end of this bizarre story was coming, and when Ida finished, the chances of Regi surviving were very slim. She started inching away. If she could get down to the river willows, she might survive.

Ida inched with her, intent now on telling her everything. "Jed planned to have Clifford kill you. Said his moron son was good for something. That didn't set well with Isaiah nor me. Having Cliffy kill would have turned him over to Satan, so Isaiah took over and shot Jed."

This woman's brain was fracturing.

Stepping toward Ida, Regi tried again. "You were completely justified. I'll go with you to the authorities, and we'll get this mess straightened out."

Ida raised the double-barreled shotgun eye level. "I don't mind you dying. I just didn't want Cliffy to do it. See, we can still blame you for Romney *and* Jed's deaths, but only if you're dead as well."

An electric frisson flashed over Regi's skin. She slowly backed away. She figured if she ran, she'd get shot, but she'd take her chances. Turning to flee, Regi stumbled on a rut and fell hard to her knees.

"Regi, honey, don't be difficult."

"You really don't want to do this!" Regi said. Somewhere inside the insane woman, Regi knew the little grandmotherly lady who minded the till at the Gas-N-Grub was still there. Regi got to her feet. She brushed the dirt off her hands. "Ida, your brother Isaiah is dead."

Ida didn't move, but she was listening.

"I'm sorry. You've been through a lot the last few days. That can cause a person to have a breakdown and see and hear things that aren't there. I know about this. I read how the mind can play tricks on you when you're in high-stress situations, and, Ida, you've had your fair share the last while." Regi prayed for a miracle.

Ida cocked her head for a moment, as though she were processing Regi's words. Then with the determination of an attacking pariah, Ida rammed the gun barrel against Regi's breastbone. "I don't want to, but Isaiah says it has to be done. You have to die."

TWENTY
DIVE

CLAUDIA FELT SOMETHING WET ON her cheek. Opening her eyes, she found Oscar standing over her as she lay on the ground. How did she get here, and where was Wakanda?

Pushing Oscar away and raising up, she found the old woman kneeling by her side. "You're okay?" Claudia asked.

Wakanda nodded.

Relieved, Claudia swiped a hand over her face and found blood. Her cheeks and forehead had scrapes from the airbag. Her head throbbed. Glancing around, she saw her car—her Caddy. She'd hit a boulder about the size of Oscar. The right front bumper was shoved against the wheel. They weren't going anywhere.

Just then a gunshot echoed through the night, causing them all to jump. Claudia's heart pounded against her ribs. Had someone fired at them? "Was that a gun?" Claudia stared at Wakanda, hoping she'd say no.

Wakanda nodded.

The terrifying sound had come from the south. Dark foreboding curled its fingers around Claudia.

"Your sister needs us." Wakanda stood and reached down to help Claudia up.

Grabbing ahold, Claudia rose. Panic pulsed within her. They had to get to Regi, but how? Where was she? For that matter, where were *they*?

Straining to see the terrain in the dark, Claudia made out thick trees all around them. She stared at Wakanda. She was the wannabe Indian; maybe she could guide them out of here. But she seemed as bewildered as Claudia. They stood in silence. Oscar brushed past her. Claudia grabbed the dog's collar and, with her other hand, took hold of Wakanda's arm. "We'd better follow him."

As they left the cluster of trees, Oscar led them north. Did the dog really know where they were going? After all, he was only a dog. But a dog that had gone to the river with Regi many times in his life before his leg had become a burden and before cataracts had blurred his long-range vision. The canine was their best hope.

The wind picked up as the moon peeked from behind a cloud, giving them light to see where they were going. Grateful she'd worn her parka, Claudia pulled the hood over her head and wondered if Wakanda was cold under her animal-skin coat. As they neared the crest of a small hill, Claudia and Wakanda crouched down on hands and knees and slowly peered over the top into a small valley where the river ran through.

Across the river, Claudia could make out several silhouettes. Someone large sat on the ground holding something—or someone. A short figure appeared to be talking to a taller one. They stood there for the longest time. The short person seemed to be doing all the talking. Claudia was too far away to tell who they were. But deep in her soul, she knew one of them was Regi. Oscar stood beside Claudia, giving her comfort. She was grateful for his company and keen memory, though she was glad the old dog had cataracts and couldn't see very far. From this distance, he couldn't pick up Regi's scent, either. If the dog knew his master was over there, he would bark up a storm.

Claudia had to get closer. To do that, she would have to slide down the hill and crawl through the barbed-wire fence without being seen.

Not saying a word, Wakanda took off, doing exactly what Claudia had thought. Breathless and terrified, she followed, keeping her hand on Oscar's collar, grateful the dog was with them. Keeping low, she pushed back branches and tore through brambles as she struggled to stay on her feet and remain inconspicuous. Afraid to pause and see if they'd been spotted, she forced her aching body to keep going. Her chest tightened. Her hands shook. But Claudia willed her feet to follow Wakanda.

Coming up to the fence, the woman slipped through then paused a moment to help Claudia. Oscar was right beside them. Wakanda peered across the river. Following her gaze, Claudia could tell no one had seen them.

"That one is Regi." Wakanda pointed. "The other is gossip woman."

Claudia strained to see now that they were a little closer. Her heart stopped as she realized Ida held a gun on Regi. The old woman rammed the barrel into Regi's chest, forcing her to step back.

"That witch is going to kill her." Claudia grabbed Wakanda's arm.

"Not yet." Wakanda grabbed Claudia's hand and pulled her down. "The river has the answer." She motioned Claudia to follow.

Desperate for her sister and yet not knowing what to do, Claudia trailed behind, keeping Oscar close. As they neared the rushing water, a flash of the day when Regi had saved her from drowning in the ditch came to mind. Well, it was big sister's turn to do the saving.

Checking to see what was happening, Claudia found that Regi and Ida had moved. Ida was forcing Regi, at gunpoint, to the river. Wakanda and Claudia ducked and ran down the riverbank behind some willows. Oscar escaped from Claudia's grasp, running up the hill away from them. Dang. If Ida saw him, there was no telling what she'd do.

At any moment, Ida's rifle could go off.

At any moment, Regi could die.

Upon arriving at his father's and finding not only Regi's truck but also Jed's, Samuel knew something bad was going on. No one was in the house. He and Morgan started following the tracks leading from the front door when a heart-stopping gunshot rang out. Anger and fear pumped through Samuel—anger because he hadn't found Regi and fear because something unthinkable may have happened.

Soon the tracks they were following split up. One set went north, three started south, but then one of the three headed north after the first one. "We'd stand a better chance of catching them if you follow that set of tracks—" Morgan pointed north. "And I'll follow these. Looks like they're stalking her and driving her to the river." He unsnapped his gun from its holster.

Samuel held a flashlight. He should have grabbed a weapon, though he didn't know if he could actually use it against his family. However, he knew he would if they threatened to kill Regi. He nodded to the sheriff.

Morgan took off, gun in one hand, flashlight in the other.

Samuel sprang into a run, his feet pounding the ground.

Terror seeped through him, pulsed in his veins, breathed in his lungs as he raced to follow the tracks.

He stopped for a moment, trying to gain a fix on his position. If they continued on this course, it would lead them to where Romney was killed. He sucked in long drags of cold air and thought of Regi.

His Regi.

Why was this happening? Jed, his own brother. Somehow he'd been involved with Romney and was now after Regi. Would Jed kill her just to steal happiness from Samuel?

Taking off again, Samuel saw a reel of images flicker through his mind. Regi, covering her ears as the fire alarm went off in his kitchen; Regi, fear on her face after throwing the pie at him; Regi, in his arms as he carried her from the wrecked Jeep to his truck; and Regi, whose lips he had kissed for the first time in years just hours before. She had to be all right. Just this afternoon she'd come to him for answers, and the only answer he could give her was claiming his own innocence. And then he'd argued with her over praying. She believed in a higher power and that God would help those who asked.

Out of his mind with worry and desperately needing divine intervention to save the woman he loved, he wondered if a prayer from him would help. He'd quit believing in such things long ago, never thinking he would ever find himself in a dire situation so completely out of his control that he would need help from above.

Whatever was happening to Regi at this very moment was beyond Samuel's grasp . . . and Morgan's. Only the God Regi believed in could save her. Samuel knew she was praying. If he added his prayers to hers, would God listen?

As he sprinted through the trees, he prayed with all his might and soul that God would forgive him his trespasses and intervene. Regi needed His help.

So did Samuel.

His fingers were frozen to the flashlight. He could no longer feel his cheeks. With every thud of his footsteps, a prayer traveled on Samuel's lips.

The moon lit the sky and cast purple shadows on the forest, making the trees look like ghouls. They were laughing at him, making fun of his attempt to pray. Still, he continued trying to believe in his heart that God would help him find Regi and keep her safe.

Out of the darkness, an animal came at him. He shone the light on red fur and knew it was Regi's dog, Oscar. The setter jumped up on Samuel then took off as if to say, *follow me*. The setter led him to a barbed-wire fence. Oscar slipped through. Samuel hopped over. That's when he saw light across the river. There were people over there. Until he knew who it was, he flipped off his flashlight, hoping he hadn't been spotted. He heard movement in the willows down the slope near the river. Peering in the direction of the sound, he saw two silhouettes. Then he made out a pink parka.

Claudia. And Wakanda beside her.

He crept to them, with Oscar leading the way. The dog nudged Wakanda's hand as he neared. She looked up and saw Samuel. She grabbed Claudia's arm, alerting her to his presence.

Claudia clamped hard onto him as if holding on for dear life. She leaned close, trembling. "They're going to kill her." She pointed across the river.

Ida was forcing Regi into the water. Samuel had to get over there and fast. But he couldn't with these two tailing him. Plus, they might get themselves killed. "The sheriff is coming from the other side. Sneak up stream 'bout a quarter mile. The river is shallow there. Cross and meet up with Morgan."

"But—" Claudia started to argue then stopped. "You love her, don't you?"

"Always have."

"Keep her safe." Claudia hugged him.

Wakanda tugged on Claudia's arm and nodded to Samuel. The old woman knew what he was doing and saw the wisdom. Claudia grabbed Oscar's collar, and the odd threesome disappeared into the willows.

Samuel stepped into the icy water separating him from the woman he loved and stopped. Horrified, he watched his aunt ram the barrel into Regi's chest, tripping her toward the river.

His breath caught. He couldn't reach Regi in time. Ready to yell and draw his aunt's attention, he suddenly stopped as a feeling overcame him to stay hidden among the willows. It was almost as if something or someone was pulling at him.

Why? He didn't know. But Samuel turned his panic to save Regi into determination as he followed the urge to stay concealed and ducked down.

"Ida, if you shoot me, Clifford will see you kill. You don't want that." Regi prayed her words would reach Ida's motherly tendencies. But Ida kept pushing her with the gun barrel, forcing Regi closer to the water.

The crazy woman's eyes gleamed with every thrust of the gun. "No he won't. You're going in the water."

Regi stopped at the river's edge.

Ida jabbed her hard. Pain coursed through Regi's chest where the gun's barrel had repeatedly hit her. "I'll do what you want. Just tell me, and I'll do it." Regi stepped into the bone-chilling river.

"Go downstream to the middle where the current is strong, and stay there. Don't get any ideas, 'cause if you try to run, I'll kill ya just like I did Jed."

Regi knew Ida would do it too. Slowly, she made her way deeper into the frigid water that stole her breath.

Ida watched with gun ready. "Hypothermia will get ya. Might take a while but then again might not. Once the numbness claims your body, you won't be able to fight the current, and you'll drown. Seen it happen many times with animals."

Regi had no choice. But if she held on long enough, maybe help would arrive. Maybe Samuel . . . Tears came to her eyes. He didn't even know where she was.

No one knew.

Ida eased her hold on the gun a little as she hollered, "Sorry it has to be this way, but since you know what Isaiah and me been up to, you've left us no choice. This makes things all tidy and nice." Ida kept the gun aimed at Regi. "Get farther out there!"

Regi stepped forward. Water crept past her legs to her waist as she waded deeper into the current. Coursing water fought against her, churning . . .

Swirling . . .

Singing . . .

Whispering . . .

River whispers.

"*Dive*," the whisper beckoned.

The word tumbled over and over with the river flow, mesmerizing Regi into submission, or was it answering her prayer?

Dive. Earl's voice? Or was she just as crazy as Ida?

Regi's foot slipped on a rock, and she slid into water up to her chest. Her coat became an anchor.

Ida was right. Hypothermia would soon set in. But what Ida hadn't realized was that Regi had already been chilled from the river. Though the water was cold, it was not as cold as the air had been on her wet pants. Somehow Regi felt shielded. But that would not last for long. Soon the cold would overcome her muscles.

"*Dive.*" The whisper again.

Regi suddenly felt the calming peace she'd been praying for and knew the Lord was guiding her. She wasn't alone.

She let her head slip under the black, swirling water.

The shock of her body being completely submerged in the bitter cold was almost too much. A frantic second of doubt filled her as water pressed her ears and sought her nose. Determined to fight the natural instinct to pop to the surface, she maintained control, tugged off her heavy coat, and dove deeper, swimming as if the devil chased her.

"*Dive.*" Regi followed the whisper.

She was now in the Lord's hands.

Using the willows as a shield, Samuel glimpsed Ida forcing Regi into the river. As they yelled at each other, their voices carried on the water's surface.

The ugly truth his aunt told nearly tore him apart. Jed was dead. *Not my brother. Lord, help us.* His heavy heart drummed against his chest and leaped to his throat as he watched Regi submit to his demented aunt's demands. Regi's voice became thready as she pleaded for her life.

She was giving up.

Samuel knew the icy-cold water was paralyzing her. He needed to do something and now. About to step from the willows and draw his aunt's attention away from Regi, Samuel stopped as a strong impression once again held him back.

He stared up the shore as if to find a reason for this feeling. Claudia and Wakanda had disappeared.

Regi was in the middle of the river, near the big swell. The treacherous current inched to her armpits.

Without warning, she went under.

Shocked, he could hardly breathe.

The perpetual sound of water running over rocks and earth echoed the terror throbbing in his head.

In an instant, Samuel knew what he must do, why he'd been prompted to wait. The current would pull Regi under, and she would surface near him. *I'll catch her and swim beyond the point where Ida can't see.*

Nearly out of his mind, Samuel waited.

As Regi fought to stay underwater in that dark lonely world, icy fingers clawed her flesh until she became lethargic. The inky-black water world tumbled in suspended time.

Drowning wasn't so bad.

Her mind drifted, and she saw sunlight sparkling on the water. Earl squatted beside her, tying her fly on her leader line. She'd forgotten how long his sideburns were, how his hair fringed his shirt collar. He stopped before he finished and handed the fly and line to her.

"You can finish, Regina. You know what to do." He smiled. She loved how his dark eyes twinkled, how the starburst of fine wrinkles creased at the sides of his face.

Help me, please. I can't do this alone.

"Yes, you can. You're strong."

I'm not strong! I need you!

His image evaporated among the willows, and a vision of Samuel took his place.

She tried to go to him, but the smothering water paralyzed her arms and legs. Her head hit a rock, jarring awake a willingness to fight one last time.

Gathering every shred of strength, Regi turned upright. She prayed for God to give her strength as she kicked against the river's bottom and jettisoned upward.

Breaking the water's surface, she gulped life-giving air. All too quickly the water's magnetic pull grabbed her. The will to fight still clung, but her body would not respond.

Again, the rushing river pulled her under.

Where was the strength Earl said she had? Why was it failing her? She could beat this. She had to. But hopelessness overcame her once again.

Why fight? Her children were grown. Claudia could handle the bed-and-breakfast. No one actually needed Regi.

No one . . . except Samuel's face came to mind.

"He needs you to fight." The words were clear. *Please, God help me. I followed Your prompting, please.*

Suddenly a strong hand latched onto her arm. And she saw him.

Samuel.

Her Samuel.

Coughing and sputtering for air, she felt as though it was an eternity until they reached the other side. Finally, he dragged her up on the riverbank into another stand of willows.

Hugging her to him for a minute, Samuel madly rubbed Regi's arms and legs. He whispered through chattering teeth. "It's okay. I've got you now. No one's going to hurt you." Samuel cradled her to him, stroking and kissing the top of her head. "I know you love to fish, but this is ridiculous."

Regi weakly smiled. Clinging to Samuel, she was overwhelmed by a flood of tears. She sobbed quietly against him.

A sound came on the other side of the thicket. They'd landed on the same side of the river as Ida. She was still out there, waiting.

Regi fearfully stared up at Samuel. He put his finger to his lips, signaling her to be quiet. He wrapped one of her arms around his neck and slung his other about her waist, helping her to walk. She couldn't feel her legs or feet. Still, she tried the best she could. Together they threaded their way through the reeds and up a steep embankment. Peering over the ridge, Regi saw Ida searching along the riverbank.

She was heading their way.

TWENTY-ONE
RIVER WHISPERS

SAMUEL HELD REGI TIGHTLY. HER entire body shook; her teeth chattered. He could hardly believe she was safe in his arms. He marveled about how he'd felt the prompting to wait as he watched her dive into the water. At that moment, he had known exactly what he had to do; Samuel knew he'd had help. That God of Regi's, He'd guided Samuel, and he could never deny it, nor did he want to. He leaned next to her, kissed her cold, wet cheek, and whispered, "You okay?"

She nodded.

He knew she wasn't. She'd been submerged in ice-cold water. He now had to fight the enemy of hypothermia. Samuel knew he had less than an hour to get Regi's body temperature up. Wanting to give her encouragement, he spoke softly to her. "Morgan is making his way to us. Wakanda and Claudia are probably with him by now. We're going to make it."

Regi hugged him back.

Together they watched Ida search the willows they'd just left, drawing closer to them.

"Where's Cliff?" Samuel asked.

Regi pointed a trembling finger toward him. Oddly enough, because of the sharp bends in the Snake River, she and Samuel had ended up not far from him. Clifford sat on the ground, rocking Jed in his arms. A powerful ache came to Samuel's heart for his dead brother. Samuel would never be able to make peace with him, never be able to tell him he loved him and that he was sorry.

A movement caught Samuel's attention. Ida would be upon them in a matter of seconds. Samuel scanned the area, hoping to see Morgan.

No sign of him.

Regi was in no shape to run. Samuel knew what he had to do. He needed to distract Ida and stall until Morgan found them. He glanced at Regi. Even in the moonlight, her face looked deathly pale. Her body temperature must be phenomenally low.

She needed a doctor. He started to rise.

"What are you doing?" Regi's voice quavered as she looked up at him, visibly fighting the cold by hugging her arms about her shaking body.

"Going to wrangle that shotgun away from her."

Regi cupped her hands together and breathed into them. "How will you do it?"

There was no time to explain. "Stay put." Samuel glared at her, hoping she realized he was serious. "I mean it!" For all Ida knew, Regi had drowned in the river. Samuel wanted to keep it that way.

Regi grew quiet.

Samuel was surprised that she readily accepted his order. It wasn't like her to give in like that, but he didn't have time to question.

He kissed her soundly on the lips and left.

Cold.

Mind-numbing cold.

Regi blinked several times as she fought the arctic chill avalanching her. She wanted to lie down, curl up in a ball, and just rest. But she knew better. She had to fight and help Samuel. She watched as Samuel put himself between her and danger. He'd get killed. She was not going to watch another man she loved die.

"You lose something, Ida?" That was Samuel. Regi couldn't stand it.

Ida was less than fifty feet away. The old woman's little head jerked up as she studied him through the darkness. She immediately raised the shotgun to shoulder level, taking aim on Samuel as she walked toward him. "Sammie?"

"Yes. Not nice to point a gun at someone unless you plan to use it. You're not going to shoot your own nephew, are you?"

Regi knew full well the woman would kill Samuel. She had to help him. Ida had passed Regi, where she lay hidden in the willows. The woman's back was toward her.

"Should have known a bad penny would turn up. Looking for that woman you've fancied all your life, are you? Well, you're too late again. She's gone."

Shaking violently, Regi tried to stand, but her legs weren't working. She couldn't feel them. A dizziness swirled her vision.

I've got to . . . help.

Regi crawled on her hands and knees. Through blurry vision, she saw a tree stump close by. Crawling to it, she somehow dragged herself to her feet.

Ida had the gun on Earl . . . no, it was Samuel.

He can't die!

Daggers of pain shot down her legs to her feet as Regi gritted her teeth and step by wobbly step crept up behind the old woman.

Almost to her.

"You can join her." The old woman cackled, preparing to fire. "This is your fault, you know."

"My fault?"

"You left Jed alone with your father." Ida's finger tightened on the trigger.

Any second there would be a blast.

Any second a life could be taken . . . again.

Too far away. Regi knew she wouldn't reach Ida in time. Needing to do something to save the man she loved, Regi screamed, "Ida!"

The old woman swung around, aiming the double-barreled shotgun directly at her.

Samuel's heart jackknifed when he heard Regi and watched Ida turn around to face her. In a split second, he caught sight of a large form steamrolling toward Ida, colliding with her. And then, horror of horrors, the deafening sound of gunfire erupted. Flash and fire lit the night.

The scent of spent gunpowder coiled over them. On the ground at Samuel's feet, Clifford wrestled the gun from Ida. He jerked the weapon free and rose.

Ida hugged her arms over her head as though afraid he would hit her or shoot. Clifford huffed a few times as he glared down on his aunt. "Hurt no more." Then he turned around and flung the weapon into the river. He looked at Samuel for only a moment and then hurried back to his father's side.

"Isaiah!" Ida had regained her feet. "Where are you?" She paced as she stared off into space, wringing her hands.

Samuel knew his aunt needed help, but he had to see to Regi first. Frantically scanning the area, Samuel spied her lying on the ground like an abandoned rag doll. His heart leaped to his throat. Fear tore him apart as he neared. She lay so still, so deathly still. Had she been hit?

Bending down, he drew her cold body to him, feeling her arms and legs, searching for an injury. No blood. "Regi, Regi, answer me!"

She gasped, trying to catch her breath. "Sam . . . uel?"

"Thank goodness." He cradled her to him. He realized that her shivering had stopped and knew this was a very bad sign.

"Sam, Earl . . . was here." Her voice was thready.

She was delirious. He had to get her warm and fast. Holding her tight against him, he stood.

From behind, he heard Ida talking to Clifford, who sat on the ground beside Jed's body. "So much to do." Her voice sounded too high, too light. "Isaiah was wrong." She became stern. "Should have loved Jed. Don't know where to begin. Sam has the flu. Threw up on my waxed floor. The smell is always there." Ida had suffered a full breakdown.

Samuel sorrowed for her and wanted to help, but Regi's life was in danger. In Ida's state of mind, she was no longer a threat to anyone. Clifford would keep her out of trouble. Samuel had to save Regi.

As he hurried past them, pain pierced his heart for the loss of his brother and the tragedy that had befallen his entire family. It seemed his father still had a stranglehold on them, even from the grave. Would the shock of this horrible night never end?

Hugging Regi tight and drawing strength in the knowledge that she was at least alive, he kept walking.

He heard someone rushing toward him. "Everybody okay here?" Morgan raced up the hill, gun drawn. Wakanda, Claudia, and Oscar brought up the rear. Water dripped off all of them.

"Is she dead?" Claudia reached for her sister.

"No. But we've got to get her warm."

Wakanda immediately tore off her animal-skin coat. "Animal skin holds heat in." She wrapped it around Regi as though bundling a baby, even folding the top over her head.

Grasping Regi in his arms, Samuel turned to Morgan. "Regi's in bad shape. I've got to take care of her. Ida's gone crazy. Clifford saved Regi and me, but Jed . . ."

Morgan motioned for Samuel to leave. "You three go on. I can take care of things here."

Holding Regi to him, Samuel hurried to his house with Claudia, Wakanda, and Oscar close on his heels. With each footstep, he prayed for guidance.

As soon as they reached the ranch and were inside the house, he laid Regi on the couch in his den. Wakanda took over. She seemed to have a sixth sense about what to do. She ordered Samuel to get out of his wet clothes and find hot water bottles and warm blankets.

Dashing to his room, he quickly changed into sweats then tore through the house grabbing blankets. He filled the water bottles, making sure they were nice and hot. When he returned to the den, Claudia rose from lighting a fire in the fireplace. Regi's wet clothes lay on the floor. Wakanda sat on the couch with Regi in her arms, bundled in the sofa throw. Wakanda motioned for Samuel to take her place while she placed the bottles on Regi, and then she wrapped the blankets Samuel had brought around them both.

"Samuel, where's your phone?" Claudia was looking around the den.

"In the kitchen." Samuel began to rock Regi as he stroked her face.

"I'm going to call Karen." Claudia left.

"Regi needs sugar water." Wakanda followed.

Samuel called after Wakanda. "There's orange juice in the fridge."

Regi's dog lay near Samuel's feet, staying near as though to watch over his master.

Samuel glanced down at Regi and was surprised to find her eyes open.

"Sam . . ." she whispered.

He looked down and saw her green sparkling eyes staring up at him. "I heard it."

She was delirious, but he'd play along. "Heard what?"

"The still, small voice."

"What?" He didn't know what she was talking about.

"God was with us tonight, guiding me, guiding you." Regi reached a trembling hand to his face, touching his cheek. "Did you hear Him?"

Immediately, Samuel thought of how he'd had the premonition to wait at the river. He didn't come up with that. No, he'd wanted to charge forward, but something—some higher power—told him to wait, nearly forced him to wait. And then when he'd seen Regi dive into the water, he knew immediately what he had to do.

"Yes, I did." He nuzzled her hand and kissed it.

She smiled warmly, and love shone from the depths of her eyes. Samuel could see all the years of bitterness, all the years of hurt, melt away. By some miracle, God had sent Regi back to him, and he was never going to let her go.

EPILOGUE

REGI GAZED OUT THE FRONT window of the Raindancer Bed-and-Breakfast. It had snowed through the night. Two feet of fluffy white lay on the ground, and the weatherman was forecasting another foot today. Regi loved Christmas Eve snow.

Oscar lay near the heat vent where the warmth could seep into his pinned leg. Earlier in the day, the Irish setter had gone with Regi and Wakanda to cut down their Christmas tree. They'd tied the Douglas fir to the back of the snowmobile and dragged it home. Oscar had run beside them, snow flying about his face. He had acted like a puppy again. Now he was paying the price.

After shaking off all the snow, Regi and Wakanda had placed the fresh pine in the living room corner. Its pungent scent filled the bed-and-breakfast. Claudia had dragged down all the old Christmas ornaments from the attic. Some were hers, some Regi's, and some were from their childhood. Wakanda had brought several bird nests she'd found to add to the collection. They were going to wait until the twins and their other guests arrived before decorating the tree. This year it seemed right that everyone be part of the ritual since they'd been through so much together.

Wakanda sat cross-legged on the couch as she worked to string popcorn and cranberries into a garland. She wore a red Christmas sweatshirt that Regi had given her, the face of Santa Claus imprinted on the front. Wakanda had taken up permanent residence in the bunkhouse, which was all right with Regi. She considered Wakanda part of the family.

The Raindancer was closed for the holidays, even though Christmas was their busiest time of the year, with people flocking to the park to snowmobile. But Regi didn't want any intrusion from outsiders for the next couple of days. Claudia agreed. She was cooking a blowout Christmas Eve feast: orange-glazed Cornish game hens, steamed veggies, potato casserole, fruit compote, and her famous orange rolls.

Wakanda growled. "Need help here!" She studied a cranberry before stabbing it with the needle. "Cranberry, popcorn chain was your idea, not mine."

"Sorry." Regi pulled herself away from the window. She found a space beside her beloved friend and picked up the needle and thread she'd abandoned from the coffee table. "I'm just so excited that I can't sit still."

Wakanda looked as her as if to say, "Oh, brother."

Regi glanced at the floor. The small heap of broken popcorn kernels at her friend's feet had grown larger. Wakanda may have patience enough to braid buffalo hair, but working with fragile popcorn was a different story. To make her friend feel as though all her hard work was going to a worthy cause, Regi said, "You know, the birds are going to love this garland on the tree."

Wakanda gave her a doubtful glare.

"It's true. See, after Christmas day we're going to take our fancy do-dah ornaments off and put the tree outside with all sorts of treats on it for the birds. Claudia knows how to make Christmas balls with bird seed stuck on them She has a plan."

As if on cue, Claudia hustled in, wiping her hands on a towel. "Any sign of them yet?" The mouthwatering aromas of cooking game hens and simmering oranges followed her. Claudia went to the bay window. Oscar raised his head. His tail thumped the floor.

Even though she'd just sat down, Regi bounced up to join her sister. They'd grown closer through the ordeal of finding Romney's killer. Regi had never told Claudia that at one point she feared her sister might have murdered him. Claudia'd had enough grief in her life without knowing everything that had crossed Regi's mind during that trying time. Things had worked out. Regi took her sister's arm in hers, and together they peered through the window, anxious for their company to arrive.

"Think anyone might have had an accident? Looks awfully icy out there." Claudia gazed at the white winter wonderland.

"You forget that country folks are more laid back. No one wants to arrive first. Our friends will be here any minute." Regi squeezed her sister's arm.

They'd invited quite a crew: Cameron and Melissa Elliott; Morgan, Hannah, and Effie; Stew and his brother; and Samuel and Clifford. After the truth had come out about Jed and Ida, Regi had wanted to celebrate life, not only with family but with friends as well. There were a few obvious invites to the party, but Regi wanted to mend some bridges too. Superintendent Elliot had stopped by the Raindancer on a regular basis with one excuse after the other. Regi knew he'd taken a liking to Claudia—even though her sister seemed to think they were just good friends—so she wanted to give him a fair chance, and she couldn't invite him without Melissa.

Regi had been a little concerned about how comfortable Lisa would be around Melissa, so she'd asked her daughter before inviting them. Lisa was fine. She was never one to hold a grudge; besides, Romney had hurt the Elliotts much more than he had her.

And Elliott had done his part to help repair what had happened. He had profusely apologized for the way he'd treated Claudia. In fact, he'd confessed that before Romney's death, he himself had come across some evidence that Romney was trying to take advantage of the Park's proposed land sale. He'd confronted him, but Romney had denied it. When his son-in-law turned up dead, Elliott suspected related foul play, did more investigating, and found the DVD Romney had made of Congressman Osborne. Turned out Romney had learned of the sale long ago and had wanted to guarantee that Osborne would go along with the sale, so he'd set a trap for him. In the end, Elliott didn't say a word to the media and gave the DVD to Claudia, promising that he wouldn't tell anyone. He also told her that he'd confronted the girl in the DVD and told her she would probably go to jail if the plot was leaked to the press. Upon Elliott's recommendation, Congress tabled the Park's land sale until things quieted down. Regi couldn't think of any other reason for Elliott to do all of that except that he was trying to impress Claudia.

When Regi invited the Morgans, Thomas thought going to the Raindancer to celebrate would help Hannah. And Effie didn't have anywhere to go this year, so she was happy to tag along with them. Stew and his brother were more than welcome, especially since Stew was bringing his famous chocolate cream pie.

"They'll be here," Regi said, nudging her sister. "Samuel was going to pick up Clifford from the care center, so that's probably why he's delayed, and the twins . . . well, Jack rarely looks at his watch, and since he's bringing Lisa, she'll be late too."

"With all we've been through, I just want everything to be perfect." Claudia caught sight of Wakanda struggling with the popcorn and cranberry chain. "Let me finish that for you, Wakanda."

"But if you're doing the garland, who will cook?" Regi asked. Then, as if struck with a brilliant idea, she answered her own question. "I could do it."

Claudia and Wakanda looked at each other and burst out laughing.

Regi folded her arms and huffed. "You both find my cooking that funny? Well, I have news for you . . ." Regi had wanted to tell her sister and friend something for a while now but didn't know exactly how.

"Yes . . .?" Claudia's eyebrows rose as she leaned closer. Wakanda kept working on the popcorn, but Regi knew she was listening too.

"Well, Samuel has been giving me cooking lessons." There, now the door on the subject had been opened . . . a little. Of course, they knew that since Ida's meltdown and Regi's near drowning, she and Samuel had been spending more time together, but she'd never told them how she felt about the man.

"There's more." Wakanda stopped working on the garland and looked up at Regi. "Samuel's giving you love."

Regi smiled. "Yes, he is, and you know what? I love him."

"Finally!" Claudia hugged her sister. "What are you going to do about it?"

"I don't know." The love Regi felt for Samuel was strong and felt right, and yet it didn't.

Since joining the Church, Regi had set a goal to go to the temple. But now . . . now she'd developed these feelings for Samuel and he wasn't even a member. Since saving her from the river, Samuel had gone to church every Sunday. But she didn't know if he planned to be baptized, let alone go to the temple. She looked at Claudia and Wakanda. They were both just beginning to investigate the Church. Would they understand her dilemma?

"Do you feel as though your love for Samuel is somehow being unfaithful to Earl?" Claudia put her arm around Regi's shoulders.

Regi remembered how Earl's image had come to her while she'd been under the water. He'd told her that she would know what to do, and then his image had turned into Samuel's. At first she'd thought the reason Earl's image had faded was because Samuel was really there, but as she had pondered what she'd seen, she had realized Earl had actually stepped aside, allowing Samuel to take over. "No, I'm not worried about that. Earl would understand."

"Well then, tell Samuel how you feel. It's Christmas, the best time of the year to say what's in your heart." Claudia touched her forehead to Regi's. "You're always telling me to quit worrying. Now I'm telling you. Quit worrying and tell him." She gave Regi a hug and then retreated to the kitchen, humming "Jingle Bells" as she left.

If only it were that simple.

When the guests arrived, they ate dinner and then decorated the tree. Everyone enjoyed themselves immensely. The hour had grown late, and most everyone had gone home by the time Regi and Samuel had found themselves alone on the couch with Oscar lying near their feet.

Regi had convinced Samuel that he and Clifford should spend the night. Since there were no paying guests, there was plenty of room. Samuel had agreed. He, too, had probably noticed what a good time Clifford was having with Jack. Maybe Regi's son *could* think of someone else besides himself. She knew his father would have been proud. She could hardly wait for Jack to open his Christmas gift. Regi'd found Earl's knife and decided it was a fitting present for their son. Plus, she knew Earl would have wanted him to have it.

Samuel got up, sidestepped the dog, and added a log to the fire. Hungry flames crawled over the dry wood. It hissed and sizzled. He rubbed his hands together and then held his palms up to the heat. "Thanks for inviting Clifford and me. With Jed gone and Ida locked up, I knew Cliff would be missing his family and that I should do something, but I didn't know what. I've always dreaded Christmas because I've been alone. But being here with you and your family has been great. I didn't know it could be this way." He came over and sat next to Regi again.

Their eyes locked, and Regi knew she needed to tell him how she felt. "Samuel, I . . ."

"Well, the kitchen is cleaned." Claudia walked into the living room, pulling down the sleeves of her golden-colored silk shirt. She immediately looked at Samuel and Regi sitting on the couch and seemed to realize she'd interrupted an important moment. "And I'm dead tired, so I'm going to bed. Remember what I told you, Reg?" She didn't wait for a reply. "Have a good night, you two." With that, Claudia disappeared up the stairs.

"What was that about?" Samuel asked as he scooted closer.

"She thinks I need to tell you something." Regi glanced at his face. The fire's glow enhanced his rugged cheeks and long nose and made his black eyes mesmerizing.

"Before you say anything, I want to ask you something." Samuel pulled a little black velvet box from his pants pocket.

Regi knew exactly what it was. Joy, elation, fear, and then joy again streaked over her skin in one big swoosh. She hardly dared to breathe.

Was this really happening?

Could it be possible that Regi had found happiness once again with a man she loved more than words could express?

But . . . the temple.

"I spoke with Bishop Caldwell," Samuel said, as his gaze became more intent, more serious. "I've set a date to be baptized in February. The bishop said he'd marry us civilly the day after if you say yes. I know you want to marry in the temple, but we'd have to wait for a year after I'm baptized. I don't know if I can wait that long. We've wasted so much time. We've known each other all our lives, and now it's our turn. And a year after our civil wedding, we can go to the temple and be sealed together for time and all eternity." Samuel opened the box. A radiant diamond smiled up at her. "What do you think? Should we do this?"

A warmth overcame her, breathing over her skin and filling her soul. One word slipped from her lips. "Yes."